A DETECTIVE INSPECTC

CW00517178

KILL YOUR DARLINGS

NEW YORK TIMES #1 BESTSELLER **TONY LEE** WRITING AS

JACK GATLAND

Hooded Man
MEDIA

Published by Hooded Man Media.
Cover photo by Paul Thomas Gooney

First Edition: July 2023

PRAISE FOR JACK GATLAND

'This is one of those books that will keep you up past your bedtime, as each chapter lures you into reading just one more.'

'This book was excellent! A great plot which kept you guessing until the end.'

'Couldn't put it down, fast paced with twists and turns.'

'The story was captivating, good plot, twists you never saw and really likeable characters. Can't wait for the next one!'

'I got sucked into this book from the very first page, thoroughly enjoyed it, can't wait for the next one.'

'Totally addictive. Thoroughly recommend.'

'Moves at a fast pace and carries you along with it.'

'Just couldn't put this book down, from the first page to the last one it kept you wondering what would happen next.'

Before LETTER FROM THE DEAD...
There was

Learn the story of what *really* happened to DI Declan Walsh,
while at Mile End!

An EXCLUSIVE PREQUEL, completely free to anyone who
joins the Declan Walsh Reader's Club!

Join at bit.ly/jackgatlandVIP

Also by Jack Gatland

COVERT ACTION

COUNTER ATTACK

STEALTH STRIKE

DAMIAN LUCAS BOOKS

THE LIONHEART CURSE

STANDALONE BOOKS

THE BOARDROOM

For Mum, who inspired me to write.

For Tracy, who inspires me to write.

CONTENTS

PROLOGUE

HUNT ROBINSON WAS NOT HAPPY.

In fact, if someone asked him if he was okay, or if they asked where, on the unhappiness scale of one to ten he currently was, he'd most likely go for their throat.

The news had come out everywhere while he was in a war zone – a war zone, of all bloody places. Television presenter Lucy-Rachel Adams, she of the "I'm so important I need two first names" brigade had been outed by her assistant of five years – no, scratch that, her *recently fired* assistant of five years – as a serial kleptomaniac. Explaining in a tearful tell all about how she was ashamed to have lied to her partner of ten years about her urge to stick things down her dress and nick them, and how being publicly shamed in a Tesco's was a life-changing moment and yada yada yada.

He'd torn up the newspaper he'd been reading at that point. He knew the whole "my assistant outed me" narrative was bollocks. Someone else had outed her. And he knew damn well who.

Lucy-Rachel was in his files; he had known about her

secret for the last fifteen years, ever since she was a runner on some ITV daytime show. But he'd sat on it and waited, knowing that at some point he'd be able to use it – maybe in a memoir or something along those lines. Or, maybe he could have used this as leverage on her, to get something really juicy on her co-hosts, in particular the ones the public actually gave a shit about. He'd even guessed that something was going to happen soon, as there'd been rumours that a couple of super injunctions were floating about, but you never knew exactly how, who and what these bloody things were involving, as that was the point of the bastard things.

He'd written the piece, too, but his coward of an editor had spiked it. And then, completely unrelated, his paper had sent him out into a war zone, to give a human side of the conflict. Younger Hunt would have snapped it up in a second; this, for his younger self, was the chance to live the life he wanted as a journalist – to go into war zones, and give a story about situations that people rarely saw. A humanised conflict, proof that, as ever, no matter what the flag, or the colour of your skin, all wars were as brutal and pointless as each other.

Older Hunt couldn't give a shit.

Older Hunt wanted money to pay for his lavish lifestyle, his mistresses and his growing drug habit.

But still, at the end of the day, although he'd lost one of his potential future scoops, one from his "little book of secrets," the trip back to the UK in his business-class seat – which, to be perfectly honest was nothing more than a normal seat with a space between him and the snoring German beside him – was spent in bitterness and annoyance. Finding out he'd been scooped was one thing, but knowing he couldn't even get on the Wi-Fi to fix things until he landed was something else. And by the time he reached Heathrow's

Terminal Five, he'd already had three arguments in his head, and had worked out what he was going to do, who he was going to speak to, and which people he was going to kill when he found them.

Lucy-Rachel Adams had been *his* secret. No one else was supposed to have been able to get even close to them. And besides, the super injunction he knew she'd put out a good year or two back should have stopped this. He needed to check with his legal team and find out why they hadn't alerted him to any problems.

They needed to explain why he was reading it in a bloody war zone rather than selling it to *The Sun,* once he faced down his editor and quit his useless paper.

Bunch of ungrateful, good-for-nothing pricks.

Immigration had been as painful as ever. Hunt, annoyingly, had a name that, although uncommon, seemed to be the same as someone else on a UK Government watch list, which meant the e-gates never seemed to work for him. And as he tried fruitlessly to get through, optimistically hoping this was the time before being refused, he sighed and walked up to the customs officer who, smiling, checked his details, welcomed him back to the UK and passed him through.

Hunt knew the customs officer recognised the name; after all, even though there was some kind of terrorist using his details, he wasn't a nobody. But, as he was waved through, it was both annoying, but also refreshing to not have the customs officer ask him questions about his job. Was it true that he'd been to Davos the day the local babies went missing, and the conspiracy theorists claimed they were eaten by billionaires? Or was it true that he'd once pretended to be part of the Welsh International Football team just to attempt to "out" half the players?

Hunt hated telling the stories, but when he wasn't given a chance to, he found himself annoyed that he *couldn't* tell the stories.

Now past customs, he had his usual paranoid thought that perhaps he wasn't the same name as a terrorist. Maybe this was a deliberate attack on him, purely because he'd once forced a Government Home Secretary to resign.

Well, two, even.

But no, surely even they weren't petty enough to do that to him, even if he was petty enough to do it to them. And then the thought faded away, replaced with renewed anger at the loss of his story as he bypassed baggage claim. Only idiots who wanted their luggage lost checked their luggage in; he'd had too many occasions over the years where the luggage had been out of his sight, where governments, intelligence agencies or even rival journalists had placed items into his luggage to either identify his destination or to stop him entering it.

There was a time in the nineties when a journalist for the *News of the World* had even snuck in to Heathrow as a baggage handler, and had placed various suspicious-looking-items of technology into three of their rival journalists' bags. It wasn't a prank; it was knowledge that, when the rival arrived at the location three hours later, the conference they were attending would now give the mischievous, bag-tampering journalist an exclusivity they wouldn't have expected beforehand.

Mainly because the other three journalists would have been taken by security at the airport, and were very much unlikely to be attending in any journalistic context, let alone walking straight after the various cavity searches.

Hunt hadn't been one of the three, but he knew two of

them, and as far as he was concerned, they bloody deserved it, the self-righteous pricks.

If he was forced to admit it, the last trip out had been the straw that broke the camel's back, and he had realised, as he arrived, he wasn't enjoying this anymore. There was a time when he'd been a name, a story in his own right, but these days, with every moron with a keyboard claiming to be a journalist, regardless of NUJ membership or, you know, actual bloody training, all Hunt wanted now was to "stop the world – I want to get off."

Luckily, while festering on a plane and going through his notes to work out the next steps, he knew exactly what he was going to do.

Walking out into the main arrivals area, Hunt stared blankly at the men and women waiting along the barrier, all with iPads, or A4 sheets of card, with various names on. He was guaranteed a car for the way home; it was the reason he agreed to do this job. He wasn't a fan of catching the underground, and then *overground* trains to where he lived, even if it was quicker, and he was sure as hell not going to leave his car in some long stay car park. After all, he'd written exposes on half of them, and the opportunity to have Hunt Robinson's car, even for a few days, would probably be enough to screw it over.

People might have said Hunt Robinson's suspicions were nothing more than paranoia, but it was only classed as that when they *weren't* out to get you. When you'd spent decades making sure they *were*, then you only had yourself to blame.

There was a man, a young Somalian in a white shirt and tie, black trousers pressed sharply, smiling at every man who walked past, on the off chance that they were the name written on his piece of paper.

HUNTER ROBINSON

Hunt Robinson sighed, walking over. A cheerful bloody driver and a mis-written sign was all he wanted today.

'Mister Hunter Robinson?' the man smiled.

'Hunt,' he replied irritably. 'Hunter's not my name. I wasn't christened it, I've never been called it and I'd appreciate it if you told whoever gave you the details, they gave you the wrong ones, and I'm not impressed.'

The man kept smiling, nodding happily, as if this really wasn't the most important thing in the world – which Hunt realised, in the grand scheme of things, and having just left a war zone, it probably wasn't.

'Come, please, I am upstairs in the short stay car park,' the driver said, offering to take Hunt's satchel, but Hunt waved him on, almost hugging his bags in horror at being parted from them. And, with the driver taking the hint, Hunt followed the smiling man up to a car that had been parked where all the other Uber and Addison Lee cars were. Placing his wheeled hard case into the boot of the car, Hunt settled into the back seat, his satchel beside him. It was a good hour and a half's drive back to his house in Kent, and, pulling out his laptop, he decided he could get some last-minute work done using his phone as a hotspot.

The man who had named himself as Yusuf explained, while randomly speaking at him about a variety of things Hunt really wasn't paying attention to, that there was free Wi-Fi onboard the car. But again, Hunt decided not to use it; he didn't trust public Wi-Fi. And there was every chance, although this man was completely legit, that he could take the details of Hunt's computer and use it against him, even hacking in and stealing his data, like they did in the films.

It was one reason why his secrets hadn't been digitised in any way; just written and kept safe.

Yusuf also passed him a bottle of clear water, explaining there was "plenty more in the cool box," as he nodded at a container on the other side of the back seat well. Hunt nodded, placing it aside for the moment. He was thirsty, but first he needed to check his emails, a chance to settle in and find out what was going on with the Lucy-Rachel Klepto-mania story. He knew it was Karen Pine who'd broken the story, and he knew how she'd done it. He'd trusted her, but now he needed to decide what to do about her.

But Yusuf seemed intent on speaking at him. And so, as they hit the M25 heading anti-clockwise, Yusuf would look up into the rear-view mirror, nodding at the man in the back.

'So what do you do, Mister Robinson?' he asked.

'I'm a journalist,' Hunt replied.

'Oh? Newspaper or television?'

'Newspaper.'

'Is it something I would have read?'

Hunt shrugged, realising work wasn't happening until Yusuf shut up.

'I don't know,' he replied. 'Nobody seems to bloody read newspapers these days. I'm starting to wonder if I'm actually pointless. I mean, there's a website portal that people read, so there's that. But, over the years I've worked for *The Guardian*, I've done stuff in the *Mail on Sunday*. I've written for most of Rupert Murdoch's little rags over the time, I'm working with *The Individual* right now. It's a new paper, aimed at straddling both sides of the political system.'

'Ah,' Yusuf nodded with the look of a man who had no clue what *The Individual* was, and it wasn't an unfamiliar look. *The Individual* was a renamed national tabloid; a chance

to change things up in the same way that the *Metro* newspaper had a few years ago. In fact, *The Individual* was very
similar to that, having just inked a deal to be given out at
stations on the Queen Elizabeth line.

As far as Hunt was concerned, though, all it meant was
the people who read his work didn't care that much about
him, just the free paper they gained for the commute, left on
carriage seats the moment they reached their destination.
Still, he didn't care as long as the salary still arrived in his
bank account.

After all, those mistresses weren't going to pay themselves, annoyingly.

Opening the bottle of water, he drank heavily from it. The
business class he'd been on didn't seem to want to give water
out, even though they'd paid through the nose for his seat,
and he could feel his dehydrated body grasping for every
drop, already reaching for another in the cool box before
he'd even finished guzzling down this one. And, as they
drove, Yusuf, not guessing Hunt didn't want to answer any
questions, for some reason kept talking.

'So where have you been?' he asked.

'Southern Ukraine.'

'Oh, I thought it was hard to go there.'

'Well sure, if you're looking for a city break, it's a bit of a
bastard,' Hunt mocked. 'But not if you're a war correspondent
having a closeup look at a war.'

Yusuf's eyes widened, and Hunt assumed the driver was
excited by this, now filled with thoughts of surviving in a war
zone. It probably gave him excitement, a sense of adventure.

'Have you ever been through a war zone?' Hunt
continued.

Surprisingly, Yusuf nodded.

'I grew up in one,' he said. 'Before my family brought me here.'

'Oh,' Hunt replied, wondering how he could bring an end to the conversation. He knew this was an opportunity for Yusuf to talk about himself, and the last thing he wanted right now was to listen to other people tell him their sob stories.

And so he nodded, mumbled that he got little sleep, and shut his eyes, putting on his headphones, set to full noise cancellation to really hammer down the point he didn't want to talk to this man. As he finished his bottle, placing it beside him and shutting his eyes, Hunt Robinson finally relaxed – until he felt a vibration from within his jacket pocket.

Frowning, he leant forward on the car seat, pulling out his phone. He'd expect it to be a text message from his editor, once more apologising, or trying to argue the case for why he hadn't put the piece out when he'd been told to, or maybe from the secret someone he was supposed to be meeting this coming week – but instead, it was a text from an unknown number, which, in a way was familiar.

It wasn't the first text he had had from an unfamiliar number over the years; it was a common way for people to shout at him, or threaten him when he'd exposed them for something, or simply written a story they didn't like. But even though the number was unknown, he recognised the syntax of the message, as his bowels turned into water while he read the anonymous message.

> I'm still waiting, Hunt. I want those pages.
> You have a week before I go public on you.
> And my book is better than yours.

Feeling a slight cold sweat on his forehead, Hunt turned

off his phone, placing it back in his pocket, trying to shake away the feeling of impending dread he now had. Forcing himself to relax he shut his eyes. He knew where this came from. Doug had found out.

It was Westminster.

It was the *Government* trying to silence him.

He could wait until tomorrow to sort this, he thought to himself.

Yes. Tomorrow.

———

MARJORIE LIKED TUESDAY MORNINGS AT ST BRIDE'S BECAUSE they were always a little quieter than usual. The morning prayer was at eight fifteen, before work, and this meant she had to be up and into the building by seven, if only to tidy everything up, but she didn't mind. She wouldn't be the churchwarden if she did.

Marjorie loved being in the church when nobody else was; it gave her a sense of history, as the church had been on Fleet Street since the sixth century, when it was founded by Irish missionaries in the name of Saint Bridget, a Patron Saint of Ireland. Of course, the church she now stood in bore no resemblance to that, as the church itself had been destroyed multiple times over the centuries; the Normans had built a new church on the spot, where King John had later held a parliament inside; and then it was replaced by an even larger church in the fifteenth century, which burnt down in the Great Fire of London, was rebuilt by Sir Christopher Wren, and was then gutted by fire-bombs dropped by the Luftwaffe in 1940. Only the Medieval lectern had survived the bombs, and the rest had been rebuilt, as close to Wren's original designs as possible.

But, even though the church was effectively fake and made to look as if it was the original, Marjorie still felt the history, especially while passing a tribute to the Pilgrim Fathers; the parents of Virginia Dare, the first English child born in North America, born on Roanoke Island in 1587. He had been married here, and the tribute was displayed within an oak reredos, a gift from Edward Winslow, who served as governor of Plymouth, Massachusetts three times. Winslow was a leader of the Mayflower voyage of 1620, and his parents were also married in the church. However, young Edward had more than a passing knowledge of the church, as he served as a Fleet Street apprentice – although the stories stated he broke his contract and left, so perhaps the rederos had been a kind of apology.

Walking down the aisle, with the pews facing in from the side, Marjorie liked to imagine who would have stood where she now stood; John Milton, as he wrote *Paradise Lost*, perhaps? Samuel Pepys? Ben Johnson?

At the north-east end of the church was the Journalists Altar, once known as the Hostage altar, and now more of a memorial table, dedicated to the memories of journalists and staff who died in the course of their work, around the world. Although this wasn't why people came here. Many of the tourists came to St Bride's because it was the "wedding cake" church, the slightly staggered spire above, giving the impression of a wedding cake.

In fact, the legend stated an apprentice baker fell in love with his master's daughter, and asked for the young woman's hand in marriage, which her father granted. He wanted to create a very special wedding cake to celebrate the marriage here at St Bride's, and, looking for inspiration, he looked up at the tiered steeple of the church, which prompted him to create a wedding cake in tiers, each one smaller than the last. Now people from around the world came to take photos of it, never even entering the church itself, and missing the secrets, many far better than a boring wedding.

One of the biggest secrets had even been discovered thanks to the Luftwaffe, and that was where she now headed.

In 1940, when the church had been gutted, there was an excavation before the rebuilding, and this revealed a crypt under the church, including the church's original sixth-century Saxon foundations, as well as more than two hundred lead-lined coffins, holding plague and cholera victims from centuries earlier. Today, the crypt was known as the Museum of Fleet Street, and many actual visitors of the church came down the stairs to look at the ancient relics on display, while not knowing some of the more gruesome secrets behind them.

And, at the end, along a narrow pathway that led past various gravestones and even a Victorian iron casket, dating from the days of "Body Snatchers" Burke and Hare, which promised "safety for the dead" by deterring those who earned money by exhuming bodies, was the main crypt chapel. This was a medieval crypt long hidden under the church, and restored in 2002 as a memorial to the Harmsworth family, and the staff of Associated Newspapers who lost their lives in the First and Second World Wars. It was here where the service of morning prayer would be heard, complete with prayers, silence, and the Bible readings set for the day, where the attendees would remember journalists who had died recently, as well as those in danger, held hostage, or who were in any kind of need, as part of the Church's ministry to journalism.

Marjorie didn't like this part. As she turned on the lights, she could feel the cool air hit her. You could romanticise about the history of the church upstairs, but down here you could physically see and touch it.

What Marjorie wasn't expecting was to hear it.

The sound was soft, nothing more than a groan, and for a moment Marjorie had the belief she could hear a spirit in torment, before a hefty dose of rationalisation went through her. It wasn't a ghost; it was probably a homeless person, or someone in need who required her help.

It was coming from the chapel so Marjorie picked up her pace, hurrying to the wrought-iron door that led into the whitewashed chapel, and opening it, she looked down at the floor in horror—

On the ground, lying on his back and with his arms outstretched as if in a Christ pose, his head aimed away from the altar, was a man. A battered, bleeding man, with a deep wound in his side, bleeding out onto the chapel floor. His hands had been bound with silk and looped around the base of the convex seats at the back of the crypt, stretching him out, and stopping him from moving. He was stripped, except for his trousers and socks, and he looked over at the horrified Marjorie.

'Please ... help ...' Hunt Robinson said, before his eyes glazed over and his head slumped back.

1

YOU HAVE THE RIGHT

THE ARREST WAS SUPPOSED TO BE A QUICK ONE.

However, nothing seemed to be as easy as believed at the Last Chance Saloon, Declan thought to himself as he sprinted down some alleyways near Fenchurch Street, following Sam Mansfield as he ran for his life in front.

It had been a favour to a DCI in Bishopsgate's Command Unit. There had been a series of art thefts within businesses in the city, with a forger managing to swap several originals for superb copies. The Temple Inn Unit, finding themselves at a loose end, had been brought on board to assist. Also, it had been quiet for several weeks now since the end of the last major case, so they had the capacity – but Declan was aware his time was ticking out.

Sam tripped on the edge of the kerb, but straightened himself as he continued to run in the vague vicinity of Leadenhall Market. He'd been caught at the latest of his many heists, a FinTech company based near Aldgate. He had a particular modus operandi, one that involved convincing companies he was there to restore or fix some problem with a painting they had in the building. This wasn't that unnatural, if all was said and done, as many of the companies in the City had paintings, ones on loan from museums, or from private collectors, and it wasn't uncommon for restorers, or assigned curators to attend the company premises to check up on the items. Unfortunately for the FinTech company in question, Sam Mansfield wasn't a curator; nor was he a restorer.

What Sam was, in fact, was a world-class forger; no older than mid-thirties at best. And over the last three months, he'd gained five or six masterpieces from companies across the city, arriving with his kit in a folio bag, and, after showing his also forged identification he'd take the paintings into a side room for around ten minutes or so – just to check them over for damage, or any markings that needed to be fixed – before bringing them back. Of course, in that time he'd swapped the original for his own excellent forgery, so they were returned a damn sight less original than they were when he retrieved them. Sam had been quite good at this, and right now, although only five or six had been discovered, Declan believed the number was closer to ten, maybe even fifteen.

However, it wasn't his case. And it wasn't his capture. They were just providing an assist.

He had other reasons for doing this. First, Declan needed allies in Bishopsgate, if he wanted to try to stay in the City of London. It'd been five weeks now, since both Anjli and Billy had been promoted: Billy to Detective Sergeant and Anjli to Detective Inspector. The problem with this, however, was even though he was also a DI, there wasn't a budget in the Last Chance Saloon for two DIs in the building, which meant

either the just-promoted Anjli or Declan needed to change
their immediate situation. Declan's options were to be
promoted to DCI in the next seven days, which seemed
unlikely, or to find a way of providing enough budget to keep
him, which, even *if* they could do so, was a little problematic,
as even though he had seniority, Anjli could be quite forceful.
And, as they were technically the same rank, there could be
conflict, something he really didn't want.

The other option, although unthinkable, was that
Monroe would be promoted up to Detective Superintendent,
or, God forbid, *died* - and Declan moved up into the now
spare DCI role via "dead man's shoes."

This however, seemed unlikely, as current-DCI Alex
Monroe didn't look as if he'd keel over any time soon, and he
was more hated by the suits than Declan was.

Which meant the final option, the one Declan didn't want
to think about, was that he would be leaving Temple Inn very
soon.

In the grand scheme of things, Declan had moved many
times. When he had started under his father, he'd been in
London as a Metropolitan Police officer. And he'd spent a
good decade in Tottenham, North London. He'd even had a
brief stint at Mile End, although that hadn't gone down too
well when he'd arrested his superior, DCI Ford.

Temple Inn was a place he'd only been at for a couple of
years now. But in that time, it had become home, and the
thought of leaving concerned him. He had a family here,
almost literally, with Anjli now living with him in Hurley, but
all good things often came to an end.

As Declan sprinted across Leadenhall Market, past the
confused stallholders opening up for the morning, Sam in

front of him, folio bag flapping at his side, Declan was very aware that within a few days, he would have to either transfer to a new Division, or he'd be resigning.

It also wasn't the first time he'd considered resigning as well. If it hadn't been for Alex Monroe and the Last Chance Saloon, he probably would have left a good couple of years earlier. Even after he handed in his notice after the Queen's Dinner affair, they'd kept fighting for him.

But now he wanted to stay. He wanted to fight for this.

Sam was slowing now as Declan kept close on his heels. For the last couple of years, Declan had been running park runs on weekends, or trying to keep to a good five or ten kilometre route when he ran in the evenings around Hurley. He wasn't as regular as others, he knew, it was just enough to keep him fit.

Fit enough, in fact, to be able to chase down the slightly younger but more sedentary man in front of him, grabbing Sam, the two of them stumbling and crashing to the floor.

'You've got nothing on me!' Sam cried out. 'I'm just doing my job!'

'And what job's that exactly?' Declan asked politely, pulling out his handcuffs. 'Because the company you claim to work for hasn't heard of you.'

'It's an administrational problem,' Sam whined, sitting up now, pulling out a wallet, showing an ID. 'Look, I'm part of a secret Government unit. See?'

Declan looked at the ID.

'I know that unit,' he said. 'I'll give them a call.'

'Oh, you do?' Sam muttered, cuffs attached to his wrists now. 'I want my rights.'

'You want your rights?' Declan smiled. 'Let me tell you

your rights. Sam. You have the right to shut the hell up. You don't have to say anything, but it may harm your defence if you don't mention, when questioned, something which you later rely on in court. Anything you do say may be given in evidence. Are they enough rights for you?'

Sam glared at him, accepting that, for the moment, his own journey was finished. As Declan clambered to his feet, pulling Sam up with him, the sound of police sirens could be heard approaching.

'I hear you're leaving,' Sam muttered as they waited for the cars to arrive.

'Oh, yeah? Who told you that?'

'Everybody knows,' Sam smiled coldly. 'You work in the City in any kind of way, it's all over the place.'

Declan grimaced. When Sam said "you work in the City," he didn't mean legally. He meant every criminal or off-the-books enterprise run in the City was probably filled full of happiness and glee because of this news. He'd done enough over the last year or so to put the fear of God into most of them, and the Last Chance Saloon's arrest ratio was superb, even if the unit was filled with the misfit toys that were too good to be fired.

Declan clipped Sam around the ear.

'I'm here for the duration,' he said. 'I'll still be here when you get out.'

'They might give me a couple of years for this,' Sam suggested. 'If I'm even guilty, of course. That's no admission of guilt. But, hypothetically, two years from now? I think by that point you'll be in Scotland. Or some strange little place in the middle of nowhere.'

He smiled.

'Maybe you'll do what they do in *Death in Paradise* and

piss off over to Barbados to do some work.'

Declan actually grinned at this. The thought of the *Death in Paradise* plan of a Detective Inspector spending time in a tropical paradise had interest. But watching the TV show, the fact he'd have to wear a suit all the time was too much for him to even consider. It was probably also the reason half the actors kept leaving the show at the end of seasons.

'No, I think I'll stay in England,' he said. 'Definitely London. I don't really know much else.'

He passed the fake ID back to Sam.

'You know, if you're going to pretend to be someone, you need to have a better ID,' he said.

Sam shrugged and reached into his pocket, pulling out a cheap plastic lighter.

'Yeah, better if I don't have it,' he said, and before Declan could stop him he lit the edge of the ID; it burst into nothing with a flash of light, leaving behind a Network Railcard.

'Flash paper,' Declan nodded. 'You forge on that? Dangerous if the printer overheats.'

'Dunno what you mean,' Sam replied innocently. 'It's always been a Railcard. Are you okay, DI Walsh? Maybe you do need some time off.'

'I'll have all the time off I need when I retire, a long way from now,' Declan replied, pushing Sam towards a waiting squad car. 'Have fun in Bishopsgate.'

He tried to make his voice sound light, but at the same time he was very much aware he had no say in the matter of whether he stayed until retirement, unless somebody found money or a promotion fast.

Detective Inspector Declan Walsh was soon to be an ex-Detective Inspector.

———

Monroe was first from the Temple Inn Unit to the scene, mainly because he'd been travelling in the other direction on his way back from something else; probably one of the many meetings he'd been taking over the last few weeks to find Declan somewhere new to hang his hat.

'You look happy,' Declan said.

Monroe didn't, and frowned at him, making a face.

'Aye, laddie,' he said. 'I've been dealing with people, talking about you. Surprisingly, nobody seems to want you in their unit. Mainly because you keep bringing trouble to the door, probably.'

'I bring troubles to the door?'

'Aye,' Monroe smiled. 'Just look at the cases we've had since you've turned up. We've had the Queen almost murdered. We've had Prime Ministers in jeopardy. We've had serial killers being killed by police officers, gangland wars, illegal duelling clubs, serial killer mechanics, the list goes on.'

'And you think this is all *because* of me?'

'Well, one or two are definitely on your lap,' he smiled. 'Or did you forget the serial killer was *your* mechanic?'

Monroe puffed his cheeks out as he looked around the scene.

'When Batman came to Gotham, the crazies weren't there,' he said. 'But after a while, the costumed bad guys turned up. "Like" matches "like" and all that.'

'Are you actually comparing me to Batman?' Declan laughed. 'Because seriously, I think you need to find some new reading material.'

There was a commotion to the left, and Declan saw DS – no – *DI* Anjli Kapoor walking towards him.

'You all right?' she asked.

Declan nodded, and Anjli looked over at Monroe before replying to Declan.

'I was talking to the boss, not you,' she said, before turning and walking away without saying anything else.

'I see she's still pissed at you,' Monroe observed.

'Yeah,' Declan replied morosely. 'Things aren't great at home.'

The main reason for this issue, however, was because Declan hadn't told Anjli her promotion would likely cost him his job when she gained it. She deserved the promotion, though, and he'd realised a few weeks before that a lot of the team had been holding back on their own promotions, knowing it could cost Declan his own job. So, he'd made the decision at the end of the last case to make sure promotions were given, and now Anjli and Billy had fulfilled their training, they were both officially promoted and fully qualified for the roles.

To save the immediate hassle, Declan had made out there was a budget for two DIs in the Unit, but last week there had been a conversation between Declan and Monroe that Anjli had overheard. And now she knew he'd been not only lying to her, but looking for new postings.

Suffice to say, she hadn't been happy about this.

Monroe, watching Anjli across the street, sighed, absent-mindedly scratching at his beard.

'I get what you're saying, laddie. But she'll come around, eventually.'

'I hope so,' Declan said. 'Because once I move, and let's be honest, Guv, I'm going to be moving, we're going to spend a lot less time together.'

'Well, that might not be a bad thing,' Monroe suggested. 'Absence makes the heart grow fonder and all that.'

Across the street, Sergeant Morten De'Geer, who was examining the stolen goods with his latex gloves on, looked up from the folio bag Sam had been carrying, now discarded on the pavement, another forensics officer beside him.

'Detective Inspector?' he shouted.

'Yes—' Declan turned half a second after Anjli replied the same answer.

De'Geer looked uncomfortable as he nodded towards Anjli.

'Sorry. I meant the other Detective Inspector, Guv.'

Declan motioned that he understood, smiled, and turned back to Monroe.

'Tell me you have something up your sleeve,' he said.

'Unless you want to go see our Prime Minister friend, see if you can blackmail him some more, I think we're a little bit stuck,' Monroe pursed his lips. 'Don't worry, laddie. I'll keep going to the very end.'

Declan didn't nod. Didn't say thanks. He didn't need to. He'd had this conversation more than once over the last couple of weeks. And Monroe knew very much he was starting to worry. Anjli, having spoken to De'Geer, walked over to them.

'So the expert's checked the painting, and it's the forgery,' she said. 'Sam hadn't swapped.'

'He hadn't?' Declan frowned. 'He went into the company, did his little "investigation" where he swapped the paintings, the whole thing. The receptionist has already given her statement stating as much.'

'Well, he has the forgery still, and unfortunately, there's

no crime to walking around the streets of London with a forgery in your pocket.'

'Shit,' Declan sighed. 'That gives us two options. One, he didn't do it because he knew we were watching, which means somebody tipped him off. Not us, but someone in Bishopsgate is going to have to take a long, hard look at themselves. Or ...'

'Or the painting in the building lobby was already a forgery,' Anjli grinned, forgetting for the moment she wasn't happy with Declan. 'Now that would be fun to discuss with them, once the CCTV from inside the building has been checked by Billy. Because if he swapped his forgery for another forgery ...'

'Whatever happens, it's their problem, not ours,' Declan said, pausing as Monroe's phone buzzed.

Looking down at it, the old Scot frowned.

'Alright,' he said. 'We're moving on.'

'Are we?' Declan was surprised by the abrupt turnaround. 'I thought you'd be looking into this forgery?'

'As you said, laddie, it's Bishopgate's problem,' Monroe looked around. 'We've got a new case. Back on Fleet Street, in fact.'

'Murder?' Anjli asked.

'Surprisingly not,' Monroe was already texting the others as he spoke. 'We do have somebody who many people probably *want* to murder though, found stabbed in a basement of St Bride's church.'

His statement and his texting finished, he looked up at Anjli and De'Geer, now walking over.

'Anjli, stay here for the moment. Finish up anything that's needed, then meet us at St Bride's. De'Geer, once you're finished, go help Doctor Marcos. She's already there.'

As Anjli and De'Geer walked off, already on task, Monroe turned to Declan.

'Come on then, let's go have a chat with a priest,' he said. 'I know how you love that. And if you punch them out, then your entire career at the Last Chance Saloon finishes with a nice, neat circle.'

2

CRIME SEEN

'So, what do we have?' Monroe asked the moment he walked into St Bride's, Declan following a couple of steps behind him. The church had been closed to the public, and the vicar stood nervously to the side, while a woman in her sixties was talking to Doctor Rosanna Marcos, the Unit's divisional surgeon. She wasn't in her custom grey PPE coveralls, instead in a pair of jeans and a tweed jacket over a T-shirt, and Declan wondered whether she simply hadn't placed them on yet, or even if she'd forgotten them for once.

'Not a lot to see up here,' Doctor Marcos said, noting Declan and Monroe and, after a farewell nod to the woman, she walked over. 'The victim, Hunt Robinson, was found in the crypt around seven-thirty this morning, in a small chapel at the end.'

'Maybe he was praying really early?' Declan suggested.

'They open for a service there every morning around eight, but I think he wasn't there by choice.'

'Aye? How so?'

'Well, for a start, he was tied to the floor, stabbed, and poisoned.'

As she waited for Declan and Monroe to digest this piece of news, Doctor Marcos looked around.

'Church usually opens by eight on a weekday, but people rarely come straight down to the crypt. The churchwarden set up early for the service of morning prayer, in the main crypt chapel. If the prayer had been cancelled, as it sometimes is, there's every chance Hunt would have bled out, and be found, well, less breathing than he is currently.'

'Where is Hunt Robinson now?'

'Ambulance took him away five minutes ago,' Doctor Marcos clicked her teeth with her tongue. 'To be honest, there wasn't much. He had marks on his wrists, likely from rope burns. He claimed he'd had some kind of poison, we need to check into that. The stab wound, in his side—' she motioned to her own side, around the kidney area '—and the blade that did it were the only major clues down there.'

She started walking towards the steps that led them down to the crypt and museum.

'Interesting thing, though,' she added. 'When found, he was incredibly confused. According to Mister Robinson, he was flying home from Ukraine yesterday. He'd been reporting in a war zone, and was absolutely exhausted. His newspaper had arranged a car for him – mainly to get him home in one piece – and while in it, he shut his eyes and the next thing he knows, he's waking up in the basement of a church.'

She nodded at PC Esme Cooper, waiting for them at the top of the stairs.

'PC Cooper has the fun part, though.'

Monroe raised his eyebrows at this.

'Oh, aye? Do tell.'

Cooper started reading from her notes.

'So, the car drove him directly home, according to the firm. We're checking into the flight, but Mister Robinson lived in Kent, so they'd have used the M25 from Heathrow, rather than driving through London. The only thing Mister Robinson would say, when he was being taken to hospital, was that he believed the water he had drunk inside the car had been drugged.'

'His own, or from the driver?'

'The driver offered him a bottle. It's quite standard with a lot of chauffeur-driven cars these days,' Cooper continued to read. 'You get free Wi-Fi, and water to drink. The last thing they want is you being pissed off and giving them less than five stars.'

'So what's the fun part?' Monroe frowned at Doctor Marcos. 'So far we have a man get in a car, get driven home, fall asleep and then wake up the following morning in a crypt.'

'It's Tuesday,' Doctor Marcos grinned. 'What day was his flight, Esme?'

'Sunday, Ma'am.'

Monroe nodded.

'So, we have a known and hated journalist, kidnapped on a Sunday night, kept God knows where all Monday, and then found tied up, poisoned and stabbed on a Tuesday, maybe as a sacrifice of some kind, in a chapel underneath the journalists church, but missing an entire a day,' he mused.

'How do we know he's known and hated?' confused by the comment, Declan asked, and Monroe was quite surprised by this question.

'Have you never heard of Robinson?' he asked, genuinely

amazed by this as Cooper stepped to the side so they could walk down the steps into the crypt first.

'Should I have?'

'He wrote a couple of hit pieces on you,' Monroe replied with a smile. 'Called you the "Charles Baker's go-to copper" in one of them.'

Declan grimaced.

'Well, he's not wrong, but yeah, now I know who you mean,' he said as they walked along a narrow pathway, away from the museum area, and with gravestones to their left. 'This is a bloody happy place, isn't it?'

'Boots and gloves from here,' Doctor Marcos replied, pulling her own on. Declan had realised now she hadn't worn her custom PPE suit because there'd been no body to examine, but at the same time she'd been wearing the gloves since they arrived. Declan just hadn't realised because he was so used to seeing them on her.

The crypt was tiny, and easier to observe from the door. To the right was an altar, a cross on the whitewashed wall behind it, and two glass images on either side giving the impression, lit from behind, of stained glass windows. On the left were the "pews" of the chapel, or, rather, a white, convex half circle bench, made from marble or stone, with eight glass "chair backs" behind eight black cushions. The bench was held up by six supports, and around the furthest of these to the left and right was looped a silk rope, long enough to travel to the middle of the crypt on either side, where, next to the bloodstain, each looped end once held a wrist.

'Churchwarden found him with his head facing the seats, arms spread,' Doctor Marcos explained. 'Knife was a folding one, and had been tossed behind the altar, no attempt to hide it, the iron gate closed.'

Monroe looked around the scene.

'How tight were the ropes?'

'Not too tight, it's a slip knot on each loop, so once the hand was in, struggling would have tightened it. But it's silk, and silk gives a little.'

She pointed at the rope.

'I think they stabbed him before they tied him, and he fought,' she said. 'He has traces of blood on his hand, and the left wrist loop has traces on it.'

'The blood wiped onto the rope when they secured him,' Declan pursed his lips. 'Fingerprints on the knife?'

'Wiped,' Doctor Marcos muttered. 'Looks like they used a handkerchief or something, probably from Hunt's own clothes, discarded on the bench.'

'He was naked?'

'No, Guv, he was in his trousers and socks, but his shirt, jacket and shoes had been folded and left at the back,' Cooper commented.

Declan looked back at the bench.

'So someone drugged Hunt, brought him here, poisoned him, stripped him, stabbed him, tied him ... but folded his clothes?'

Cooper looked apologetically at Declan.

'Yes,' she replied. 'Apparently. That's what Marjorie – the churchwarden said.'

Declan looked back at the floor of the crypt.

'This feels ritualistic, Masonic even, but at the same time, there's something off,' he said, but paused as, from the back of the crypt, he saw De'Geer hurrying towards them.

'Guvs, Doc, we have company,' he said, nodding back at the main entrance. 'Sinclair's upstairs.'

'Who?' Monroe frowned, and De'Geer paled.

'I'm sorry, I meant to say Commander Sinclair is upstairs,' De'Geer replied. 'Seems this is his local church.'

Declan looked across at Monroe, seeing the same confused expression as his. The City of London Police had a slightly different rank structure than the Metropolitan Police. Whereas the Met rose from Constable to Commissioner, with the structure going Constable / Sergeant / Inspector / Chief Inspector / Superintendent / Chief Superintendent / Commander / Deputy Assistant Commissioner / Assistant Commissioner / Deputy Commissioner and finally Commissioner, the City of London had a smaller remit, and so at the top it went Commander / Assistant Commissioner / Commissioner. Edward Sinclair was therefore the third highest ranking officer in the City of London police, and for him to even venture out of his Guildhall office meant something bad.

'Do we need to call Bullman about this?' he asked. 'She's closer to Chief Superintendent Bradbury than we are, and Sinclair's his boss.'

'Aye, but Bradbury's remit straddles the Met and City line,' Monroe was already leaving the crypt, heading to the stairs. 'He's been based in Scotland Yard more than Guildhall for the last two years, so the chances are he's not up to speed either.'

Walking up the stairs and emerging into the church once more, Declan saw Anjli beside a new arrival. He was in his sixties, slim, with an aristocratic face, everything very angular and sharp. He looked like Charles Dance, if he was a marathon runner. His hair was greying, but held under a cap, and he bore an expression that screamed out "don't mess with me."

'Sir,' Monroe said, his voice showing a hint of caution as

he glanced around. 'We didn't expect you. Honestly? We never expect you.'

Commander Sinclair gave the briefest of smiles before looking at Declan.

'Walsh,' he said, holding out a hand. 'We've never met formerly. I knew your father well. He was a good man.'

Not well enough to attend his funeral or send flowers, Declan thought to himself as he shook the Commander's hand.

'Thank you, sir,' he said, resisting the urge to add how his father had not only probably never heard of Sinclair, but also didn't have a file on him.

No. Wait. There was one.

Declan must have frowned as he thought this, as Sinclair mimicked his expression.

'Something wrong?' he asked.

'Sorry sir, working through the case,' Declan lied. 'I hear you attend the church?'

'I used to, back in the day,' Sinclair nodded, looking around the nave. 'Haven't for a few years now, the Guildhall work keeps me busy. But I also knew Robinson, and I was passing by.'

Declan nodded, forcing himself not to look towards Monroe at this line. There was no way Sinclair could have been "passing by" – this was a deliberate visit.

'I've been brought up to speed on the case,' Sinclair now turned his attention back to Monroe, the senior officer on the scene. 'Was anything missing?'

'Sir?'

'Items of clothing, personal effects, anything like that?'

'Yes, sir,' Cooper spoke now, flipping to the relevant sheet in her notebook. 'His phone was missing, as was his wallet.'

'Any bags?'

'They were apparently inside a satchel, so yes, sir.'

Declan narrowed his eyes at the question.

'Sir, you seem to know something we don't,' he said carefully. 'It'd be a great help if you shared it.'

Commander Sinclair considered the request and nodded.

'Hunt Robinson, pardon my language, was a complete arse,' he explained. 'I butted heads with him many times over the years, mainly when I was a Detective Superintendent at Bishopsgate, and mainly because he was always in the wrong bloody place at the right bloody time, like a typical journalist.'

He took off his cap, as if suddenly realising he'd left it on when entering the church.

'The reason he got away with so much was his little black book of blackmails,' he continued. 'He was a solid investigative reporter when he wanted to be, but he preferred to bank these up, write them down, and use them when he needed something done. Celebrities, politicians, Olympians – you name it, if they were important, he had all their dirty little secrets in there.'

Declan started to get why Sinclair was asking this.

'He never digitised it, never copied it, that book, to my knowledge, was welded to his hip, and with him at all times. Probably so full by now he wrote in the margins, but he never replaced it, and he wouldn't have let it out of his sight.'

Monroe nodded. 'You think this is a theft?'

'I'm guessing you don't have the book then, DCI Monroe,' Sinclair replied. 'And if it's not here, when it should be here...'

'There was no book found,' Cooper helpfully added. 'Or satchel, sir.'

'You've got a radioactive death pit out there, Monroe,' Sinclair mused, looking towards the door. 'The people that book could destroy is possibly in the hundreds, not including collateral damage. And someone has it.'

'We'll get on it, sir,' Monroe straightened. 'Thanks for the heads up.'

But Sinclair had already moved on, heading down the stairs to look at the scene of the crime.

Watching him leave, Monroe grimaced.

'He's in the bloody book,' he muttered. 'Has to be. Nobody comes and takes a personal interest like this unless they've got something to lose. Not once has that bugger visited us since we opened. And now he's here, all smiles, offering whatever we need? Wee bastard's scared of something.'

'I'm guessing you don't get on, by your florid terminology?' Declan grinned.

'My florid terminology?' Monroe laughed at the comment. 'Aye, he's an alright copper. But he's a shifty one. And Patrick hated his guts.'

'Why?'

'You've now met the man,' Monroe sighed as he walked towards the main entrance. 'Imagine working beside him for years.'

Declan went to follow, but stopped as his phone buzzed. Seeing this, Monroe waved him to continue as he left for some fresh air, and, standing in the church's nave, Declan opened the text message. It was from DCI Sampson, the officer Declan had butted heads with over the Robin Hood event murders. He'd written a nice report about Jess though, so Declan had changed his opinion of him.

He hadn't spoken to him in a while, so this was a surprise.

Declan. Hear you might need a new job. DI
opening in my office if you need it. Call me.

Declan stared at the message for a long moment. Sampson was a Thames Valley DCI, and Declan hadn't contacted him. Which begged the question: how did he know about this? Monroe? Declan hadn't seen Monroe as that close to the man. But a job offer was a job offer, and in a week, he'd have nothing. So, tapping out a quick message, saying he was in the middle of a case and he'd call later in the week, he placed his phone away, looking up—

To see Anjli standing there in front of him.

'Why's Sinclair here?' she asked.

'Apparently he has a connection,' Declan replied, thrown by the sudden appearance. 'Boss thinks it's bullshit and he's here for himself.'

'I agree,' Anjli nodded as she glanced at the steps to the crypt. 'He's a prick.'

'You know him?'

Anjli nodded as they both walked towards the main entrance.

'When I was kicked out of Mile End, he fought for my dismissal,' she said. 'He wanted me gone, Declan. I'd never met the man, and he did his best to end my career for nothing.'

She stopped.

'Or, rather, because I wasn't the type of detective he wanted in his force. Not *white* enough.'

'That's a hell of an accusation,' Declan replied, his voice lowering. 'And one you might not want to repeat.'

'I'll tell you what,' Anjli forced a smile, but it was a bitter one. 'When you become my superior again, *Guv*, then you can tell me what to do.'

And, this said, Anjli turned and left the nave, leaving Declan standing alone.

'Yeah, she's still pissed at me,' he muttered to himself, before walking over to the north-east end of the church, and the Journalists Altar.

He'd been told it was here, and as he scanned the photos of fallen journalists, he paused as he spied the smiling face of Kendis Taylor.

'Hey,' he whispered, stroking the cheek of the smiling, long-dead woman in the photo. 'If you have any suggestions on what I should be doing with my life, I'd really like to know.'

This done, he gave a brief prayer, nodded to the ceiling and left the church.

3

BRIEFING ENCOUNTER

'ALL RIGHT, MY LITTLE CHICKADEES,' MONROE SAID AS HE stood at the front of the team, now in the briefing room, the plasma screen behind him. 'Tell me what we have.'

The briefing room was full – Declan and Anjli sat in their usual chairs on the right, Billy, with laptop, sat at the table on the left, while De'Geer, Cooper and Doctor Marcos were at the back. The only person missing was Bullman, who'd been out all morning.

'Hunt Robinson, sixty-four years old, found half naked, tied to the floor, stabbed and poisoned,' Cooper read dutifully from her notebook. 'St Bride's churchwarden Marjorie Boynton found him around seven in the morning, while preparing for the morning's prayers. She had no idea how long he'd been there, however, and the last recorded appearance of Mister Robinson was on the Sunday night, when he was picked up by a car from Heathrow Terminal five, after returning from Ukraine where he'd been working as a war correspondent.'

'Okay, so tell me about the scene,' Monroe looked over at Billy. 'CCTV?'

Billy shook his head.

'The church has CCTV,' he replied. 'But in the early hours of last night, there wasn't any. For some reason, the entire network was down – most of Fleet Street didn't seem to have any.'

'That sounds a little suspicious,' Declan muttered.

'It happens more than you'd expect,' Billy shrugged. 'Sundays in the City are quiet, so often maintenance is scheduled for then.'

'So no CCTV for the moment,' Monroe sighed. 'Because why the hell would we want it easy? What do we know about the driver?'

'Yusuf Mohamed, thirty-seven, has worked for the company for the last four years,' Billy read from his laptop screen as, behind Monroe, the image of Yusuf now appeared on the plasma screen. 'Somalian refugee at the age of thirteen, no priors, no problems, and he's been a British citizen for the last five years.'

'Do we have a statement?'

'Yes, Guv. We contacted the cab company, they contacted him, and he came back quickly.' Billy now read from his notes. 'He explained that Mister Robinson had been sleepy when he arrived, was stressed about something, and shut his eyes after doing some work. Apparently, he was asleep all the way to his home in Kent.'

'And then what happened?'

'Nothing,' Billy replied, shrugging. 'According to Yusuf, he helped Mister Robinson to the door as he was quite tired, and Mister Robinson opened it, entered his house and then closed it behind him. Job done, Yusuf went home.'

'Any witnesses in the house?'

'He's married, but his wife hasn't been around for the last couple of days, something to do with a Wellness retreat in Chelmsford,' Anjli spoke now, looking at her own notes.

'Robinson wasn't Yusuf's last job of the day,' Billy added. 'He also picked somebody up at Gatwick at ten that evening and took them back to the other side of London. And the cars all have trackers, so we'd see if he went back that night.'

'Not that it had to be the Sunday night,' Monroe mused aloud. 'He's disappeared somewhere between Sunday and Monday, after all.'

He looked to the back of the briefing room.

'Doctor Marcos?'

The Temple Inn divisional surgeon nodded, rising from her chair next to De'Geer and walking to the front. She nodded to Billy who, pressing some keys on his laptop, opened up an image of the victim.

'Hunt Robinson was poisoned, stabbed, tied and left for dead,' she said. 'However, not all of these were there to kill him.'

'How do you mean?' Declan asked.

'Well, the blade itself wasn't a deep cut, not what I would call a killing blow,' she explained. 'He was poisoned, but they believed it was with shellfish.'

'Shellfish?'

'Apparently, according to his Wikipedia page, Hunt Robinson is allergic to it,' Dr Marcos explained. 'Incredibly so. And toxicology just came back with a report; it looks like he'd ingested about four grams of chitosan supplements two hours before he was found, so around five in the morning. It's often used as a weight loss aid, as it's believed to help block the absorption of dietary fat and cholesterol, improving cholesterol levels and reducing inflammation. Very easy to get hold of over the counter.'

'Let me guess, chitosan uses shellfish?'

'It's a supplement derived from chitin, a substance found in the shells of crustaceans such as shrimp, crab, and lobster, so yes,' Doctor Marcos nodded. 'My hypothesis is they – whoever "they" are – forced these tablets down his throat, and expected him to have some kind of anaphylactic shock and die.'

'Then why stab him?' Declan frowned.

'Purely because they didn't like him, I'd assume,' Doctor Marcos replied with a slight smile. 'Or maybe they hoped by doing this, it'd weaken him, maybe help the poison go through his system. Unfortunately, they hadn't realised his allergy to shellfish was nothing more than an over-statement.'

She waggled a finger.

'Never blindly trust Wikipedia,' she intoned ominously. 'His editor informed us he simply didn't like eating shellfish, it sometimes gave him a bad stomach, so there was a minor allergy, but nothing too serious, but Robinson decided he'd rather tell people he was fatally allergic than repeatedly explain why he didn't want to eat it.'

'Makes sense,' Anjli said. 'I've told people I was allergic to aspects of their cooking before.'

'Like what?' Billy asked.

'Pretty much anything my mum cooks for a start,' Anjli replied, to a chuckle of laughter from the room.

'So, let me get this right.' Declan was writing in his note-book as he spoke. 'Hunt Robinson was "poisoned" by shell-fish, of which his attempted murderers believed would kill him – but it did nothing more than give him a bad stomach, and he was stabbed because they wanted to weaken or hurt him, and *that* did more damage?'

'Pretty much, yes,' Doctor Marcos replied. 'They didn't even catch anything vital. Most rubbish murder attempt ever. Well, since someone tried to ram Monroe's head through a window, anyway. That was a pretty rubbish attempt.'

'Tell me about the knife,' Monroe asked, wincing at the memory.

'Well, to be honest, there's not much to tell,' Doctor Marcos replied sadly. 'It's a butterfly knife, a folding-out one. You can buy them at a million stores in the UK, probably bought online, or maybe even bought in a small military shop over the counter with cash.'

She nodded to Billy, who clicked another photo onto the screen; this time a sketch of Robinson, laid out, with the blood spatter marked onto it.

'They stabbed him while he was standing,' she said, pointing at the blood on the sketch. 'You can see here that the immediate blood flow was brought downwards by gravity, which wouldn't have happened if he was prone. They then wiped the blade down, removing the fingerprints, and tossed it behind the altar.'

'Do we know what they wiped it down with, Ma'am?' Cooper asked.

Doctor Marcos nodded to Billy, and another photo appeared on the screen; this time it was a crime scene photo taken earlier that morning, showing Hunt Robinson's crumpled shirt.

'This is the shirt we found folded over on the pew, the seats, whatever you want to call them – the weird half circle of marble that people seem to want to sit on,' she replied. 'As you can see here, it has blood on it. I believe once they stabbed him, they wiped their fingerprints off the hilt with the shirt, tossed the knife to the other end of the crypt, folded the shirt, and left.'

'Do we have fingerprints or DNA on the shirt?' Declan asked.

'We're checking,' Doctor Marcos nodded. 'There's also traces of blood on Robinson's left hand, which might have been from some kind of defensive fight, and this was passed onto the silk rope when they secured him.'

'Do we know anybody who had reason to do this?' Anjli asked, looking up from her notebook.

'Take a number, sit at the back of the queue,' Monroe replied, now rising from his position of leaning against Billy's desk and returning to the front of the room. 'He wasn't liked by anybody.'

'In fact, even his own editor wasn't impressed with him,' Billy added. 'We spoke a few minutes ago, and he said he had to fight tooth and nail to get Robinson to even *go* to the war zone, when ten years ago he would have jumped at the chance.'

'What's changed in that time?'

'He's got older,' Monroe replied, holding a finger to stop Declan from continuing. 'Before you speak, poor Esme at the back has been jiggling about like a coke-head leprechaun, waiting to speak.'

Cooper blushed as she stood back up, checking her notes before speaking.

'It was just one thing,' she said. 'When I was at the scene, when they were taking Mister Robinson to the hospital, he became incredibly agitated.'

'Well, if I'd been stabbed and poisoned, I think I would as well,' Monroe smiled. 'What stuck out for you?'

'He wanted to know where his bag was,' Cooper continued. 'He said he had a satchel, and in the satchel was a book. He was very distraught when he realised it wasn't there.'

'I bet he was,' Monroe looked at Declan. 'I believe it wasn't so much the satchel as the book itself. And there was nothing at the scene of the crime?'

'No sir,' Cooper continued. 'Only the shirt, shoes and the jacket had been placed at the back. The trousers, pants and socks were still being worn by Mister Robinson. Everything else was missing, including his wallet, his phone and apparently this satchel.'

'To be clear, he might not have had it on him anyway,' Declan suggested. 'I mean, he had it on Sunday, but we don't know what happened in the time between.'

'Aye, but we do know the bag, or more likely the book inside it is important,' Monroe said. 'Sinclair climbing out of his spider's web was enough to see that, and we know the book is – what was the term we were told? Oh yes, a "death pit," something with enough ammo within to destroy people.'

'Maybe this was why Mister Robinson was taken? Somebody getting revenge?' De'Geer suggested.

'Or, maybe they took the book because they want to destroy it,' Declan suggested. 'If you had a secret in there so bad it could kill your career, maybe even end your life?'

Monroe nodded. 'Anything else before we continue?' he asked, before turning to Billy, currently holding his hand up. 'Billy, I've told you a dozen times you don't have to put your hand up, laddie.'

Billy shrugged. 'I like being polite,' he replied with a hint of a smile. 'It stands me out from the rest of you.'

'Go on then, out with it,' ignoring the jibe, Monroe waved a hand.

'When I spoke to Robinson's editor, he said he'd spoken to Robinson in Ukraine on Sunday, before the flight, and he said Robinson was angry at him.'

'Oh, aye? And why would that be?' Monroe leant closer, eager to listen.

'Apparently he'd been scooped on something he claimed was his,' Billy checked his own notes again. 'Lucy-Rachel Adams, some soap actress, reality star, singer – you know, the whole shebang. Something came out this weekend in the *Mail on Sunday,* claiming she had been a serial kleptomaniac for years. It was a bit tawdry, but it was a story Hunt Robinson had been sitting on for a while, and felt *he* should have broken. And the fact it came out while he was in a war zone made him think it was deliberate.'

'Do we have the name of the journalist who broke the story? Maybe there's a link there?'

'I can check into that,' Billy noted down the request. 'His editor said he'd been told by Robinson to print it, but he'd "spiked" it, held back on it.'

'And the reason why?'

'Possibly because of the paper's audience, sir,' Billy shrugged. 'The paper's called *The Individual,* and it's aimed a little left of the slightly right wing *GB News* market. Probably felt something the *Mail on Sunday* would put in their "sidebar of shame" wasn't what he wanted to print. But Hunt Robinson was suitably annoyed about it.'

He flipped a page.

'And there were the attempts to steal it,' he added. 'Two attempts over the last year to gain the book, or at least his satchel. The first about eight months ago, when Robinson claimed someone had burgled his house but, after turning everything over, they hadn't taken anything, including his expensive television and games system. And then a few months later, he had his satchel taken by two men on a moped while walking down the street.'

'That's a common thing these days, maybe not such a reach—'

'Yes, boss, but they found the bag a hundred yards down the road, completely intact. His laptop, his phone, everything was still in there.'

'Almost as if they wanted to find a particular item,' Declan suggested. 'The book?'

'It'd been in his office at the time, locked in his desk.'

Monroe pursed his lips, considering this.

'So now we know he has a book that's been taken, a book we know has secrets within and that he's very precious of. There's a missing day, somewhere, somebody tried to poison him, and they definitely attacked him. And as yet, we have no CCTV to explain the situation.'

'It could be one of several things,' Anjli suggested. 'It could be somebody annoyed that he had a secret on them, someone deciding to take matters into their own hand, it could be somebody annoyed at a story he's already revealed, or it could be somebody who knows there's a secret in the book, something that could hurt them, and want to get rid of it, while also getting rid of Robinson at the same time.'

'Okay, so it's attempted murder and possible theft,' Monroe said. 'Declan, I want you to go speak to this editor. Perhaps he might give you something more about what happened. Anjli, Cooper, go see Mister Robinson in hospital, see if there's anything else he can tell us. Maybe he's remembered something, or perhaps he's gained some more information from his missing time. Rosanna, check over everything. See if there's anything we've missed. Billy, find me some

CCTV. There's got to be something we can check from five am this morning. Maybe even check his phone, see if it's been on at all over the weekend, or made any calls. And De'Geer, you're with me. I want to look at Robinson's Kent house.'

As the team stood up, preparing for their tasks, Declan took the moment to walk over to Monroe, gathering his own notes.

'DCI Sampson?' he asked, watching Monroe as if the name itself would be enough to explain why he was asking.

'Am I supposed to know the name, laddie?'

'That depends,' Declan replied, 'on whether you aimed him at me to give me a job.'

'Sampson?' Monroe was surprised by the accusation. 'Wait, you mean the Robin Hood convention guy? The man's an absolute bellend! I wouldn't get him to contact you, there's better people out there! I would have gone to DCI Freeman in Maidenhead! At least that way, you wouldn't have to travel far for your commute!'

Declan held up a hand in surrender.

'Well if you didn't, who did?'

He stopped, however, as he saw Bullman lean out of her office. She had obviously returned during the briefing, and decided not to attend.

'Walsh. Office. Now.'

'Oh, it looks like you're in trouble, laddie,' Monroe smiled. 'Glad it's not me for a change.'

Ignoring the gleeful chuckles from the DCI, Declan walked over to Bullman's office, knocking on the door before entering.

Bullman was already sitting at her desk, her short white hair giving her an impression of severity, whereas Declan knew she was actually quite relaxed at the best of times, and sometimes even quite abusive in an annoying, jocular kind of way. She had a thing for giving him annoying nicknames, but seeing her expression, he was sure this wasn't one of those times.

'Ma'am,' he said.

'Got a problem, want to talk to you about it,' she said without looking up from her laptop. 'I want to talk to you about your daughter.'

'Jess?' Declan was surprised by this. 'What about her?'

'We've got her scheduled to come in for work experience from tomorrow now she's heading towards the Easter holidays,' Bullman replied. 'Is that correct?'

'Yes, Ma'am. She's coming in for two weeks.'

'I want to delay her,' Bullman said. 'She can do one week, but not two. Tell her she can come in next week instead.'

'Can I ask why?' Declan was a bit confused by the request.

Finally, Bullman looked up from her desk, staring Declan directly in the eyes.

'Because, DI Walsh, if we bring her in this week, it means that she spends the first week of her time here during your *last* week.'

Declan felt ice slide down his spine.

'You don't want her here while I leave?' he asked.

'I'd prefer not to. It's no secret I think she's a good potential officer. And I've stated many times I'd have her on my team when she qualifies. But, right now, she's a seventeen-year-old girl who's about to come in and work on a case, while her dad struggles to find a job.'

'Ma'am, with the best will in the world, it's not up to me,' Declan shook his head. 'It's up to her. She knows I'm running to the end of my secondment. I rely on her to make her own decisions.'

Bullman watched Declan for a long few seconds, as if weighing up the options.

'Fine, I'll see her tomorrow,' she said. 'But you need to go see your Prime Minister friend and blackmail him again or something, because I'd rather not be giving your goodbye drinks while she's still eager to join.'

Declan said nothing, and after another moment, Bullman looked back up.

'I'm doing what I can, Declan,' she said sadly. 'But right now, we need a miracle.'

'That's fine,' Declan forced a smile as he walked to the door to the office. 'We're the Last Chance Saloon. Miracles are what we excel in.'

4

VISITING HOURS

Unlike Declan, Anjli hadn't spent a lot of time with journalists, but she had spent enough time to know how they worked. Cooper, on the other hand, was still quite new to this. So, as they entered the wardroom to find an irritated and rather agitated Hunt Robinson watching them, Anjli knew without a doubt this would not be an easy interview.

'They aren't letting me out,' Hunt Robinson said angrily, as if Anjli or Cooper had the magical power to sort this. 'They stapled me together, and they've fixed me up, but they won't let me leave this bloody building.'

Anjli nodded, smiled, and tried her best "good cop" look.

'Mister Robinson,' she said. 'I'm Detective Inspector Kapoor, of the City of London Police. This is PC Cooper. We'd like to ask you some questions.'

'If it gets me out of this bloody ward, then I'm thrilled to do so,' Robinson muttered, settling back into his bed. 'This is stupid. I'm fine.'

Anjli looked at her watch.

'Six hours ago, sir, you were found in a state that

suggested you were very much *not* okay,' she replied calmly. 'You were stabbed, poisoned and left for dead in the crypt of a journalist church. I'm sorry if you think you should be able to leave, but you lost a lot of blood. And the doctors have said they want to keep you in for a night at least, for observation.'

'Oh for God's sake!' Robinson made a motion on his tray table, as if swiping everything off a desk. There was nothing on the tray to swipe off, though, and the motion was pointless. But he seemed to feel better, as he settled back onto his bed again.

'Ask your questions,' he grumbled. 'Although what I'd rather know is an update on where my bloody satchel is.'

'Do you remember where you were yesterday?' Cooper asked.

'Yes,' Robinson said, a little mockery in his tone. 'I was in a war zone.'

'No, sir. That was the day before yesterday,' unfazed, Cooper continued.

'To me, it was yesterday,' Robinson replied. 'If you wanted to know what happened, what I was doing on Monday? You should have asked.'

'I believe she did,' Anjli had already taken a massive dislike to the man, as she interrupted in Cooper's defence. 'Let's try again. Do you remember what you were doing chronologically yesterday? Not physically or mentally? Can you at least tell me your last memory?'

'Absolutely,' Robinson said, leaning a little closer as he spoke. 'I was in Ukraine, covering a war zone. I caught a British Airways flight back into Heathrow. During that time. I did some work. I came through customs, and then I found my driver, who drove me back to my house.'

He narrowed his eyes.

'He poisoned me.'

'Could you explain that, please?'

'The water,' Robinson nodded conspiratorially. 'It was poisoned, or drugged, I should say. He gave me a water bottle. I gulped it, probably too quickly. Then, after about ten minutes, I fell asleep. I don't think I even finished a second bottle.'

Anjli wrote this down in her notebook.

'Do you think you could have just been exhausted, sir?' she asked politely. 'And that you fell asleep in the car?'

'I've been a journalist for thirty-plus years,' Robinson exclaimed. 'I can sleep anywhere. But I can also keep myself awake when a story requires.'

'And did the story require you staying awake, sir?' Cooper asked now.

Robinson looked at her now, as if finally acknowledging her presence.

'I was drugged,' he repeated. 'And then I found myself in a crypt, tied up, stabbed and left to die.'

Anjli politely nodded for a second time.

'I get that, sir. And we're trying to work out who did this,' she said. 'But you're making it a little difficult for us, by not knowing where you were on the Monday.'

Hunt Robinson folded his arms, wincing a little as the action tightened the muscles around his stomach.

'Well, I'm so sorry that I've been causing you problems with your workday,' he replied snarkily. 'I'd so hate to be the burden of bad news.'

Anjli ignored the comment as she carried on writing.

'Okay, let's look at what you do know. Did anything happen on the plane?' she asked. 'Was there anybody there who could have passed you a drink that was drugged instead?'

'Perhaps it was in your system before you got in the car,' Cooper added helpfully.

'Only the flight attendants, and to be perfectly honest, they were as rubbish as usual.'

Robinson looked over at Cooper.

'You made the right choice becoming a copper, love. Flight attendant is a shit job. They never give you what you need, they never treat you as you should be treated.'

'And how's that, Mister Robinson?'

'If you pay a lot of money for business class, you expect a service comparable to the amount you pay,' Robinson grumbled, the issue obviously still eating at him. 'The Wi-Fi was rubbish too. I couldn't get on it for the entire flight.'

'Yes,' Anjli wrote this down in her notebook. 'Your editor said you'd been angry over a scooped story, and weren't able to talk about it while you were flying.'

'Scooped story?' Robinson shook his head. 'That dopey prick. It was more than a scooped bloody story. I'd had it for years. He knew I wanted to put it out somewhere – it was tabloid gold. I'd written it in full and stuck it on his desk.'

'Not emailed?'

'I don't do emails. I do it as proper journalists do. Hard copy,' Robinson snapped. 'It was ready to go. And that coward damn well sat on it.'

He looked away, his face reddening with anger.

'I bet he talks about it now, though,' he growled. 'Now the *Mail on Sunday*'s put it out, I bet he's all over it.'

'Are there any other stories out there you'd written that hadn't happened? Stories from your black book, perhaps?'

Robinson smiled.

'Ah,' he nodded now, understanding. 'You've worked out why I was attacked.'

'It's a line of inquiry, sir, nothing more.'

Hunt Robinson relaxed, strangely calm now that the book could be mentioned.

'I have a book that has secrets about people,' he said. 'I've got enough enemies who'd want to take it, but at the same time, I don't think they'd do what someone did to me. Most of them wouldn't lose their careers, and they'd know better than to cross me, because even though I've lost the book, a lot of it's still up here.'

He tapped the side of his head for emphasis.

'When was the last time you saw your book? Was it on the flight?'

Robinson nodded, as if silently confirming the story with himself.

'I had to check it, after I realised the story had got out,' he explained. 'It was in my satchel when I got into the car, but it wasn't with me when I woke.'

'Could it be at home?'

'Why would it be at home?' Robinson said. 'Remember that American Express card advert? "American Express – don't leave home without it?" Well, that's my book.'

'Yes, sir. But as we've already worked out, you have a missing day where we don't know what happened,' Anjli was fighting the urge to strangle the injured journalist. 'Could you, hypothetically, have left your house without it?'

'And my phone and my wallet?' Robinson shook his head. 'Jesus Christ. I thought the police were supposed to be intelligent these days. How about you find me some Met Police? Maybe they're better?'

Anjli was angering now, but forcing herself to keep her face calm.

'Why a silk rope?' she asked to change the subject.

Hunt Robinson went to snap off a sarcastic reply, but he'd had an answer planned for a different question and now paused, his face frowning, his mouth opening and shutting a couple of times.

'What do you mean?'

'The rope they used to tie you up was silk,' Anjli continued, enjoying Robinson's discomfort. 'Do you think it was some kind of ritualistic accessory? That being left to die in a crypt under a journalist church, a silk rope tying you up was some kind of Masonic execution?'

At this, Hunt Robinson paused, frowned again, and then laughed.

'Oh my God,' he said. 'You're serious, aren't you? Masonic connection! You've been reading too many bloody Dan Brown books. There's no Masonic connection here. I'm a freeman of London.'

Anjli and Cooper both knew what being a freeman of London meant, as they'd dealt with a couple in a recent case.

'I get what a freeman is,' Cooper looked at Anjli for help. 'I don't understand the silk rope part?'

'A freeman of the City of London has the right not to be hanged with a normal rope,' Robinson replied. 'Instead, they're hanged with a silk rope. It means there's less marks around the neck when they're pulled down.'

'So basically, the silk rope is purely for cosmetic effect?'

'I suppose so,' Robinson accepted this.

'But you weren't being hanged,' Cooper added. 'You were tied to the floor.'

'I was still being executed,' Robinson argued, and Anjli

almost felt there was a hint of pride, of arrogance in the fact that somebody had deemed him important enough to execute. Like he'd made it somehow. 'So perhaps I was being executed with a silk rope, as befitted my station?'

Anjli wrote this down in her notebook.

'How well known is it you're a freeman of London?' she asked.

'I've attended Stationer's Guild meetings for over twenty years now,' Robinson shrugged. 'I'm guessing people out there know I have the freedom of the city. I don't really shout it out, though. It's not on my Wikipedia page, or anything.'

'But it's out there,' Anjli mused as she tapped her pen against her lips. 'That could narrow down the list of suspects. If they've given you a silk rope to die with, it means they know you're a freeman of London; and if they know that, it places them in a slightly higher category than some random killer who's been told to murder you.'

Robinson looked a little nervous at that point.

'Have you had death threats recently, sir?'

'No, none at all. Well, the usual ones, I suppose,' Robinson replied. 'I mean, I've just come from a war zone. So I had quite a few people trying to shoot me.'

'And from the UK, for instance?'

Robinson didn't reply.

'Sir?' Cooper pressed.

'No,' white-faced, Robinson shook his head vigorously. 'Someone who's trying to kill me, or threatening to kill me? I would remember.'

Anjli leant closer to the bed.

'Mister Robinson, if you are deliberately holding something back, you are deliberately obstructing the course of justice,' she whispered sweetly; the paling of his face hadn't gone unnoticed. 'This might be a witness statement, but it could quite easily turn into an interview once they let you out.'

'Then you'll have to interview me,' Robinson snapped back. 'With my solicitor sitting beside me, which she should be doing here, because this is turning into a bit of a witch hunt. You don't like my work, I'm guessing. You seem to have decided already that somebody wants me killed for personal reasons, but what if I've stumbled on some massive conspiracy? What if Westminster themselves want me dead, because I'm getting too close to some terrible, election-destroying secret?'

Anjli watched Hunt Robinson dispassionately for a few moments.

'Are you?' she asked.

Robinson didn't answer this. Instead, he waved his hands, backtracking.

'The point I'm trying to make is that you don't know anything, *Detective Inspector,*' he replied. 'And if you don't mind, the one o'clock news is about to start, and I'd like to see if I'm on it.'

Anjli nodded to Cooper, and the two of them moved to the ward's door.

'Don't go anywhere,' she said, almost mockingly. 'We might have some more questions for you.'

'Put them through my solicitor,' Robinson replied, staring away from them. 'I'll get her to call.'

'Can't wait.'

The conversation now over, Anjli and Cooper left the ward in silence, only speaking once they were certain they were out of earshot.

'Thoughts?' Anjli asked as they walked down the stairwell.

'Professional or candid?'

'We're always candid in the Last Chance Saloon,' Anjli smiled. 'Thoughts?'

'He's a prick, Ma'am,' Cooper replied. 'An arrogant, self-entitled prick. But, he's terrified.'

'Being stabbed does that.'

'No, it's more than that,' Cooper opened the doors for them to pass through as she continued. 'He's terrified of something else. The wound, the missing time, it almost feels like to him it's an inconvenience, an annoyance. But the moment you asked about people having issues with him, he paled and tried to poo-poo it away.'

'I saw that too,' Anjli nodded. 'Almost like he knew someone was after him.'

'So what's the next step?'

Anjli shook her head, walking out of the hospital entrance and heading towards the car park.

'I think we need to check into Mister Robinson a little more,' she said. 'He might be the victim here, but I think there's more going on than he's letting on.'

―――――

BACK IN THE WARD, HUNT ROBINSON LEANT BACK ONTO THE pillow behind him and shut his eyes, forcing himself not to let the panic overcome him. He'd been taught breathing exercises years earlier, and he used these now, forcing air into his lungs for the count of four, holding for seven and then exhaling slowly for eight. He'd been told once this was a way the military went to sleep anywhere, as you were effectively starving the brain of oxygen, and forcing it to stop worrying about shit that wasn't important.

And more than anything, Hunt Robinson needed to stop thinking.

One of the nurses popped her head through the door.

'You okay, Mister Robinson?' she asked.

Opening his eyes, and irritated she'd broken his count, Robinson glared at her.

'Do I look okay?'

'Well, you look better than you did when they brought you in,' the nurse smiled, not bothered by Robinson's bad mood. 'Hey, we didn't want to interrupt while the police were here, but you had a message.'

'I did?' Robinson frowned. Nobody knew he was here, except for Janine. 'Was it my wife?'

'I didn't take the message so I don't know, but I believe it was a woman,' the nurse said, pulling a piece of folded paper from her pocket which turned out to be a post-it note. 'It simply says, "Get well soon, but remember what you owe me."'

She frowned.

'Doesn't sound very wife-y.'

Robinson fought down the utter terror as he nodded, forcing a weak smile.

'Personal joke,' he said, nodding. 'Thanks.'

The nurse smiled and left, and Hunt Robinson stared up at the ceiling.

He had a week.

Luckily, he'd *started early.*

5

EDITORIAL REVIEW

'I HAVE TO SAY, DECLAN, I EXPECTED A COUPLE MORE STORIES out of you before you trundled off into the sunset,' Sean Ashby gave a grin as he sipped at his double-strength coffee, facing Declan across the table. 'You sure you don't want any of the sausage roll?'

Declan smiled in return and shook his head, taking a mouthful of his flat white. At least he thought it was a flat white as he'd ordered a flat white, but considering the road-side cafe they were in, he didn't even know if they understood what one was.

He glanced at the mug; it read WORLD'S GREATEST DENTIST. He didn't want to ask why such a mug was in a cafe off the M25 so he placed it back down.

'You sure you don't want a pasty?' he asked. Usually Sean had a Cornish pasty in his mouth when they met, and it felt a little like the editor was cheating by eating a sausage roll.

In response, Sean flipped him a middle finger as he bit into the end of the roll, flaking it, as ever, onto his jumper.

'Have to say, I was surprised when I heard you moved to

The Individual,' Declan half chided. 'Did your computer in the *Guardian* offices burst into flames when you told them? Like the devil walking into a church?'

'Hey, I was just the features editor there, while here I run the whole show,' Sean said, his mouth still half-filled with pastry. 'Well, for as long as it'll last, anyway.'

'You don't think it'll last?'

'It's a vanity project by some vaguely right-leaning, centrist billionaire, so who knows,' Sean shrugged, washing his lunch down with his coffee. 'And yes you don't need to say anything. I know Kendis would have been ashamed of me. But shame doesn't pay the mortgage.'

He winked.

'And it's a big mortgage,' he finished.

'I'm not here to judge, God knows I've made enough mistakes in my time,' Declan replied. 'And Kendis always did say you were a self-serving, devious bastard with no soul.'

At this, a hungry look appeared in Sean's eyes, and he leant closer.

'Is this what this is?' he asked excitedly. 'The tell-all from the Queen's favourite copper before he leaves the force?'

He looked up and made a cross.

'God rest you, your Maj,' he muttered. 'Let me guess. Charles isn't a fan. You're unable to get a royal decree from him?'

'Stand-up comedy's loss is journalism's gain,' Declan deadpanned. 'And no, I don't want to give a tell-all.'

'Saving it for the memoirs, like your dad was going to do with Kendis? Good idea,' Sean nodded wisely, as if in on this assumed secret that even Declan wasn't privy to.

'And no bloody book.'

'Shame, the things you've done, it'd be a bestseller,' Sean

held his hands up, as if looking at quotes on the wall. 'I can see it now. "I couldn't go to sleep until I finished it!" "Declan's life story is the stuff of movies!" "I thought it was derivative shite!"'

Declan raised an eyebrow at the last one.

'Well, I can't blow too much smoke up your arse,' Sean leant back on his plastic chair, his lunch demolished. 'Go on then, this is about Hunt Robinson, right?'

He gave an impish grin.

'You know what we call him in the office?' he asked. 'It's very simple, we change a letter in his first name and suddenly the name fits his personality perfectly.'

'So, you're not a fan then?'

'Christ, no.'

'Enough to—'

'Oh, no!' Sean held up his hands. 'I've not heard the full story but I've heard enough. I don't need to do all that shite to make his life hell. Jesus, I sent him to a war zone to get shot, but the cockroach keeps breathing.'

'Still sounds a little like motive,' Declan said as he passed across his phone.

On it were crime scene photos.

'Good God,' Sean whispered as the full extent of what had happened to Robinson hit him. 'Can we use any of these?'

Declan quickly whipped the phone back.

'If you hadn't posted a crime scene pic of Montgomery Pryce with an arrow in him last year, I'm sure we could have talked,' he said. 'But since you did, you're on Monroe's shit list. So no.'

'And how do I get off this list?'

'Assist with my enquiries.' Declan pulled his notebook out, giving up on the coffee.

Sean grinned. 'I'll scratch your back if you scratch mine,' he replied. 'And my scratching might actually be pleasurable.'

Declan wasn't sure where the conversation was going here, so he settled for a frown rather than a confused expression.

'Explain?' he asked.

Sean shifted in his seat for a moment.

'Look,' he eventually spoke. 'You're about to fall on your sword, and nobody knows why. You could have used a dozen favours in Whitehall, and you haven't used any. By the end of the week, you're gone. Not even to a provincial post, from what I hear.'

'And your point is?'

'Come work for me,' Sean said, as if it was the most obvious suggestion in the world. 'Seriously. We could use an investigator like you. You know the world, you can get answers when needed ...'

'And I know the Prime Minister on a first-name basis?'

Sean made a face at this.

'PMs come and go,' he replied. 'Sooner or later, their secrets come back and haunt them.'

'I'm no journalist,' Declan leant back on his chair. 'Why the offer?'

'Because you put your neck out to find Kendis's killer, for a start,' Sean leant closer, arms on the table as he gave his pitch. 'You've been someone quite public, and at the same time never being caught with your pants down, no matter who you've been seen with. You rub shoulders with billionaires—'

'Yeah, I saw the piece you did about me and Eden Storm at the Royal Albert Hall.'

'You did?' Sean smiled. 'Tell me, then. Was it a hit piece? A fluff piece?'

Declan considered the question and shook his head.

'No, it was actually well laid out,' he admitted.

'Damn right it was,' Sean smiled. 'I wrote it.'

He picked up a pen and wrote something on a napkin.

'Look, just think about it,' he said. 'I took on this role not because I'm right-wing like my critics say, but because I want a paper that sits in the middle ground. However, to do that I need unbiased journos, and some of them are green, unable to find a way out of a wet paper bag if I gave them a pair of scissors. Someone like you, who could do the deep diving. It'd be worth a lot to me, and the publishers.'

He passed across the piece of paper.

'That much,' he said.

Declan took the paper, looked at it, and nodded.

'Double my salary, give or take,' he replied.

'There's no giving or taking at all,' Sean gave a wolfish smile. 'It's exactly double. To the penny. And that's nothing compared to the advance we'd give for serialising your adventures in the paper. We even have a literary agent who reckons they can get you a seven-figure deal for your memoirs – when you write them, of course.'

Declan rubbed at the back of his neck as he considered the offer. It was the last thing he'd expected today, but it was something new, something that could be his own.

'How long do I have to decide?'

'Until, say, the end of the week,' Sean kept the smile. 'I know you're on a case right now. I'm not going to screw around with that. And my source said you'd not take it immediately.'

'Your source?'

'Sorry, fell into journalist mode. I mean the … well, the recruiter, a – um, well, I suppose you could say a colleague of yours, who suggested you for the role.'

'Who is it?'

'Can't say,' Sean held his hands up. 'Confidential privilege and all that. Besides, she said not to give her name until she was ready to give it.'

Declan frowned. *She*. Could this have been Anjli finding him a way out?

His pitch given, Sean now sat back on his plastic chair, watching Declan.

'So, now I've scratched your back, what do you need from me exactly?'

'I was told you fought with Hunt Robinson,' Declan pulled his notepad out. 'Something about a scoop?'

'Bottom feeding, that's what it was,' Sean replied irritably. 'And not the sort of stuff I want to be peddling. So a celebrity likes to steal things? It's news for the other rags to tear apart. If I printed it, what'd be next? Public indecency? I'd be nothing more than a high-class gossip mag. Hunt's "secrets" varied along a very long scale, you see. On one side, they were career ending. The other, they were tittle tattle for the *Daily Mail* side bar of shame audience.'

'All of his secrets were like that?' Declan looked up. 'Because someone looks to have decided something he had was worth killing for.'

'Okay, yeah, that one came out of left field. But then what I knew of it, I wasn't impressed.'

'What you knew?'

Sean shifted in his chair as he opened his laptop, scrolling through a list of files.

'He gave me a list of his five top juicy scoops about three months ago,' he said, clicking the trackpad. 'I'd just started, and he was looking to prove his worth and all that. He was annoyed you beat him to Andy Mac grooming boys. But I think he was more pissed that Andy hanged himself before he could do anything.'

Declan wrote this down.

'Do you have the list?'

'I'll email it when I find it.' Unsuccessful, and now checking his pockets, as if to magically find the answer, Sean looked back at Declan. 'To be honest, I think he thought by doing this, he'd stop me from firing him.'

'You would have?'

'Let's just say he has a history and a reputation,' Sean smiled with joy as he pulled out a half-eaten sausage roll from his pocket. 'Forgot I had that there.'

'How long has that been in there?' Declan asked, horrified as Sean started eating it.

'Don't wet your knickers, I put it in there when I had a meeting this morning,' Sean grinned, before pausing, staring at the sausage roll for a moment and then placing it down.

'No, I remember why I didn't finish it,' he muttered through his half-full mouth. 'Vegan.'

Declan fought the urge to chuckle as Sean swallowed down the remnants of his food.

'Is Hunt liked?' he asked.

'Robinson? I don't think anyone likes him,' Sean mused. 'Some people say he's on the spectrum, you know? But I think it's just he's a massive prick. No, a massive self-righteous prick.'

He looked as if he wanted to spit.

'I know what you're aiming for,' he continued. 'You want to know if Robinson had enemies, people who wanted him dead? Well, pretty much everyone he ever met felt that way about him. The guy's a cancer, Declan. Only reason I'm still hiring him is I'm terrified I'm in the bloody book.'

'Do you have reason to be?'

'Don't be a fool, everyone has!' Sean laughed, but it was a nervous one. 'Ever been unfaithful? Or caused someone else to be? Ever say the wrong thing, spill the wrong secret? Drink the wrong thing before driving? Steal things for kicks? That's all it takes.'

Declan didn't say anything; Sean's words cut deep. He was one of the few people who knew Kendis had slept with Declan the night before she died – told by her, rather than by his journalistic skills, however.

'Did you ever see the book?'

Sean nodded.

'Just a peek, but I saw enough. He was showing off, waving it about at an event once, Pandora's book, people called it. You open it up, read any page, and you'll see secrets you didn't want to know. Black thing, looks like a Filofax. Probably adds pages when he needs to destroy more lives.'

Declan noted this down.

'Someone did this who knew him,' he said. 'They knew the flight number.'

'That's if he's not lying.'

Declan paused, placing the notebook onto his lap.

'Go on.'

Sean shifted uncomfortably on his chair; it was obvious he hadn't meant to speak aloud.

'Look, I have contacts, right? I know what happened this morning. How he was found, *two days* after he went home.'

'He claims he was drugged.'

'And what, kept unconscious for all of Monday? Are you seriously believing this?'

Declan shrugged.

'It's what we're working on. But off the record? No.'

'So you think he knew his attacker?'

Declan narrowed his eyes.

'All of this is off the record,' he said. 'All of it.'

Sean made another theatrical sigh and nodded, settling on his chair as Declan continued.

'Hypothesis. Either Robinson was awake or not. If it's the latter? Then sure. His story checks out. He was knocked out, kept out, and woke up stabbed in a crypt. Or there's door one. He was awake throughout. Which means he was either threatened to keep quiet, or he's chosen to keep quiet.'

'And why would he do that?' Sean was smiling now.

'Maybe someone has a book on him, too?' Declan suggested. 'Why the bloody grin?'

'Watching you investigate, it's incredible,' Sean replied. 'I mean, your eyes narrow, and you do that whole "Sherlock Holmes" stare, it's fascinating. Did he mention about the attempted thefts, by the way?'

Declan nodded.

'Do you believe him?'

'Christ no. Man's a flake.'

Declan watched Sean for a moment before returning to his notes.

'So you think he did this himself?'

Sean shook his head, as if realising he was digging a hole.

'Look, this is more your thing than mine,' he replied. 'But

still, I wouldn't put anything past him. He's a slippery little bastard. When I spiked his story, he tried to go above me, get me fired. Just because I said it was crass.'

'Do you have the story still?'

At this, Sean's smile flickered for a moment.

'No,' he said. 'I lost it. The bloody fool doesn't email, he prints and sends. It was on my desk, now it's not. It'll turn up, though.'

He paused, his expression altering slightly, as if a memory had just crossed it.

'That said, there was something,' he added. 'Around Christmas, so a couple of months back. Way before he went to Ukraine. There was a shindig, big Westminster thing. You probably had an invite or something.'

Declan thought back; he'd been at one of Charles Baker's Christmas bashes. It was where he met Shaun Donnal and learnt of a killer with a fetish for Father Christmas hats.

'Possibly,' he said.

'Lots of police, MPs, journos there, big announcement being made. Hunt went in all piss and vinegar, claiming he was going to "do one on the establishment," but then came out like he'd been neutered.'

'What happened?'

'Nobody knew,' Sean shrugged. 'The other journos I had there weren't really keeping an eye on him. But I heard he'd been mouthing off about the Roman story.'

'Roman story?' Declan shook his head. 'Like the empire?'

'Ish.' Sean was rummaging through his pockets again. This time, however, he didn't pull out a sausage roll. 'About twenty years back, there were these two MPs. Brothers; one in Labour, one on the other side. Both coming into Parliament in their late twenties and early thirties, they were nicknamed

Romulus and Remus, as in the two brothers that founded Rome, and there were mutterings their plan was to get one of them into the hot seat and then try to merge the parties together. You know, unite the country. But then there were others that said they were in some kind of high-stakes pissing contest, and would do anything to stop the other.'

'Names?'

'Jason and Alfred Bannister, but they went as Jay and Alfie.' Sean was typing on his laptop now. 'Jay Labour, Alfie was Tory. Alfie was two years senior, but you couldn't really tell. This was the file we had on them in *The Guardian*. I, um, acquired it when I left.'

He turned the laptop to show a single folder on the screen.

'Go on, click on it.'

Declan opened it to find it empty.

'Yeah, it surprised me, too. But that's anything of note, meat wise. Sure, there was MP stuff, but I was features. I had people like Kendis doing the grunt work. And she found out Hunt had something on them.'

'In his black book?'

'Yeah. Either Jay or Alfie had done bad things. Really bad.'

'Like what?'

'No idea,' Sean sighed. 'They both died in a helicopter crash ten years ago. Hunt was all over it, said he had the true story of excess, blackmail and most of the other deadly sins. But he was at *The Telegraph* at the time, and they killed it. Killed it so bad he lost his job in the process.'

'And after that?'

'Nobody cared. They were dead, it was sad, move along. You don't see anyone talking about Andy Mac or Susan

Devington these days, do you? Or that guy from *Alternator*? You punish the living, Declan, and the dead can rest in peace.'

'But he brought something up at Christmas?'

'Apparently. Who knows? I heard there was talk of some kind of tenth anniversary memorial to them announced at the bash. He was told the details. Probably by Digger Doug.'

'Sorry who?' Declan frowned.

'Nickname,' Sean replied. 'Douglas Gregory. His go-to private investigator. Worked with him for years, and to be honest, they probably knew each other better than they did their wives. If Doug even had a wife. I never bothered finding out.'

'I'm guessing Doug was the one who found the secrets?'

'Probably. I don't know. You'd have to ask him. Maybe he spoke to Hunt yesterday.'

Declan placed his notebook away.

'Nobody else spoke to him yesterday?'

'Not that I know of, but I'll ask about.'

'And any major enemies?'

'As I said—'

'Yeah, everyone thought he was a dick, I get that, but was there anyone who stands out as a potential killer?'

Sean rubbed his chin.

'Kathy Pine might be someone to talk to,' he said. 'She posted the story that got him into a tizzy. Maybe he kicked off at her? I know they hated each other.'

'And how do you know that?'

'Because when they both worked at the *Mail*, he was shagging her behind his wife's back,' Sean grinned. 'And it exploded spectacularly at a fundraiser gala where she got pissed up and told everyone within earshot, including his wife.'

Sean gave a wry smile.

'I wonder if his buddy Doug knew he was cheating on him with her?' he asked innocently.

Declan nodded thanks and rose from the chair.

And then, as if an afterthought, he looked back at Sean.

'You saw inside the book, right?'

'I saw the book, and a few flicked pages, sure.'

'You ever see anything about Commander Edward Sinclair in them?' Declan asked carefully.

'Why?' Sean straightened, the sniff of a story too irresistible to miss. 'Is he?'

'Between us and off the record?'

Sean nodded.

'In that case, I don't know, but he was bloody quick to the scene, and he never leaves Guildhall,' Declan replied. 'He fed us some tale of butting heads when he was a Detective Superintendent at Bishopsgate, but I got the feeling he was more interested in the book than the man.'

'Everyone is,' Sean replied. 'Whoever has that book can write their own ticket.'

Declan didn't like the sound of that.

'Hey, between us,' he moved closer to the table, finishing the frankly awful coffee. 'The colleague who gave you my name, who was it?'

'I said, she—'

'I know, she said not to give her name out,' Declan leant onto the table now. 'But let's be honest, Sean. I just gave you gold. The moment I leave, you'll be sniffing out Sinclair's file, looking for a way to link him without breaking the "off the record" allowance you gave me. And as it's a job offer and not a big bloody secret, how about being a mate?'

Sean winced, as if offended by the suggestion.

'Fine,' he muttered. 'Like, "colleague" might have been a bit high, but you did work together.'

'Who.'

'She wanted it to be a surprise.'

'Who, Sean. Or I walk over to the *Daily Mail* right now and offer them the serialisation of my memoirs.'

'You said you didn't—'

'Who.'

Sean made a grumbling noise, clenching his fists as he relented.

'Theresa Martinez,' he eventually stated.

Declan straightened.

'Tessa Martinez? *Magpies* Martinez? She's in Send Prison.'

'Not anymore,' Sean explained. 'She got out. Appeals and overturned verdicts, a distinguished prior career—'

'She murdered someone!'

'A car accident, even if she felt she wanted to kill them, a fugue state brought on by pain medication and ten years' worth of PTSD,' Sean shook his head. 'Used by people she thought wanted to help, frustrated at the lack of help from the legal system, already done a year's worth of time, yada yada.'

Declan stared at the editor behind the table.

'She used us,' he said.

'And yet you were still her character witness,' Sean said with a smile. 'She came recommended by a friend. She's a bloody good detective, started with me about a month back. Does background mainly.'

His expression brightened.

'You should probably talk to her,' he finished. 'She dealt with Hunt, too.'

Nodding thanks again, Declan walked to the door of the cafe.

'Can I use any of this?' Sean asked hopefully.

'No,' Declan looked back with a grin. 'But if and when I ever write my memoirs, you're the first person I'll contact.'

6

HOUSE CALLS

D<small>E</small>'G<small>EER HAD BEEN IN A SULK ALL THE WAY TO</small> M<small>EOPHAM</small>, <small>JUST</small> south of the A2 in Kent; Monroe hadn't wanted to ride pillion on De'Geer's motorbike, while De'Geer moaned that traffic on the M25 would be unbearable this time of day.

Monroe had retaliated with the reminder they had a siren. And blue flashing lights.

De'Geer hadn't been impressed.

Now, they pulled up in a squad car down a single lane cul-de-sac, facing a wide, red-bricked house. There was a double garage to the right-hand side, two white doors on it, a front door with a portico in the middle and two large windows either side, reached by a small, paved driveway. Monroe couldn't see much, but it appeared like the property looked out over a selection of fields.

It was a better view than his own one, that was for sure.

There was already movement behind the curtains of the house to the right, and Monroe gave it a little wave as he walked towards the front door, De'Geer following.

'Well, if anything happened here, that's someone who'll

know,' he said, nodding at the house. 'Let's chat to Janine Robinson, and maybe you can pop over and have a wee chat with whoever that is in a minute.'

De'Geer nodded, pressing the doorbell and stepping back. After a minute, a flustered slim woman with short, spiked, dyed-black hair, and a Barbour coat half-pulled on, glared out at them through rimless glasses. She was middle-aged, maybe sixty at best, but her eyes looked tired and stressed.

'Janine Robinson?' Monroe asked. 'I'm DCI Monroe, this is Sergeant De'Geer. We're—'

'I know why you're here,' Janine pulled her coat fully on. 'And I already told you I didn't need a lift.'

Monroe paused, frowning.

'Ma'am, we're not anyone's "lift," I'm afraid,' he said. 'We're—'

'Here because of Hunt, I get it,' Janine was irritated and quick to snap, but Monroe understood the reasoning. 'Look, I just got back from Chelmsford to get a message from you about Hunt.'

'You didn't get it this morning?'

'I was at a Wellness retreat; we turn the phones off.' Janine was pulling trainers on now. 'I only remembered to turn it back on halfway home. That's when I heard. I then spoke to some officers on the phone who caught me up to speed, and now I'm unpacked and about to go see my husband.'

'Perhaps you could stay a little longer?' Monroe smiled. 'We'd like a wee chat if possible, inside?'

'My husband is hurt. I should—'

'And yet, on gaining the news, you didn't head straight to the hospital, which would have been far easier, as your house is a good hour in the opposite direction. Instead, you drove back here and unpacked,' Monroe's smile had faded now. 'So aye, there's a lot of things you should be doing. First and foremost is helping us catch his attacker.'

Janine went to argue, blew out her cheeks, and then stepped back, allowing them entrance.

'Ten minutes,' she said. 'And then you can lead me to the hospital with your blue lights on, save me having to hit the rush hour traffic. Deal?'

'Aye, Sergeant De'Geer just loves doing that,' Monroe said as he stepped past her. 'He'll even use the sirens, too.'

THE HOUSE WAS LARGE; A FOUR BEDROOM WITH AN EXPANSIVE hall in the middle, with rooms to the left and right, and a red-carpeted staircase at the back. On the wall were framed newspaper front pages. Checking one, Monroe realised they were all headlines written by Hunt Robinson throughout his career.

'Come through to the sitting room,' Janine waved them to the right-hand door. 'There are seats in there.'

De'Geer and Monroe followed Janine in, allowing her to take the armchair as they both perched on the edge of a brown leather sofa against the wall. The walls were magnolia coloured, the rear end of the room opening up into a conservatory, and like the hallway, the walls were festooned with framed front pages.

'I'd offer you tea, but we're not staying long,' Janine replied. 'I'll keep this short. I hadn't seen Hunt for weeks, as he'd been on his war tour—'

'War tour?'

'It's just what I called it. And he was supposed to be back in a week, so I went to a Wellness retreat in Chelmsford. Thursday to Thursday.'

Her expression gave Monroe the impression of a woman more annoyed she'd lost out on a holiday than concern over her husband.

'So you weren't here at the weekend?'

'No. I was in Chelmsford. And before you ask, the phone was turned off, so no ping. All you have are the people I was with as witnesses, and the Dart charge payment thing probably showed me crossing the Dartford bridge.'

She nodded to herself.

'I need to pay that tonight, too, or I'll be fined more,' she muttered, taking a notepad from the side and writing something on it.

'Handy, having that there,' Monroe nodded at the paper.

'Oh, we have notes and post-its all over the bloody house,' Janine replied dismissively. 'Never know when the *Auteur* will have his next genius thought; don't want to lose it.'

Monroe sensed a note of sarcasm on this, and decided to press on.

'You think he's an *Auteur*?'

'Apparently everyone else does,' she replied, waving around the room, indicating the frames. 'Although there's been a distinct lack of them over the last few years.'

She cocked her head at one behind Monroe; it was a piece on John Major, from 1992, with an image of him on a wooden soapbox, speaking to a crowd on what seemed to be a village green.

'That was taken during the election,' she said, almost with a hint of pride. 'Major turned up at our local cricket club, doing his "standing on a soapbox" schtick. We'd only just moved in here. Hunt heard about the event and rushed over with a disposable camera. It was an impromptu one, everyone was caught off guard except for Hunt. Got him a front page, and a raise.'

She smiled.

'And it made every resident of the village hate us for about a year, after he wrote the hit piece on John Major,' she continued. 'Major's a patron of the cricket club, after all.'

'This seems to be a repeating trend,' Monroe replied. 'Doing great but shooting himself in the foot at the same time.'

'He's nothing if not consistent,' Janine mouth-shrugged. 'But recently, I have no idea what he's been up to. We live separate lives, really. I do bell ringing and run the parish council. He ... well, he tries to be good. Fails, but tries.'

'Tries to be good?' De'Geer was writing this down. 'Ethically?'

'I think he's realised that with the life of excesses he's had, he needs to really suck up if he wants to go to Heaven,' Janine smiled, but it was a mocking, humourless one. 'Especially as he's got fewer days in front than behind. And he's got a lot of sins to make up for. Shagging around for a start.'

'Affairs?'

'Sure,' Janine rose from the chair now, walking to the sideboard and pouring a whisky for herself. 'Purely medicinal. I'm in shock for my poor darling husband.'

'Aye, we can see that,' Monroe nodded. 'Mister Robinson claims he was taken from the airport and has no memory of since then or Monday. Is there any way we can confirm he was away?'

'Oh, he wasn't,' Janine looked back, shaking her head. 'He'd put his laundry in the basket. I mean, he hadn't actually done the washing or anything, that would be menial work, my domain, but he'd definitely come home, unpacked, and ordered takeout. It was in the bin.'

Monroe looked at De'Geer, who'd also understood the meaning here.

'Mister Robinson claims his phone and satchel were taken,' De'Geer said, rising from the sofa. 'Do you know if they could be here, and he hadn't remembered?'

'No idea, I've only just got in.'

'But you saw his washing?'

'Only because I dumped mine on top.' Janine was getting irritated now. 'If it's anywhere, it'll be in his office. But I never go in there.'

'Could we go in there?' Monroe joined De'Geer in rising. 'Just a wee look around, and then we'll take you into London? Blue lights and everything?'

'Upstairs, first right,' Janine sat back in the chair, whisky in hand. 'You can't miss it.'

JANINE HAD BEEN RIGHT; THERE WAS NO WAY YOU COULD MISS Hunt Robinson's office; for a start, it seemed to be the only room in the house with dark-coloured, non-magnolia walls. And, weirdly, it seemed to be the only room not covered in newspaper headlines. In fact, apart from a couple of photos of Hunt with various dignitaries, there wasn't anything on the walls promoting him at all.

To the side was a metal filing cabinet, a sticker with "OLD STORIES" written with a marker pen on it. At the back of the room, the window behind it, was a desk. It was a green-leather-topped mahogany one, with drawers either side.

However, this wasn't an antique one, as two of the "drawers" on the right were one door, which, when opened, showed a desktop computer.

'Likes to look the part, it seems,' Monroe said as he tapped a keyboard, hoping the monitor would burst into life. It didn't.

'Another notepad,' De'Geer said, holding up a pad of paper. 'This one's headed.'

Monroe took the pad, checking it, and went to place it onto the desk – but then stopped, and took off the top five sheets, placing them carefully in his pocket.

'Need tissues, sir?' De'Geer asked, amused.

'Don't have the time to bugger about on it with a pencil,' Monroe replied, already checking the drawers and then the cabinet. 'Locked. Surprising for a home office.'

De'Geer shrugged.

'Sir,' he said, crouching beside the desk, and rising back up, a leather satchel in his hand. Monroe reached across and took it, opening the bag up.

'Where was this?' he asked. 'Was it hidden, or just discarded?'

'It was wedged at the back, sir,' De'Geer looked back at the desk. 'I don't know if it was deliberate or not.'

Monroe *hmm*ed as he looked into the satchel. Inside was a phone, either turned off or out of battery. Next to it was a cable charger and plug, a notebook, and some business cards. A check of another pouch showed a digital recorder.

'Should we listen?' De'Geer asked.

'No, we're not here with a warrant,' Monroe sighed, but not before flicking through the half empty notebook. 'Well, it looks like his satchel and his phone are here, but no black book of career-ending disaster.'

'His wallet's here, too,' De'Geer plucked a leather wallet from the shelf. 'With his house keys.'

Monroe placed the satchel back on the floor.

'So we know he came home, dumped his washing, came in here, placing his bag and wallet down, and then ordered take out,' he mused. 'Still doesn't give us anything for Monday.'

He tapped at the phone, but it didn't start.

'Phone's dead,' he said. 'I'd say take it to Billy, but—'

'But we don't have a warrant, and this is just a chat,' De'Geer nodded.

Walking back down the stairs, Monroe paused at the bottom, staring across the hall. Janine Robinson was watching out of the window, as if unaware of their presence.

'Did you find what you wanted?' she enquired politely, not averting her gaze from the glass.

'Aye, he left many of his missing things here,' Monroe walked across the hall. 'I, um, used some notepaper. To write a note down. That okay?'

'Sure.'

'But his black book is missing.'

Janine nodded.

'Of course it is,' she sighed. 'That's what you really gave a damn about, wasn't it? Someone send you here? Sinclair? One of his flunkies?'

'And how would you know Edward Sinclair?' Monroe asked.

At this, Janine Robinson finally turned from the window.

'Because I had an affair with him,' she said matter-of-factly. 'Twice, actually. We had a dalliance years back, before either of us were married, and then we ... well, reconnected late last year. I'm sure he'll say otherwise, but it wasn't a great time for me and Hunt, we'd both had, well, dalliances we were ashamed of. And, when I found out he'd been dipping his wick into another candle, some secretary called Lesley, I – well, I threw myself on Edward at a Christmas bash in town.'

She smiled, before looking from Monroe to De'Geer.

'Is that what this was about?' she asked. 'To get the book? To save your boss?'

'No,' Monroe shook his head. 'To find out what the hell actually happened, because I'm starting to think your husband is a wee bit of a bullshitter, if you'd pardon my language.'

At this, Janine laughed, waving her hand around the walls of the hall.

'Look at all these headlines, these newsworthy pieces,' she snapped in reply. 'All of them bollocks, made up with snippets of gossip taken from disgruntled employees and Civil Servants, and created to form the story required by his editors. That one there? Hates the Government. The one beside it? Praises them. The difference? The name of the paper.'

She walked to the front door, opening it.

'My husband sold his soul to anyone that paid him,' she said, standing in the doorway. 'He'd write whatever you needed, whatever audience you wanted. He knew he'd never be given a big job in news, so he scrabbled around for the biggest paydays, no matter how ethical.'

She grabbed a large handbag, looping it over her shoulder as she grabbed her car keys from the side table.

'Because of this, everyone hated him, and if it wasn't that, it was the book,' she said. 'And when I say everyone, I mean *everyone*. So, if you're done snooping around, I'd really like to visit my husband before he pisses everyone in the hospital off, and they euthanise him.'

She smiled.

'Because that's my job. I've earned it. And no two-bit whore is taking it from me. Shall we?'

Quietly, and thinking through everything Janine Robinson had just said, Monroe walked with De'Geer out of the door, heading to the squad car.

'And don't worry about the escort, I'm sure you have better things to do,' Janine climbed into her own car, a Ford Focus parked at the side. 'See you soon, I'm sure. Say hi to Edward for me.'

Monroe watched her drive off before getting into the car. De'Geer was already behind the wheel.

'That's an angry woman,' he said, starting the engine. 'And she was very unkind to the journalist he was having an affair with.'

'It wasn't a journalist,' Monroe frowned. 'She said Lesley, a secretary.'

'Check your phone, boss,' De'Geer pulled out into the street. 'DI Walsh sent a message. Apparently, Hunt had an affair with a rival journalist. But he says that was Karen Pine.'

'Well then, laddie, who the hell is this Lesley?' Monroe stroked his beard. 'I'm starting to think this whole story's as unreliable as the narrator, or Mister Robinson's appetite is more voracious than we realised.'

'Back to the office?'

'No, laddie,' Monroe settled back into the passenger seat. 'You are, after you grab that neighbour's number in case we need it, but I want to have a wee chat in Guildhall first.'

7

FAMILY TIES

THERE WERE JOBS THAT BILLY LIKED. AND THERE WERE THE ones Billy hated.

Weirdly, when Billy sat in front of his computer system in the Temple Inn office, it wasn't the jobs where he *couldn't* find the data that annoyed him. Those jobs were the interesting ones, where he had to delve deeper into the internet, tantalisingly stroking the dark web to get it to comply with his needs, to find the things he asked for.

This was true detective work as far as he was concerned.

The jobs he didn't like were the ones where there was *too much* information out there; where the snippets he needed, the titbits of important data that led him to the next, vital clue were drowned within a sea of pointless, useless numbers.

It was a standard tactic in social media when a celebrity, or even a Government, knew something bad was about to break out about them – for example, they were about to be outed, or an affair was about to be made public, or half a dozen other things in a similar vein – they'd usually employ a crisis management team to drown the immediate news cycle with something new, so that if you went into a search engine, or Twitter, or whatever browser of choice you used and typed in their name, these things would come up instead of the bad news. In the industry, it was known as "deadcatting"; the act of throwing a dead cat on the table, so it'd be all anyone would talk about.

There was even a reverse angle, that if something big was about to come out, maybe a new film, or a new, popular Government bill, you'd "dead cat" the bad news at the same time, knowing it wouldn't gain traction, as people would shy away, when there were better things to focus on.

It was a workable tactic, and if it wasn't broken, there was no need to fix it. But what it did do was it made people like Billy, hunting for nuggets of gold in gravel, find himself on a much larger quarry.

Hunt Robinson was such a name.

Usually a journalist was nothing more than a byline, somebody who wasn't really known unless they had awards, or were well respected. If you ask the average person on the street to name their favourite paper, they could do so. Or rather, depending on their age, they would give their favourite news outlet, as many people would read it digitally now, or watch on TV, giving their favourite news station: BBC, Sky, GB News, whichever they gained their stories from.

But once you started moving down the list, the questions became harder. "Who's your favourite newsreader?" was easy, as people remember faces, but "who's your favourite journalist?" was a question that most people couldn't answer. Sure, there were the Vox Pop columnists brought in for star power. But the regular byline journalists? They weren't known. They were enigmas. They were faceless. Only devout readers would recognise the byline names.

Apart from when you were someone like Hunt Robinson, because over the years Hunt had been a part of enough stories involving himself, to drown out anything that he'd done.

He'd had affairs, he'd had fights, he'd had arguments, publicly drunken ones, where he'd be escorted out of gala dinners and such like, all of which gave a wealth of information, including photos and headlines, that didn't really help Billy in drilling down his investigation. Sure, every public meltdown Hunt gave, every argument Hunt had, gave another suspect for his attack. But really, would any of these people have done such a thing? Was a drunken spat at the BAFTAs enough to stab a man in a weird, semi-ritual manner?

What Billy really needed was information on the *book*.

But surprisingly, although Hunt was everywhere, the book was barely mentioned, almost as if it was nothing but an urban legend.

Billy, taking a break, leant back from the monitors, staring around the office. He didn't understand how the book worked. Was it one book, like a Filofax, where you could add sheets of fresh paper? Or a series of books? Was it something else? Twenty years of gossip and secrets wouldn't fit into a normal-sized book.

Surely there had to be more.

Sighing, Billy decided to try a new tactic here. It seemed his computer work wasn't going to help; it also didn't help that the Fleet Street CCTV was being a pain and most of the places he needed to check had maintenance work scheduled on the night in question, which meant he couldn't check any of the footage. He had checked Hunt Robinson's car, and ANPR hadn't revealed it driving anywhere over the Monday, which meant it was probably still parked in Kent. Monroe had texted, saying Hunt's phone was still at the house, but it'd been turned off, or out of power, likely for the whole day.

That didn't help him either.

Now he had to resort to looking into trains, buses, any kind of public transport that could have helped. The chances were, living in a village in the middle of Kent, that if Hunt came into London, he either had to be brought in by car, or make his own way.

And then there was the conundrum of the silk rope.

Anjli had sent a text explaining that it was something to do with his position as a freeman of London, but this wasn't a secret Billy could dig into; it was even on his Wikipedia page.

Billy decided to move away from the keyboard and play his trump card. And, reluctantly, he picked up his phone, dialling a number.

After a moment, the booming voice of Chivalry Fitzwarren answered.

'Billy, my boy,' he said. 'You're calling during office hours? You must need something.'

'Afternoon, Uncle Chivalry,' Billy smiled. He liked Chivalry. After all, he was the only member of the family who still spoke to Billy. It'd been a couple of years now since he was effectively ostracised by the Fitzwarren clan. And only Chivalry had stood beside him. He had helped the Last Chance Saloon a couple of times as well, which made Billy feel a little more comfortable in outsourcing to him.

'I've got a question,' he said. 'Hunt Robinson.'

'That's a name I hoped never to hear again,' Chivalry

replied. 'Although having seen the news, somebody tried to kill him, or something – is that right?'

'Something like that,' Billy agreed. 'Am I wrong, or did we have a problem with him?'

'When you say "we," I'm assuming the family?' Chivalry's voice had a lighter edge to it, and Billy knew on the other end of the line, the older man was smiling. 'You want to know whether he's had it in for the Fitzwarrens, and you can't ask anybody else, can you?'

'No, and I will point out you promised to get me back in with them.'

'I am, dear boy, but it's a slow case. They've warmed a little to your plight, but you still managed to arrest one of their own.'

'One of "our" own, don't you mean?'

'Well yes, if I was talking about myself, then sure. But when talking from your perspective?' Chivalry let the obvious answer hang. 'They don't class you as one of the family, still. But I'm on it. Don't worry. We'll fix things.'

There was a moment of silence, and Billy knew Chivalry was now changing gears, turning his attention to the subject in hand.

'But, as for Hunt Robinson ... yes, that devious little toe rag tried a hit at us.'

'When was it?'

'About five years ago, I think,' Chivalry replied down the line. 'I wasn't involved. I was abroad at the time. Which is amusing in a way, because you'd have thought if he was going to make a play to take us down, he would have gone for me. I am the most public and obvious choice, after all. I'm frankly insulted.'

Billy grinned. Chivalry was definitely the black sheep of

the Fitzwarren family. His interests had been the reason he'd helped the Last Chance Saloon earlier the previous year, too, in a case that involved occult rituals and stolen antiquities.

'We're trying to find out who attacked him,' Billy explained. 'There seems to be a massive list.'

'Oh, there is,' Chivalry replied. 'Most people who've met him probably want to hurt or kill him. But, that said, most people don't want to lay him out in the middle of a crypt with silk rope.'

Billy paused.

'We haven't announced the rope,' he said.

Chivalry laughed.

'Good God, William! Dear boy, do you honestly think that you're the only police source I have? I heard everything. I've had an old friend from Bishopsgate contact me, asking me if I could explain the occult symbolism to a man found in a crypt, tied like Jesus, and stabbed in the side.'

'Bishopsgate isn't taking the case,' Billy frowned.

'Well, you should tell Commander Sinclair that,' Chivalry replied. 'Because he's pressuring them to check into it.'

Billy noted this down. It had been pointed out from the very beginning that Sinclair had a definite interest in the case, leaving his gilded Guildhall throne to attend. It just hadn't been explained how *much* of an interest the man had.

'What did you tell them?'

'What I'm telling you right now. There's nothing occult about it,' Chivalry's voice was tight, as if he was working out something as he spoke. 'Sure, he was splayed out on the floor, tied with a rope. Yes, it was a crucifixion pose. But I don't think they were trying to make a Christ-like martyr of him. If anything, it seems a little too staged. Too conspiratorial.'

'How so?'

'You know – okay, if I was going to kill him, I'd shoot him in the head or have his car crash or a dozen different other ways, maybe even fake a suicide, rather than try to create some kind of symbology that would cause the police to run around in circles.'

'You think this is deliberate?' Billy was noting this down as he asked.

'If I wanted to send you off on a wild goose hunt, dear boy, I would do exactly what happened here,' Chivalry explained. 'I would strip Robinson down to his trousers, like the Freemasons, I'd stab him in the side; a small wound, something that wouldn't hurt. I'd poison him, but not enough to kill, and I'd place him in a spot that has some kind of mystical symbolism – a journalist church, for example.'

He paused.

'But I'd also leave a message,' he finished. 'And, from what I can work out, there was none left for you. No smoking gun that diverted you from the true story.'

'Which is?'

'Haven't the foggiest, dear boy. But even if I was doing this, if I was to go for anybody, it wouldn't be Hunt. It'd be digger dug.'

'Sorry, did you just say digger dug?'

'No, *Digger Doug*, D-O-U-G, short for Douglas,' Chivalry was speaking now as if he was getting frustrated with the idiocy of his nephew. 'Douglas Gregory, weaselly little private investigator, worked a lot with Hunt.'

Chivalry laughed.

'You think Hunt is some kind of genius investigative journalist, who can gain all this information on celebrities? Guess again,' he explained. 'God no – he hired Digger Doug to go in and get these things. That's how he got the nickname; he was the digger, the person sent to mine the data, and he'd do whatever it took. He'd bribe employees, stake out houses, even go through rubbish when that was relevant. These days, I think he employs cyber nerds like you to go hack into systems.'

Billy ignored the jibe as Chivalry, on a roll now, continued.

'It was believed he was part of the phone hacking inquiry that happened a few years back as well. Horrid little man, weaselly little shit.'

'You seem to have a real thing against private investigators.'

'No, I don't mind them. God knows I've hired enough over the years when I've looked for trinkets for my collection. I just have a thing against traitors,' Chivalry snapped. 'You see, Hunt hired Doug, but Doug liked an easy life as much as Hunt does. So, whereas Hunt decided he wanted to take down the Fitzwarren clan, Doug realised we could make life difficult if we realised he was an enemy, and so he came to us and asked us how much we'd give him to *not* find anything.'

'Was there anything to find?'

'You're ostracised from the family for sending one of us to prison, so what do you think?'

Billy reddened, glad Chivalry couldn't see him.

'How much did they give him?'

'Five times what Hunt offered him, I believe. As far as I know, he went back to Robinson and said he couldn't find anything. Sure, it annoyed Robinson, but he soon moved on to somebody else.'

Billy understood well why Hunt Robinson had moved targets; it was most likely because the Fitzwarrens, through

Doug, gave him a different target to aim at, in the process solving a problem of their own.

'Do you know if he still works with Doug?'

'No idea, dear boy. I haven't heard about the man for years. But I'd say he's definitely an option to look at, because if Hunt Robinson was landing in the UK from a war zone, and trying to find out what was going on with his stories, I can guarantee Digger Doug was his first call.'

Billy didn't bother asking how Chivalry knew about the stolen scoop; even if Sinclair hadn't told him this, there were enough people Chivalry could have heard this from.

'Thanks, Uncle,' Billy said, finishing up the call. 'And give my love to the family.'

'Oh God, no,' Chivalry laughed down the line. 'If I even mention I've been talking to you, I get into the shit as well. Just let me keep working on them. We'll have something soon; at least they've reopened your allowance. But if you're serious about looking for people who want Robinson dead, you might want to try St James's Palace.'

Billy was about to disconnect the call, but stopped.

'Wait, you mean the Royal Family?'

'Maybe not the family themselves, but definitely the grubby little office spods and hangers-on who hang out at the Royal Court,' Chivalry replied. 'They wanted his head a decade back. And I heard they've been looking into him again recently. So brush up your national anthem and have a chat there.'

Billy didn't reply to this, instead giving a brief "see you later" and disconnecting the call. He was already typing the name of Doug Gregory into the computer before he placed the phone on the desk.

It seemed that Doug was a known commodity to the City

of London Police, having been brought in many times over the years, in connection with various cases – but nothing had ever stuck on him. But there was an address, at least. Billy noted it down and started continuing down this new Royal Court rabbit-hole line of enquiry.

There was every chance that "Digger" Doug was someone who could help, or that someone in St James's could help him with what the hell was going on …

But, for the moment, he still needed definite proof why Hunt Robinson was attacked, and by whom.

Sighing, he returned to the CCTVs. Maybe they were working now.

They weren't.

8

MEMOIRS AND STORIES

AFTER FINISHING WITH SEAN, DECLAN MADE HIS WAY BACK TO the Temple Inn unit. It was close to rush hour by now, and Declan noted the evening was drawing in; the clocks had recently changed, going forward, but this didn't help the general feeling of a darkening evening at clocking-off time. Declan didn't usually worry about rush hour, as he was often working until well past it, but that was different today though; there was something that had been bothering him since the morning, and he needed to check into it, back at home.

On arrival, he found Billy on his own and had spoken briefly to him, but Billy had mentioned something about his uncle and the Royal Family, and Declan always knew to steer clear of conversations involving Chivalry Fitzwarren. And so, as Billy was amid checking security footage and didn't seem to be in the best of moods, Declan took this as an opportunity to pack up his things and leave for the day.

Anjli had driven in separately that morning, so he knew he didn't have to wait for her to return for a pickup; that said, she'd gone to the hospital to speak to Hunt Robinson and still hadn't returned by the time he arrived – and if he was being brutally honest, their conversations hadn't been the most cordial of late.

Especially once he told her Tessa Martinez had suggested him for a new job. Tessa Martinez, who Anjli knew he once had a childhood crush on.

Yeah. Maybe best not to tell her.

No. That's keeping secrets. And you promised you wouldn't.

But she'll kill you.

Maybe. Maybe not.

Either way, she wouldn't be back for a while, and this meant he had time to investigate a different lead, something a little more personal.

He'd arrived back at Hurley around six in the evening, having received a message from Anjli while driving – she'd arrived back at the office with Cooper, but was looking into something; she suggested they meet later in the *Olde Bell* to compare notes. It sounded like a date, but the "compare notes" line gave him the distinct impression she was being cordial, more than flirtatious.

He grabbed himself a glass of water and walked out to the garden shed, where, placed in air-tight boxes, his father's notes were.

Patrick Walsh, while working as a police officer, had made copies of every official document he'd worked with over his career. Every case he'd been involved in, every suspect, every transcript, every photo, had been meticulously copied and filed away for safekeeping, whether it was for his own records to work from at home, a lack of faith in the digitising of the proposal process, or even if it was purely for his own memoirs, something that Declan knew he'd been working on before he died. Either way, it'd been a gold mine, and had helped Declan with a couple of cold cases.

Now, he hoped the spectre of his father could help one more time.

He started flipping through "contacts," a folder his father had put together about people who he'd been working with, and, as he flicked through, he smiled triumphantly to himself, while pulling out a slim, folio folder with a name written on it.

Edward Sinclair

He'd been sure this existed, as he remembered seeing it when he'd been working with Jess to digitise the papers, but at the time, he had paid little attention to it. He'd never worked with Sinclair, bar the occasional nod when passing. Sinclair, back when Patrick was alive, had been of roughly equal rank to him, a recently made Chief Superintendent – although Patrick was Met while Sinclair was City Police. And, over the years, although currently Declan's boss's boss's *boss's* boss, Sinclair had been a ghost, leaving the grunt work to his subordinates, and hadn't really affected the team – especially when he became Commander, and Bradbury moved up into his role.

But now Sinclair was turning up at crime scenes and asking questions. Too many questions for somebody vaguely connected, and Declan was convinced there had to be something, somewhere, that explained why.

But, as he opened the folder and read through it, frustration slipped in. Page after page flipped through showed notes and reports, but realistically, there was nothing of note on Edward Sinclair. It gave his career; his background, his university, even his Hendon test scores, but didn't really give any data on the man himself. In a way, it was almost like it had been deliberately redacted, although Declan knew this couldn't be the case.

Unless Monroe had removed some things. It wasn't the first time he'd done that.

Placing the folder back on the shed's workbench, Declan frowned. He knew he'd seen something else about the man, and if it wasn't in Sinclair's folder, then it had to be somewhere else.

Annoyed at the roadblock, he paced around the shed, trying to remember where this conviction of something else came from. When had he read last about Sinclair? It was shortly after he'd moved into the house, and a day or so before Karl Schnitter had broken in and stolen his father's Mac, convinced there was data on it that could incriminate him, unaware his prey had a secret room behind a chunk of shelving and plasterboard. But what was the context? If it wasn't a file, then …

The manuscript.

Patrick Walsh had been writing his memoirs. A solid "tell-all" about his time on the force, it had been half-finished when he died in a car crash. Kendis Taylor had been helping him with it. Of course, she too was dead, killed in an unrelated attack, but this meant he couldn't ask either for their help, unless he had a Ouija board and a couple of top-rate mediums.

But Declan now remembered where he'd seen the mention of Edward Sinclair. And even though the document the manuscript had been written in had been on the stolen and then destroyed hard drive, a copy had been on an external cloud drive.

Picking up his phone, he texted Jess, asking if she knew where the file would be.

And within seconds, a message from his daughter came back.

God, Dad, you're a Luddite.

He smiled as a second text appeared with a link, but the smile faded as he considered Bullman's words. In a matter of days, he'd be leaving the force unless something came up, most likely to be paid an obscene amount of money to scavenge hits for a national paper. And Jess would be there, knowing it was the last thing he wanted to do.

He didn't do the job for the money. He knew, even before Sean had said it, that he could sell his own memoirs for six, maybe even seven figures. He was the guy who'd saved the Prime Minister's life on multiple occasions, after all. But that didn't mean he wanted to do it. Even Patrick Walsh hadn't looked for a deal before writing his own.

Which probably pissed Kendis off incredibly.

Closing the physical files back up, he left the shed, walking back up the garden and into the house. In the living room, Declan sat on the sofa, his own laptop on the coffee table in front of him as he opened it up.

Following the link details from Jess, he went into his network settings, finding the cloud folder Jess had set up for him, opened the manuscript document, and moved to the search bar.

He stopped as the page scrolled down past the title page, showing a simple dedication.

For Declan – I hope you'll be a better man than I was.

It was a dedication he'd read before, but for some reason, these words resonated hard with him this time.

'Sorry, Dad, I failed you again,' he said as he typed. Putting "Sinclair" into the search bar, he found there were seven mentions of Edward Sinclair within the book. As he scrolled to each one, he saw that five of them were just generic conversations where Sinclair had been in the room. Patrick had seen Sinclair at a police gala, for example, and he'd kept away from him because he knew Sinclair would moan at him about Monroe ... and similar.

But then there was one passage that stuck out, from around ten years earlier.

I hadn't worked with Monroe for a couple of years by this point, and Declan was newly positioned in Tottenham when Detective Superintendent Edward Sinclair came to visit. He wanted to discuss Declan; said he was a little concerned that the kid had moved up so quickly. In return, I pointed out I hadn't given any help at all, and that Declan's career in the Royal Military Police had given him what he needed to become a Detective Constable. Sinclair didn't believe me, but I was aware he was under a lot of pressure. The Bannister case was weighing on him, and he needed to find an answer for the Government. And there were rumours the Royals were muscling in, too, but God knows why.

However, at the same time, I was aware there was a coverup going on. The brothers hadn't been the only people who died that day. Emily Kim, the television presenter had also been on the helicopter when it crashed, and nobody knew why. Still, it wasn't a question for me to answer, and so I left it. I knew Sinclair would find someone to blame eventually. But why he was so personally involved, I did not know. Then he left, and I forgot all about it.

Declan was coming over because Derek Salmon had got himself into trouble again.

Declan sat back from the laptop, reading the passage a second time.

Jason and Alfred Bannister had been in Hunt Robinson's black book. And Sinclair had been investigating their deaths.

He recalled Sinclair's words; that he'd been "butting heads" with Hunt. Was it because of this?

He went to pause, but then noticed a *comments* tag was beside the piece. Someone had highlighted the text in the Word document and commented on it, currently hidden. Opening up the comments bar, Declan read the message left.

It's good to see Declan mentioned. You should do more with him in the book. If only because writing about him reminds me of happier times. KT

KT. Kendis Taylor.

Declan stared at the message for what felt like minutes, but was more likely a few seconds. This had been written before his father's death, and when Kendis and Declan hadn't been in contact. And, reading the words again, Declan felt a pain in his chest as his heart hammered against his ribs.

Kendis, beautiful Kendis. How many more ghosts come to haunt me before I leave?

Shaking himself out of the melancholy, Declan googled Jason and Alfred Bannister's death, seeing that it had been a helicopter crash in the Pennines, and that the two of them and a pilot would have died instantly. There was, however, no mention on any of the pages of Emily Kim.

Had this been something Hunt knew? Had Sinclair made sure nobody knew she was there? And if so, why?

His stomach rumbled, and Declan sighed, rising from the sofa. It was almost eight now, and he needed to grab something to eat.

So, grabbing his jacket, he headed to the pub.

MONROE HAD BEEN SITTING IN GUILDHALL FOR A GOOD HOUR and a half before Doctor Marcos turned up.

'What are you doing here?' he asked, confused as she sat herself down next to him, giving him a grin and passing him a small silver carton of Capri Sun she'd pulled out of her bag.

'Bored,' she said. 'There's nothing to do when there's no body; I can't poke or prod anything, and Hunt Robinson seems to be getting better, unfortunately, so the morgue is being gravely under used.'

Monroe stared down at the Capri Sun in his hand.

'And why have you given me this?'

'Thought you'd be thirsty,' she said. 'I picked a couple up on the way.'

Monroe shrugged, pulling out the straw and glaring at it.

'It's a paper straw,' he grumbled. 'That won't go through the top.'

'Oh, I've got that sorted,' Doctor Marcos replied, pulling out a vicious-looking scalpel from her pocket.

'You carry a scalpel now?'

'I'm a forensics examiner,' Doctor Marcos smiled. 'Of course I have a scalpel with me. And ever since you sent the simunition-firing revolver I stole from SCO19 back to them, a woman needs to find her own protection.'

Taking the Capri Sun from Monroe, she expertly made an incision in the top, placing the straw through.

'There you go. All done and no sticky orange juice dumped on your shirt. Well, yet.'

Monroe smiled and started sipping at the orange.

'So what did you get from the wife?' Doctor Marcos asked.

'I don't think she likes her husband,' he replied. 'She said there were problems in the past. Affairs, from the sounds of things. She apparently knew about one he'd been having with a secretary, and one with another journalist. From the looks of things, it's the same one who scooped him on the Lucy-Rachel story. Karen Pine.'

Doctor Marcos nodded.

'If they were sleeping together, then there's a chance she could have read it in the book?'

'That's what I think. It makes sense. He's sleeping with her, one night she looks at the book, sees a couple of stories. They break up; apparently it was a bit of animosity. She decides one day to use the story, possibly as a "screw you", possibly to boost her own career.'

'So we need to speak to her.'

'Oh, we need to do more than that,' Monroe reached into his pocket, pulling out the notepad pages he'd taken from Robinson's office earlier. It wasn't as clean as it'd been when he picked it up, however; now it had a light rubbing of pencil over the top, revealing indentations left from when something had been written on the sheet above, and had pressed through.

Meet KP — Tomorrow, 4pm The Albion

'KP? Karen Pine?' Doctor Marcos was surprised. 'Nice get. And look at you going all "Magpies" with your crime solving.'

'What we need to do now is work out if this is an old note or not.' Monroe carefully folded up and slid the note away, so as not to get graphite on his fingers. 'But if this was written on Sunday, then whether or not he remembers it, Hunt Robinson met with the woman who scooped him yesterday, maybe even a matter of hours before he woke up in a London crypt, bleeding from a stab wound.'

———

9

DATE NIGHT

Arriving at *The Olde Bell* shortly before eight, Declan nodded to Dave, the landlord and, seeing it empty, took his usual space beside the window after ordering a pint of Guinness, and settled down to work on his notes.

Anjli arrived half an hour later.

'Have you ordered?' she asked as she sat down opposite him, briefly pecking his cheek as she did so.

'I thought I'd wait for you,' Declan pushed the notebook to the side. 'Hungry?'

'I could eat, but I wouldn't say I'm hungry,' Anjli replied. 'I've got a bit of a sour taste in my mouth.'

'Oh?'

'Hunt Robinson. I almost wish they'd tried a little harder when they left him for dead.'

Declan raised an eyebrow.

'That good a day?' he asked.

'I've had better. How did your day go?' Anjli deflected the question.

In response, Declan grinned.

'I was offered a job by the editor of *The Individual*,' he said. 'Some kind of detective job, and double my salary.'

Anjli raised both eyebrows at this point.

'Bloody hell,' she exclaimed. 'Can you get me a job as well? Asking for a friend, who'd also like a salary twice as much as she currently earns?'

Declan laughed.

'I can ask, but I was personally requested,' he said. 'Well, more suggested by a mutual colleague.'

'I thought the only mutual colleague you had with Sean was Kendis, and she's well, you know ...' Anjli frowned.

Declan shrugged, but paused halfway through it. *She was going to find out anyway, it was better he told her.*

'Apparently he's got a new friend in Tessa Martinez.'

At the name, Anjli's amused disposition instantly disappeared, and her face darkened as she stared at him.

'Tessa Martinez,' she repeated. 'As in the *Magpie* Tessa Martinez? As in the *murderer* Tessa Martinez—'

'As in yes to all of those,' Declan interrupted. 'I didn't see her there or anything, but apparently she's done her time and made some kind of deal.'

'And she's now out?'

'I don't know everything – how she started working with *The Individual* in particular, but going on the basis that the *Magpies* had a very good press team back in the day, she probably remembers a lot of the skills,' Declan replied, realising the conversation was rapidly heading south, and regretting even mentioning this. 'Either way, he needs a detective to help with the investigations. She's been working with him, there's too much work for one person, and she suggested me.'

He watched Anjli for a moment.

'I don't get it,' he said. 'A minute ago, when you heard how much I'd be paid, you joked about joining me. But now, you're actually angry that I'm even considering such a thing.'

'I didn't think you'd be working with a murderer,' Anjli muttered.

'I've not even said if I'm taking the job,' Declan replied angrily. 'I've still got a few days left before the end. Anything could happen.'

'Oh, what, some magical ending's going to happen, is it?' Anjli snapped back. 'You're going to blackmail Charles Baker again? Or someone'll give us a ton of money? Maybe I should go speak to my billionaire mate Eden, and see if he wants to fund your job for a couple of years?'

Declan stared at Anjli for a long, uncomfortable moment.

'You know, this is all because of you,' he said. 'And Billy.'

'Don't you dare put this on us.'

'I'm not putting it on you,' Declan replied. 'I'm just pointing out it's because of you. The two of you were well past your promotion windows. The only reason you hadn't got them was because I was in the way.'

He looked out of the window as he continued.

'How could I honestly not make sure you guys had your promotions? How could I stand there and watch you languish in roles beneath your abilities? How am I the bad guy here?'

'Because this is some kind of bloody martyrdom experiment,' Anjli sighed, looking up at the bar. 'I'm ordering food. What do you want?'

Declan resisted the urge to tell Anjli that all he wanted was for her to be gentler on him and leant back on the chair.

'I'll have the usual.'

Anjli walked off, ordered food, bought herself a glass of white wine and sat back down.

'Look, I'm sorry,' she said. 'I can't help being angry. You should have told me, you should have discussed this with me—'

'No,' Declan said. 'No, and I'm sorry. But there's a lot of things I'd discuss with you. There's a lot of things I'd ask your opinion on. But when it comes to making sure that you get what you deserve, I'm not going to ask you, I'm going to make sure you get it.'

He leant forward, taking a mouthful of the Guinness before continuing.

'Anjli, when I joined the Last Chance Saloon, I was on my third life, if not more,' he explained. 'I'd punched out a priest, I'd made sure that my DCI was going to prison, I'd been seen as a traitor to the police to some, and a surprising benefactor to others. My father had been writing a "tell all" on everybody and I pissed away a half-dozen friendships, because I was convinced he had been murdered, and the police were covering it up.'

'Well, he had been murdered.'

'True, but they weren't covering it up, were they?'

The pair of them laughed at this, and Declan continued.

'Either way, Anjli, I quit the job after the state dinner, when I felt guilt, believed I'd failed everyone. And it took returning to my old haunt with the Redcaps to bring me back – and to bring me back to you.'

'I was always there, Declan.'

'I know. But me? I've had more lives than a cat. And maybe I've outrun the clock,' Declan replied. 'You and Billy, you've had your moments. The fact you're both in the Last Chance Saloon shows that, but it doesn't define who you are. And I'm sorry you're annoyed that I made sure you got a promotion.'

'It's not that,' Anjli interrupted. 'I like the promotion. Billy likes the promotion. We're glad you did it. However, it's the fact you did it without even working out a game plan.'

'I know, and I'm sorry,' Declan said. 'If it means anything, I don't want to go. This new job would double the money. Great, wonderful. I don't want it. I don't want to be digging around celebrity bins or doing the private investigation work for a journalist. I want to be here; I want to be a copper. I want to be a Detective Inspector – Christ, I want to be a Detective *Chief* Inspector. But I'm not going to blackmail my way to getting that.'

Anjli smiled. But it was a mocking, sardonic one.

'So it's okay for you to blackmail so Davey stays in, or for Bullman to blackmail the ex-PM so Monroe stays in?'

'Yes,' Declan laughed. 'And look where that got me. Davey was given her job back, and she still walked. It was a poisoned chalice, and she knew it. If I go to Baker, or anyone like that, and beg them to keep me, I'll end up owing them. And we don't know what I'll be asked in return. Likewise, if I go cap in hand to Bradbury, or even Sinclair ...'

There was something in his voice that alerted Anjli.

'Problems with Sinclair?'

Declan shrugged.

'Can we just call a truce and see what we both found out?'

'Okay,' Anjli nodded. 'I can do that. You go first.'

Quickly, and while waiting for the food, Declan explained to Anjli what he'd learned in the conversation with Sean Ashby, including the fact that ten years earlier the Bannister brothers had died, in circumstances that seemed to contradict the official story. Adding to this, he told her about the revelations he had learned while reading his father's memoirs.

Anjli listened, taking in everything with the good grace of not interrupting; at the end she bit her lip, as she considered what she knew.

'He's scared of something,' she said. 'When I saw him, he argued the toss, made out he was the victim, the wounded party, but when we started asking if there was anybody that wanted him dead, he paled as white as a sheet, and changed the subject.'

Declan leant back on his chair and was about to reply when the barmaid came over with their two meals. As Anjli tucked into her fish and chips, Declan poked idly at his steak and ale pie for a moment.

'What if this is something else?' he asked. 'What if somebody's after him, but not for the reasons we think?'

'I'll be honest, Declan, I'm not even sure that someone's after him,' Anjli looked up from her food. 'If it wasn't for the fact he'd been stabbed, and the book was missing, I'd wonder if he did this himself to gain some publicity somehow.'

There was a buzz from both of their phones; Declan was the first to pull his out, checking it.

'Message from Monroe,' he said, reading. 'Apparently Robinson's wife doesn't like him. Said he had an affair.'

Anjli chuckled as Declan ate his own mouthful of food as he thought about this.

'Sean mentioned a rival journalist named Pine,' he said, reading the rest. 'However, Monroe says here the wife complained about a secretary.'

'A secretary's a jump from rival journalist.'

'Maybe there were two? It seems Hunt Robinson had the appetite.'

Anjli placed her cutlery down for a moment.

'Sinclair was involved with the Bannisters, now he's involved here,' she said. 'Why does he ...'

There was a second buzz that cut her off, especially as she watched Declan's face as he read it.

'Now what?'

'Monroe, again,' Declan looked up. 'Apparently, Mrs Robinson also quite happily told Monroe and De'Geer she was having her own affair.'

'With whom?'

Declan showed her the screen.

'You won't believe it,' he grinned. 'When they mentioned Sinclair, she kicked off and said he was the one she had the affair with.'

'That changes things, surely?' Anjli was counting things off on her fingers. 'Sinclair has to be in the book. And he had an affair with Mrs Robinson, so he's involved. Christ, this is getting complicated.'

'I'm sure by tomorrow someone would have explained it,' Declan returned to his pie with gusto now.

'Hopefully we'll get things sorted quickly,' Anjli replied. 'Jess is in the office tomorrow, isn't she?'

'Yeah, and I'd like our last few days working together to be easy, and not filled with certain death.'

'I'm guessing Liz still isn't talking to you?'

Declan shook his head.

'Liz hasn't contacted me since the wedding,' he replied. 'I get it, I almost killed her fiancé.'

'You also saved her fiancé.'

Declan went to reply to this, but stopped as his phone rang.

'Monroe? Finally given up on texting?'

'No,' Declan frowned, staring down at the screen. It was a number he didn't recognise.

'Walsh,' he said, answering the call.

'Hello, Declan,' the voice of Charles Baker spoke down the line. 'Sorry to call you like this. I understand you're running the Hunt Robinson case?'

'I'm on the case, yes, Prime Minister,' Declan replied, holding the phone so Anjli could hear it as well. 'I'm guessing you have input into this?'

'That all depends,' Baker replied, and Declan could tell from the tightness the man was stressed. 'Have you seen the front page of tomorrow's *Mail*?'

Declan saw Anjli typing on her phone, likely already sending a message to Billy, asking him what the *Daily Mail* was putting on their front page tomorrow.

'Oh, don't worry about checking, the question was entirely rhetorical,' Charles Baker continued. 'There's a very interesting story about Tamara Banks. Remember her? Bastard offspring of Cruella de Vil and Heinrich Himmler? She was one of my rivals at one point for the Prime Minister.'

'Are we looking at a good or bad story?'

'Oh, it's incredibly bad,' Baker replied. 'It's "I'm expecting a letter of resignation soon" bad.'

'Well, I would have thought you'd be happy she was being removed?'

'You'd think,' Baker said, his voice toneless. 'The problem is I know for a fact that she didn't do the grunt work here. The name might be hers. But I've spoken to some, shall we say, more loyal friends of the party at the paper, and they've confirmed the story was definitely something Hunt Robinson knew, and had spoken about.'

'Hold on, who wrote it?' Declan had a worrying sensation in his stomach.

'A hack named Karen Pine.'

Declan looked at Anjli, seeing she'd recognised the name.

'So it's because of Pine you're contacting me?'

'I couldn't give a toss about Pine,' Charles Baker snapped. 'She's not the organ grinder, she's the bloody monkey. No, I'm more worried about where she got it from.'

Declan knew where this was going.

'This story that's just broken, that's front page news tomorrow, it's in Robinson's book, isn't it?'

There was a long pause on the other end of the line.

'Detective Inspector Walsh, I understand you're looking to leave soon,' Baker eventually spoke. 'So, for your last miracle, could you please find out how a missing book, and a secret within it, is now taking down members of my Cabinet? Maybe find who's leaking national secrets? And please, consider making a trip to Westminster your priority tomorrow morning?'

'An appointment with the Prime Minister?' Declan grimaced. 'Yeah, I've done that. I'll take a rain check if it's okay. My daughter's coming in for her first day of work experience, so I'll—'

'It wasn't a request,' Baker snapped. 'I want to meet you. Ten am, Palace of Whitehall. And if you do this, I might even be able to help you with your other problem.'

And, this ominous statement made, the call disconnected.

Declan looked across the table at Anjli.

'Curiouser and curiouser,' he said.

10

HEAVY IS THE CHECKERED CAP

'THANK YOU FOR SEEING US,' MONROE FORCED A SMILE AS HE walked into the office. 'I'm aware it's late in the evening and you probably have some very important black-tie dinner to attend, and some hands to shake.'

City of London Police Commander Edward Sinclair sat back in his chair, watching Monroe and Doctor Marcos as they positioned themselves in the chairs in front of him, and shook his head, half-chuckling as he did so.

'You know, for a DCI with one foot in the grave, you're remarkably confident when there are no other officers in the room,' Sinclair said with a smile. 'No offence intended, Doctor Marcos, but as far as I'm concerned, you're more a civilian holdover than an officer.'

He shifted his attention back to Monroe.

'But Alex, I respect that about you. I really do. Even at your last point of existence as an officer, you still feel the need to insult your superiors.'

'Are you late for any events?' Doctor Marcos asked simply, her expression blank of emotion.

In response, Sinclair checked his watch.

'I am actually, there's a charity ball I need to attend. The Mayor of London will be ...'

Sinclair trailed off.

'Very good,' he said, looking from Doctor Marcos to Monroe. 'You're quite the double act, aren't you?'

In response, Monroe shrugged.

'As you can see, sir, I wasn't mocking you – or belittling my superior, as you stated. I assumed you had some hands to shake, and a very important party to go to, as such, are the trappings of power, I understand. I was thanking you for deeming us worthy of your already diminishing time behind that desk. Today, that is.'

Sinclair's eyes narrowed as he tried to work out whether Monroe was mocking or praising him right now.

'So why do I now have the pleasure of the pair of you attending my office?' he asked, deciding not to press the matter.

Doctor Marcos shrugged in response.

'Don't ask me, I just came to visit my boyfriend,' she said. 'I'm a little bored at the moment, looking for things to dig into. Do *you* have anything I can dig into, Edward?'

Monroe leant forward on his chair, speaking quickly before Doctor Marcos could derail the conversation any further.

'I thought I'd give you an update on the Hunt Robinson situation,' he explained. 'You seemed quite concerned about it when we saw you this morning.'

'Robinson ...' Sinclair gave a faraway look, as if trying to remember what Monroe was talking about. 'Oh, yes, the crypt under the church thing.'

'Please,' Doctor Marcos sighed, holding her hands up in

mock surrender at this. 'I can take a lot today, but please don't pretend you forgot the journalist found in a crypt this morning.'

'Well, to be honest, Doctor Marcos, I wasn't there when the journalist was found,' Sinclair replied calmly. 'I was passing by on my way to Guildhall when I heard about the alert. I thought I'd pop in and see what was going on.'

Monroe wanted to continue this line of enquiry, but something in the way Sinclair spoke warned him off. Taking a moment to gather his thoughts, he continued.

'Sir, if you could, please tell me about your relationship with Hunt Robinson.'

At this, Sinclair's face darkened.

'Am I a suspect in your case, DCI Monroe? Is that what this ambush is?'

'Not at all, sir – and I don't really think the two of us, when facing someone of your rank, could be called an ambush, do you?' Monroe smiled, fighting the urge to throw the metaphorical gloves off. There was something very wrong here, and the last thing he wanted to do was dance around it. 'But you are an interested party, and that makes you interesting to the investigation.'

Sinclair looked to the side, out of the window for the moment, the blackness of London effectively creating a mirror back into the office as he accepted this.

'Look, I'll be honest, I never liked the man,' he replied. 'We butted heads. We faced off against each other over the last twenty years.'

'What was your take on the man?'

'Hunt Robinson? The guy's a barrel scraper, a bottom feeder. Wherever there was trouble, the police would arrive, and he'd be watching.'

'When we spoke this morning at the crypt, you asked about his satchel,' Monroe replied. 'Why were you inquiring about his possessions?'

'Well, you know, the body – I mean Robinson – was found with his clothing beside him, but no other items were there. I assumed they had been stolen.'

'How did you know there were other items? In particular the satchel and his mysterious book?' Monroe asked. 'We hadn't said it to you at the point you asked.'

'I must have read it in the report,' Sinclair interrupted angrily. 'I knew he'd been found, and I was informed he was claiming he'd been tranquillised in a car, waking up two days later. I also know that he claimed he had his satchel beside him.'

He smiled triumphantly.

'There. That must be where I knew it from.'

At this, Monroe pulled out a notepad, writing something down.

'Did something I say interest you, DCI Monroe?' Sinclair frowned at the action.

'Yes, sir,' Monroe replied with a slight smile. 'Believe it or not, your reply actually gives me a new direction to aim at, so thank you for that.'

Unsure if he was still being mocked, Sinclair nodded.

'Well, if it helps the case, I'm glad we had this chat.'

'Just so I'm a hundred percent sorted, sir, can you confirm over the years you've just butted heads? You've had no major incidents with Robinson?'

At this, Sinclair frowned, shifting uncomfortably in his chair at the question.

'If you've got something to ask, I'd really appreciate it if you stopped going around the houses, and bloody well ask it,' he stated.

Monroe accepted this, and in response, he pulled out his phone.

'I totally understand that, sir,' he said. 'So, let me give you a little more information on my thought process here. We've had a few interviews today; as you can understand, we're checking into a lot of things. We even spoke to Hunt Robinson himself, and we spoke to his editor, Sean Ashby of *The Individual*.'

'Great paper. Read it on the way to work.'

'That's good to know, sir, I'll pass it on. Anyway, we also spoke to his wife, Janine. Lovely lady, absolutely hates him.'

'She should join the club,' Sinclair smiled darkly. 'We have badges.'

'Have you ever met Mrs Robinson?' Monroe continued.

'I wouldn't know if I did,' Sinclair replied. 'If she hates her husband, she probably doesn't go around telling people she's married to him.'

'So that's a no?'

Sinclair must have guessed there was something more going on here, as he held up a hand, staring off, either thinking hard, or trying to give the impression of a man thinking hard.

'I do a lot of black-tie events, and I've seen Robinson at them,' he eventually admitted. 'It stands to reason one of the women I've seen him with was his wife. So yes, I probably have met her, but did she stand out? I'm afraid not.'

'Did you take your wife to these events?'

'Why the hell would you ask that?' Sinclair almost exploded. 'That's a bloody personal question you're asking there, Alex. Be wary where you're taking this.'

He tapped at his epaulettes.

'I outrank you by about five levels,' he hissed. 'They don't give these out in *Tesco*.'

'No sir, no insult meant,' Monroe didn't even bat an eyelid at the outburst. 'I was gathering context. I don't do these sorts of parties; not high enough up the food chain, you see, so I don't know if these are the sort of shindigs one brings their partner to. If it was, and you did, it stands to reason Hunt Robinson would have. If not ...'

Sinclair relaxed a little at the explanation.

'Oh, I see,' he said, a little sheepishly. 'Some are like that, yes, and I do bring my wife. But she's not a fan of them, so often finds excuses. But these events don't really care if you bring your significant other, or if you go "stag" and all that.'

'Thank you, sir,' Monroe checked his notes. 'So there is a chance you did meet her, but it wasn't enough of a meeting to stick in your memory.'

'Exactly. So, if we're done—'

'One last thing,' Monroe was still writing. 'This book.'

'Robinson's blackmail book? What of it?'

'Well, you might not know this, but as I said earlier, one of my team spoke to Sean Ashby, and he said he'd seen in the book once – and that you were in it.'

Monroe gave an embarrassed smile, holding a hand up.

'I know, I'm sure there's a lot of people in that book,' he said. 'But, during our questioning, what was very interesting was a couple of things came up.'

He shuffled forwards on his chair.

'It seems there's a very strong chance this disappearance, this *theft* of a very important book of secrets, could be connected to an event ten years ago, when two MPs died in a helicopter—'

'Oh, don't give me that!' Sinclair half rose from his chair now in anger, cutting Monroe off. 'If you're about to tell me that this is all about the Romans, then you can leave the bloody office right now!'

'Following leads, sir, nothing more. But that crash, you were connected to that, weren't you?' Monroe asked. 'The investigation, that is? Maybe you can tell me a little more about it – you know, from the ground, so to speak, as all I have is a couple of references and mentions from older cases.'

'Let me guess, this was in Patrick Walsh's bloody memoirs, by chance?'

'Oh, I was considering my own notes from the time,' Monroe smiled. 'But I guess from that you knew about Chief Superintendent Walsh's memoirs before he died?'

Relaxing slightly, Sinclair chuckled.

'I know everything, Monroe,' he said, his tone now displaying a hint of arrogance. 'I know, sitting here in Guild-hall, you might think I do nothing. But I'm the spider in the centre of the web. I am justice, and I am the law.'

'Interesting,' Doctor Marcos now spoke, re-entering the conversation. 'The only other time I've heard of a man claiming himself to be a "spider in the middle of a web," it was in Arthur Conan Doyle's *Sherlock Holmes* and that was about Moriarty – and he definitely wasn't on the side of the angels.'

Sinclair stayed standing, more calm and considered than Monroe had expected, following this conversation.

'Alex, Rosanna. It's been lovely speaking to you both, we really must do it more often,' he said. 'But as I earlier explained, I have a very expensive gala to attend. I need to get changed and then, as you said earlier, "go shake hands with

very important people." I'm sure you can go and have a ... I
don't know, a pie and eels, or something. I don't really know
what you lower ranks like to do.'

The smile faded, and the tone hardened.

'But I tell you now, Monroe, I brought you into my office
today as a courtesy. I felt bad watching you wait outside like
some kind of beggar. But if you ever come back to Guildhall
with anything less than a full report, I'd have you out of the
force faster than you were brought back in, you understand?'

'Yes, sir,' Monroe rose, nodding to Doctor Marcos to do
the same. 'And thank you for your time, sir.'

As he reached the door to Sinclair's office, he stopped, his
face showing a conflicted expression.

'Permission to speak candidly and off the record?' he
asked, looking back at Sinclair, who made a theatrical sighing
motion, rolling his eyes as he did so.

'Fine, go on – and then once you're done, piss off.'

'My team is really good at what they do,' Monroe started,
facing Sinclair. 'And they find secrets people hide for years.
And sometimes people, such as, say Janine Robinson, they
just up and out the secrets without any coaxing. Like, for
example, who she might have had an affair with, after
meeting them at a party at Christmas, and how they were old
lovers.'

Sinclair didn't speak, his lips thin as he watched Monroe.

'Now, I'm no angel, and I don't give a shite about what
anyone else does, sir, but it seems to me you're worried about
something in this book, when you should be more worried
about other things coming to life.'

'Is that a threat, *DCI* Monroe?'

'Oh, no, sir,' Monroe grinned. 'Just a heads up. She

seemed to be a woman with an axe to grind and nothing to lose. I always find they're the ones you need to watch. You understand?'

Surprisingly, Sinclair simply gave a curt nod to the question.

'Thank you,' he said.

'Anytime,' Monroe nodded. 'After all, sir, we are on the same side.'

Walking out of the door and shutting it behind them, Doctor Marcos glanced at Monroe as they walked down the corridor.

'You just gave away your trump,' she chided.

'You think that's the only thing out there?' Monroe shrugged as they walked up to the elevator, Monroe pressing the button. 'We have nothing else, but now he doesn't know what we have. After all, when you give something like that away for free, what else do you have in your pocket?'

Doctor Marcos nodded at this, the slightest hint of a smile on her lips.

'So what was it he said that made you write in your notebook?'

'Sinclair said he read the report,' Monroe entered the elevator, Doctor Marcos following. 'We hadn't written one at that point. Had you?'

He pressed the down button.

'If he was turning up at the scene, it wasn't because he was passing by, or read any bloody report, it's because he'd been told about it. And he could have said that, but he chose not to.'

As the doors closed, he looked back at Doctor Marcos, his face an expression of anger.

'So I'd like to know who he's hiding, and why,' he said. 'Because Edward Sinclair might be our bloody Commander, but he's no detective. Someone aimed him at us, and I want to know what their gameplay was.'

11

CAUGHT FOOTAGE

'WELL, THIS IS A WEE BIT UNDERWHELMING,' MONROE grumbled as he stared at the briefing room. 'Where is everybody?'

The briefing room itself was half filled on this morning. Monroe stood at the front, beside the desk and with the plasma screen behind him, Bullman was in her usual spot beside the door. Anjli was seated on a chair near the front, with Jess beside her, where Declan would usually sit, and to the back, Doctor Marcos sat beside De'Geer. She'd returned to her previous pillar-box red hair, and Monroe had already made a comment on how they didn't need lightbulbs on with her in the room.

He hadn't been wrong.

'PCs Mastakin and Cooper have gone to pick up Karen Pine,' Anjli read from her notes, 'and Declan has been summoned to see the Prime Minister.'

'Oh aye, has he?' Monroe smiled. 'Must be great having friends in high places. Still, maybe it'll give him a chance to see if he can beg for ...'

He trailed off, glancing uncomfortably at Jess.

'... some opportunities to help with the case,' he finished lamely, giving her a little smile. 'And is there a reason why Billy hasn't come in yet?'

He looked through the glass window at Billy, still sitting at his monitors, tapping furiously on his keyboard.

'He thinks he's found a lead,' Bullman replied. 'Bless his little cotton socks. Said he'll be in with us in a few minutes.'

'Oh, will he now? Well, let's just hope that by the time he graces us with his divine bloody presence, we're not finished,' Monroe grumbled. 'Okay, where are we?'

'Today's *Daily Mail* headline states that Conservative MP Tamara Banks was a signed up member of the National Front while at university in the late nineties. Attended far-right rallies too, and they have a witness who claims Tamara dressed as Eva Braun to a fancy dress party,' Anjli read from her notes. 'Not a good look for the Conservatives as you can understand. Especially as they're going through Home Secretaries like disposable napkins right now. Although, let's be honest – half the time they want the right-wing vote, so maybe dressing up like a Nazi helps?'

'Probably not in this case,' Monroe grimaced. 'Especially as the hit piece also says she owns a first edition *Mein Kampf,* and had an old friend reckons she was at a hen night in the Eagle's Nest.'

Anjli nodded as she flipped a page.

'The piece also claims over the last couple of years, Tamara Banks has been using her position in a top secret cabal known as the "Star Chamber," to remove political enemies – and by that, they mean anyone who doesn't believe in a far-right agenda.'

Monroe's eyes narrowed.

'Aye, we've heard of the bloody Star Chamber before,' he said. 'Text Declan and get him to mention that to Mister Baker, see if anything comes out.'

He looked back at Doctor Marcos.

'Anything new from forensics?'

Doctor Marcos shrugged.

'Nothing new, no fingerprints, DNA, anything that shows anyone other than Hunt Robinson being in the crypt that night. But, I know a new recruit to forensics did something super clever with some paper and a pencil last night.'

'She means you,' Bullman nodded to Monroe. 'In case you didn't know.'

Monroe leant against the table.

'Meet KP – Tomorrow, 4pm The Albion,' he intoned. 'I think we can all assume the KP is Karen Pine, and The Albion is some kind of pub somewhere. How long before we get her in?'

'I think Mastakin and Cooper had to go to her apartment in Wapping, so it could be a while,' Anjli replied. 'Remember, she's not a suspect here. Just a potential witness. We think there's a chance, based on your note, that she might have had a conversation with Robinson on the day of his amnesia, and that she printed the story raises questions of where she found it out.'

'It's probably not that great a secret, but looking at how it's stayed dormant so long gives credence to it being a tough one to prove,' Bullman added. 'But hypothetically? He either told her, showed her his book, or she may have seen it while they were …'

She finished the line with a whistle.

Monroe nodded.

'We'll cross that eye-gouging vision when we get to it,' he replied. 'What else do we have? '

'Not a lot,' Anjli admitted. 'Hunt's claiming he has amnesia, even though we know there's a strong chance he might not. Cooper and I believe he's scared of someone; that something happened that he won't talk to us about.'

'Declan mentioned something about a Westminster bash at Christmas?'

'Yeah, he's going to tug on that thread with Baker. As for Hunt, though, other things we know? His wife doesn't like him.'

'Aye, tell me about the wife.'

'Janine Robinson, married nine years,' Anjli carried on. 'Met at a Government fundraiser, works for a variety of charities, as some kind of PR or marketing person. We're looking into that. They seem to lead separate lives. She claimed she had an affair sometime after Christmas, with Commander Edward Sinclair—'

'Who claims he barely knows her,' Doctor Marcos interrupted from the back. 'Even though they apparently knew each other before she was married.'

'Do we know her maiden name?' Bullman asked. 'Maybe Sinclair didn't realise she was the same person. Maybe she looks totally different. It's unlikely, but it does give him plausible deniability and I'd rather we were ahead of that.'

'There's something I don't get though, Guv,' Anjli placed the notebook down as she looked up. 'The Wellness retreat, and how she claims she came back after hearing he'd been injured.'

'Go on, lassie.'

'Well, when speaking to you and De'Geer yesterday, she said she only realised he was at the hospital when she turned the phone on and she had a message from the police, explaining what happened while she drove home. That she only remembered to turn it on halfway around the M25.'

She looked around the briefing room, looking for help from the sparse occupancy. And it was De'Geer who answered.

'Actually, I wondered about that as well,' he replied. 'It felt wrong somehow.'

'How so?'

'Well, how did she find out about him if the phone was turned off?' De'Geer asked. 'First, I thought perhaps she saw it on the morning news, so this morning I checked with the Wellness retreat. They said that apart from the phone they used on reception, there's no technology. They don't watch television – it's classed as bad. Which means that yesterday morning, Tuesday, there was no reason for her to come home. And she had no calls that day.'

'Maybe that was her time to finish?' Jess suggested.

'She told DCI Monroe that she was Thursday to Thursday, and the Wellness retreat confirmed she arrived last Thursday,' De'Geer shook his head.

'So she left two days early,' Monroe nodded, understanding where the conversation was going. 'You think she knew in advance?'

'I think she had more knowledge than she's letting on,' Anjli replied, and she was about to speak again when Billy, overcome with excitement, came running into the briefing room.

'I've cracked the case!' he exclaimed excitedly.

'Oh, have you, now?' Monroe laughed. 'Please, Detective Sergeant Fitzwarren, show us your genius.'

Billy ran over to his usual spot in the room, connecting

his laptop to the HDMI port. The plasma screen behind Monroe burst into life as he did so.

'So, yesterday, you took some note paper—' he started.

'I accidentally acquired some notepaper,' Monroe interrupted, speaking carefully. 'I wouldn't take anything without a warrant.'

'No, sir. Absolutely. My mistake – yesterday, you *accidentally* acquired a piece of notepaper, that when rubbed with a pencil, gave a time and a location for a meeting at somewhere called The Albion,' Billy was typing frantically on the keyboard as he matched this with his speed of talking. 'So, I looked into "The Albion" to see what was out there. There's a taverna in Faversham, and a few other places with similar names, but there are three pubs named "The Albion" in London. The first is in Islington. The second in Hammersmith. The third ...'

At the press of a button, a Google Map appeared on the screen, showing a street map view of a crossroads; heading north to south was Farringdon Street, to the east was Ludgate Hill, and to the west was Fleet Street.

'... is right here,' Billy pointed.

'Well it has to be that one,' Anjli leant back in her chair.

'So I thought the same, and I started thinking about this, working out what to do,' Billy was still excitedly babbling, caught up in the moment. 'We know the message has been passed, but we didn't know who to or who from. We think KP is Karen Pine, though, so I checked around.'

He pointed at the screen again.

'Karen Pine was working at the *Daily Mail,* which has its bullpen of reporters based in Northcliffe House, off Kensington High Street. So, to get into the meeting, she would have caught the Circle Line from Kensington to Blackfriars and walked up, so I looked at the Blackfriars cameras. And at three-fifty-five ...'

Billy clicked the mouse button and a security camera photo of a woman emerging from the station appeared on screen. She was wearing a coat, but had no handbag on her.

'This is Karen Pine,' Billy explained, pointing at the woman. She was slim with long dark hair, but the image was pixelated. 'We found her.'

'You're lucky,' Doctor Marcos was checking her phone. 'The second Albion pub you mentioned was only a mile to the west of her offices.'

'I know, I ... well, I checked there first,' Billy admitted. 'But wasting time there didn't help the narrative of how great I was.'

He looked back at Monroe.

'City cameras were down early Tuesday morning, but they weren't down Monday afternoon. This camera shows Karen Pine heading towards The Albion. Knowing this, I also probably broke a few rules and asked a few favours, and ... I ... checked her credit card reports.'

Monroe raised an eyebrow.

'Billy,' he chided. 'Your new rank has got to you.'

Billy flushed.

'Karen Pine paid for a round of drinks at close to four-forty-five pm on her card,' he continued. 'That's two pints – one lager, one bitter, a sandwich, and a large wine.'

'Sounds like she was paying a tab,' Anjli replied.

'That's what I thought,' Billy said, 'And we have her leaving just before five, so she paid and left, heading back to the station.'

He showed a new CCTV picture; this time, Karen Pine had something in her hand.

'What is that?'

'I can't tell for sure, Guv, but it's book shaped, and it's covered in plastic. Like a carrier bag. But I can't get any better resolution.'

'Maybe someone gave her it?' Jess suggested.

'But here's the interesting part,' Billy grinned. 'At this point, I still didn't know for sure who she met in there. So, I started thinking about how I'd go to her if I was Hunt. He lives in Meopham, and it has a train station, so I worked backwards and checking through various train services and pages, I realised that if Hunt Robinson caught a train from Meopham around three, he could arrive at Victoria, catch the Circle line, again to Blackfriars, and be there in time for his meeting. And lucky for us, Meopham Station has cameras.'

He pressed another button on his keyboard, and the screen changed to a new image. This time it was CCTV from a provincial railway station, taken from outside. There was a man in jacket, trousers and shoes, a baseball cap over his head, hiding his features. And, in his hand, was the same colour plastic bag seen in Karen Pine's hand.

'This was taken at three,' Billy said. 'He's hiding his face to make sure we can't see him, and he didn't have his phone, so nobody could track him. But I think this is Hunt Robinson, based on the clothing we found at the scene of the crime.'

'That's definitely him,' Doctor Marcos confirmed, leaning forwards. 'I recognise the jacket.'

'But if they were coming from the same station, why not return together?' Jess asked, before reddening. 'Unless they were worried about being seen. Of course. Sorry.'

'No, I wondered that as well,' Billy clicked on the button. The same man, now without the bag, was leaving The

Albion. 'This is the same man, leaving five minutes before Karen paid her bill.'

Monroe nodded.

'It's suspicious, but if he still claims he has amnesia, he can say he doesn't remember the meeting,' he said. 'Although mixing bitter and lager is a criminal offence in its own right.'

'I agree,' Billy replied with an irritating smile, 'but I haven't finished yet. Hunt Robinson was outside The Albion at a quarter to five. Guess what closes at five?'

'St Bride's Church?' It wasn't that hard a guess.

Billy nodded.

Click.

On the screen was another image; this time of the man believed to be Hunt Robinson, cap on head, walking down a narrow street.

'This is taken from beside the FedEx shipping offices on Bride Lane,' Billy explained. 'They're in a little court to the side, but monitor both entrances. They have cameras for obvious reasons, but to be caught on them means only a couple of things, the main one being—'

'He's heading for St Bride's before it closes.'

Billy stepped away from the laptop as he looked around the room.

'I think Hunt Robinson entered before five. It's a church he knows well, and I think he quickly found a place to hide, maybe in the crypt, and waited until the church was locked down.'

He nodded at the screen.

'I think he then got rid of the cap and pulled the things he needed out of his jacket. Realistically, all he needed was a knife and a length of silk rope, right?'

'And some diet supplements to give him a bad stomach,'

Doctor Marcos was walking over to the screen now. 'He probably spent the rest of the night sitting in the crypt, killing time until it was ready to go. It's quite probable, and it explains a lot of things; for example, the blood on the silk rope.'

'How so?' Bullman asked.

'Well, when we saw it at the scene, we wondered if there was a fight. But it'd be easier explained if this was a one-man job,' Doctor Marcos was smiling now, already visualising the scene. 'He dumps the things he doesn't need in a waste bin, knowing they'll be cleaned before anyone realises. He then walks down to the crypt, takes off his shirt, ties a silk cord around his wrist, loops it round the base of the pew things, and then stabs himself with the folding butterfly knife. It's not a deep wound, and to be perfectly honest, a wound in that area wouldn't hurt immediately, with the adrenaline in his system, it probably felt as if he was being punched. He's been stabbed before, in Bosnia, according to his medical notes, so he'll know how it feels for comparison.'

She ran a hand through her hair as she continued.

'Then, with the wound now flowing, he takes the tablets, allowing them to go into his bloodstream through the stomach lining. Or maybe he's already had them. Either way, he wipes the blade on his own shirt, folds it up, places it down, tosses it onto his jacket, lies on the floor, slips his hand into the other noose and positions himself until he's held tight, arms outstretched, and waits.'

'The second hand he placed into the noose would have been used to wipe the blood off the knife and throw it, and it's rubbed onto the hand, and then the rope,' Anjli suggested.

'So Hunt Robinson did this himself?' Monroe mused.

'And Karen Pine helped him? We need to find out why he invited her along—'

He stopped as Jess held her hand up.

'Mary, mother of God, not you too,' he said. 'No need to raise your hand.'

'Did he invite her?' Jess asked. 'Sorry, I mean did he invite her, Guv?'

Everybody looked at Jess now, and she glanced to the floor, a little sheepish.

'Sorry, I'm just ... I'm coming at this quite new.'

'No, go on,' Monroe encouraged.

'Well, I'm thinking that piece of paper you had, it showed "KP" on, right? But surely, if he was organising the meeting, why would he write the note? To me, I write a note down, so it's because I've been told something I need to remember. And he's writing the note to remember to meet "KP" at four pm.'

'You might have a point there, lassie,' Monroe nodded. 'There's a chance he could work for Karen, rather than with. We'll find that out when she arrives.'

He looked over at Anjli.

'Pass a message on to Declan, let him know what's going on. And let's just see what Karen Pine has to say when—'

He stopped as his phone started ringing, noticing that as his went, so too did Doctor Marcos's, buzzing with a new message rather than a call.

'Cooper?' he asked as he answered the phone, placing it on speaker. 'Good of you to call. We need you to be a little more forceful when you bring Miss Pine in. We've got a feeling she's a lot more connected to this inquiry than we thought—'

'Oh, she's definitely a lot more connected, boss,' Cooper's

voice echoed through the phone's speaker. 'We knocked, but there was no answer. We went around the side and the back door was unlocked. We just found her in the kitchen, stabbed in the back. Like, literally. With a massive kitchen knife.'

'I'm sorry, boss, but Karen Pine is dead.'

12

WEST MINSTERS

DECLAN HADN'T EXPECTED TO BE BACK AT THE HOUSES OF Parliament before he left the Last Chance Saloon. If he was being brutally honest, he was quite hoping to never return to the place again. However, when you're called by the Prime Minister, there's not a lot you can do about it, and so Declan went through the rigmarole of the St Stephen's gate security once more.

Walking through the Great Hall, he paused as a memory struck him.

'Do you need a moment?' Anjli said, a hint of amusement on her face. 'You look like you're about to cry.'

Smiling, Declan continued up the stairs. He was going to miss working in London. Maybe even miss working as a detective.

But the one thing he'd miss most of all was working with Anjli Kapoor.

Walking down a corridor to the left, he entered the octagonal "Central Lobby," the core of the Palace of Westminster, and a place designed by Charles Barry where both houses could meet. It was here where Declan and Anjli had first waited to see Charles Baker, and Declan wondered how long he'd be there this time, when a young woman walked out of one of the side corridors, looking around nervously before spying Declan, and nodding at him.

'DI Walsh,' she said. 'The Prime Minister will see you on the terrace.'

Declan grinned. He didn't know who this woman was, but he guessed she was yet another in a long line of assistants and personal secretaries. He hoped she wouldn't turn out like the previous ones. The first he ever met, Will Harrison, ended up trying to start some kind of coup and was murdered, whilst the second, Jennifer Farnham-Ewing, had been ingloriously fired after screwing up, blocking Declan's entrance to a state dinner, where he was trying to save the Queen's life, as well as Charles Baker's himself. She had also been involved in a mistimed campaign for a crime bill, connected to a serial killer vigilante, so she was pretty screwed in relation to returning.

Although the Daily Mail said Tamara Banks was a Nazi, so who knows?

Declan followed the lady through the corridors, nodding at a couple of MPs who had seen him as he was walking through. He didn't know who they were, but they seemed to know him, so it was polite. And, eventually, the two of them emerged out onto the rear terrace. Positioned at the back of the Houses of Parliament and looking out across the Thames, it felt quite warm for the day; although early in spring, the morning was actually quite clear. The heaters were on, however, as at the back of the terrace, Charles Baker sat at a familiar table, nodding at Declan. His hair was as white as ever and blow-dried back, his skin tanned and moisturised.

He was in his late fifties by now, but looked late forties. He was sickeningly healthy, but Declan thought he could sense a hint of weight loss. Not illness, but maybe stress related.

'It's your last time here, isn't it?' Baker smiled. 'I thought we should go back to old times. You know, sitting at the table we first met.'

Unlike the first time, when he was doing his best not to be there, this time Baker rose, shaking Declan's hand.

'How are you?'

'Surprised you're being so nice to me,' Declan replied. 'We've not exactly been on good favours recently. And I wasn't expecting to see you before I went.'

'I'm hurt,' Baker grinned. 'I thought you would have at least tried to blackmail me for your job or something.'

'Did that before, didn't take. Remember?'

Charles Baker was eating a scone and as he nodded, layering some clotted cream on to the top of it heavily.

'As fun as this is,' Declan said, 'you were right when you said this is the last time we see each other. I'm on the way out, but first I'm on a bit of a deadline.'

'I heard,' Charles Baker finished spreading cream on to his scone, and took a mouthful. 'You're hunting the book, aren't you?'

Declan wasn't surprised by this question.

'We understand there's a book that he's missing, yes,' he said. 'But officially, we're investigating the attempted murder of a journalist.'

'I heard about that, too,' Baker sat back in his chair, his mouth still half full as he spoke, watching Declan. 'But as to the book, this Tamara incident is quite concerning.'

'How so? I thought your loyal right would eat it up, start polishing their medals.'

'Well,' Baker considered his lines carefully. 'The story aside, it's more the *getting* of the tale, shall we say? This is something few people knew about. Even I hadn't been told the full story about her, and I'm the bloody Prime Minister.'

'Just shows even puppet masters have their puppet masters,' Declan smiled coldly.

'But one thing I do know is that Hunt Robinson had something on her,' Baker ignored the jibe. 'Let's just say, when you're Prime Minister, you have a lot of resources at hand. And through people – unsavoury, late-night people – I know what's in that book. Well, what's believed to be in it.'

Declan realised suddenly what this meeting was actually about.

'You don't give a shit about Tamara,' he said. 'You don't care about Hunt Robinson.'

'God, no,' Baker interrupted. 'He was an odious little shit. And I'm quite glad someone gave him a battering. He's been up my arse for the last three or four years now, and since I was Prime Minister, he's made my life miserable.'

'Well, heavy is the crown and all that,'

'Yes, I know. I can't complain,' Baker smiled. 'I wanted the job. I got the job. And once you're in the job, everybody wants to remove you from the job. And therein lies the problem.'

Declan watched Charles Baker for a long moment.

'His book covers many years, I've been told,' he said. 'A good few decades, even. Are you in it?'

'How would you mean?'

Declan glanced around the terrace to make sure they weren't being overheard.

'Let's just remember, as you're all about nostalgia today, that the first time we ever talked here was in relation to a murder investigation that for twenty years you'd believed you were the culprit. For all that time you'd held a secret, kept over you by Francine Pierce. One where you believed you'd killed Victoria Davis,' he intoned. 'Could a secret like that be in this book?'

Baker considered the statement.

'He never got that,' he said. 'At least, to my knowledge, he never did. Frankie was very good at keeping her secrets to herself, even if they were other people's secrets.'

He sighed, pushing the plate of scones away, then changing his mind, opening the pot of clotted cream again.

'No, I'm more worried he has other things. Like the fact that fifteen years ago, I moved from Labour to Conservative,' he explained. 'I'd decided that I wasn't going to get anywhere, and Labour was moving away from the centrist nature of Blair. So, I made my choice to join the Conservatives.'

He waved around the terrace.

'Something I think has done quite well for me,' he smiled. 'But I think the book might have a different story.'

'Does the book, by chance, have a different reason for why you left the Labour Party?'

Baker took another mouthful of the scone, eating it slowly while he considered a response.

'Let's just say I left before I was pushed,' he replied. 'And let's just say, for hypothetical sake, that the Conservatives took me in, unknowing of certain things.'

'What did you do, Charles?' Declan asked. 'What am I going to find myself sorting out for you?'

'You won't sort anything out,' Baker snapped. 'If this book is found in time, before the stories come out, that is. Whoever's got the book will start releasing things, piece by piece. And if you fail? Well, you'll be gone, anyway, so someone else will clean it up.'

Declan thought back to his previous conversation with Sean Ashby.

'You're leaving of the Labour Party, it wasn't to do with the Bannister brothers, was it, by chance?'

At this, Charles Baker's eyes widened.

'What do you know about that?'

Declan shrugged.

'It seems the Bannisters are turning up quite a lot at the moment,' he said.

'I was friends with Alfie and Jay Bannister before they came into Parliament,' Baker admitted. 'I even vouched for Jay to the vetting committee, before the 2001 General Election. At the same time, I mentioned to friends on the Tory side that Alfie was a good bet, too. They both got in, although my side won.'

He looked away for a moment.

'I spent a lot of time with his brother in the Labour ranks. And the two of them were closer than any twins. I knew them both equally. When they died, it was a tragedy.'

'How did they die again?' Declan asked. 'Helicopter crash, right?'

Charles Baker's face darkened.

'It was a terrible accident, both of them died instantly—'

Baker stopped, shook his head.

'Actually, I don't know if they died instantly or not,' he replied. 'The accident was terrible. But there's every chance they were trapped in that helicopter, burning to death, screaming as it exploded on the side of a mountain in the Pennines.'

'How many people died?'

'Three,' Baker said, straight-faced as he said the number. 'The pilot and the Bannisters.'

'Would you like to change your answer?' Declan leant closer, placing his elbows on the table as he moved in. 'For example, would you like to add a few numbers to that?'

Charles Baker licked his lips nervously, and it seemed to be more than the act of regaining crumbs from his scone as he leant forward to match Declan.

'Six,' he breathed, his voice barely more than a whisper. 'Six people died. There was a press secretary, Penelope Hallett, there was a TV person, Emily Kim, and there was an unknown sixth body found. It was a woman, but they couldn't find out who it was, the body was too ...'

Declan leant closer, understanding now why Baker had switched parties.

'Which one of them was there because of you?'

Baker sighed.

'Emily,' he said carefully. 'I'd introduced her to Jay when he first entered Parliament. They'd started slowly, but they were shagging after five years. I was stunned they'd kept the whole thing secret for ten years. We were ... it was complicated.'

'And after?'

'People knew something was going on, they also knew I'd been involved in affairs Alfie was having. I was quite the matchmaker. Word was spreading about my party loyalties, and I was getting disillusioned with Blair ... my time was ending. Alfie saw it, and pulled me across.'

'And Jay?'

'He was the one who screwed me over,' Baker snapped. 'Saw me as a threat to his own ambitions. I loved him like a brother, but so did Cain with Abel.'

Declan nodded. None of this surprised him; he knew very

much what the Charles Baker of twenty years earlier had been like.

'So, Emily was there with Jay, but why were the other three on the helicopter?'

'Because the Bannisters were screwing around, and you know that, Declan. Stop fishing!' Charles Baker was getting angry now. 'You know better than this. Or is it true you're looking to become a private eye for a newspaper? Is this the future I see, you standing outside Number Ten with a camera with a zoom lens?'

Declan took the moment to pause.

'But why didn't people know about this?' he eventually asked.

Baker sighed, rolling his eyes, as if explaining to a simpleton.

'Look, it was a tough time when they died in 2013. The Tories were in power, but it was a coalition. They knew at any minute something catastrophic could happen. If the Lib Dems pulled out, there'd be another election, and at the time Cameron wasn't strong enough to keep it going. And there was also talk of other things happening. Big shakeups. The love affair of Clegg and Cameron wasn't as deep as people thought it would be.'

He looked out across the Thames, sadly.

'And then this accident happened; two brothers from either side of the Commons, passing away in a terrible accident. It was sad. But it was also a PR dream. For once, Labour and the Conservatives were united. They couldn't throw shit at each other in the press because they'd hurt their own. The Bannisters' deaths gave the Government something to unify behind, something that was greatly needed at that point.'

His shoulders slumped.

'The last thing we wanted to point out was that both brothers had been dipping their wicks, their mistresses had been on the helicopter, and that the pilot smashed into the side of a mountain because he was out of his box on cocaine.'

Declan raised an eyebrow.

'But Hunt Robinson had this?'

'I don't know how, but yes. And for the last ten years, people have repeatedly tried to get this bloody book away from him,' Baker grumbled.

'What was Sinclair's connection with this?' Declan asked. If Charles Baker had been expecting this question, he made a very good impression of looking surprised.

'Ed Sinclair?' he paused. 'He was a Detective Superintendent at the time. Connected to the Westminster police, ran a lot of security for Westminster. The type that threatened journalists when they went out of line.'

'He was the one who got the pages?'

'He was the one who made damn sure Hunt would never reveal,' Baker replied. 'Even now, if it came out, it'd torpedo a dozen MPs just like that. Why do you mention his name now, though? He's been in Guildhall, looking for the next ladder rung, off the scene for years.'

'Because he's all over this case, and he's never looked at our cases before. He's always been hands off.'

'Well, from what I heard about Sinclair, the term "hands on" is something he's very good at,' Baker smiled at his own personal in joke. 'If I was you, Declan, I'd consider who has the most to gain from this book. Someone in the Government? There's enough secrets in it to bring us all down. Our enemies? No, because there's enough to bring *them* down as well. He was pretty much an all-seasons blackmailer. Celebrities, politicians, he cared not about policies or political beliefs. All he cared about was how much money he could make.'

'And he held this book over you?'

'The party, not me. He never wanted to release the stories,' Baker wiped at his mouth with a napkin. 'Once you give away what you have on someone, you can't ask them for favours anymore. And Hunt Robinson asked for a lot of favours.'

Declan understood this well.

'There is one thing I know about Hunt Robinson,' Charles Baker replied. 'Something spooked him at a White-hall party at Christmas. The same one I invited you to. He'd been sniffing around recently, and I had some people look into him, check what was going on.'

'What did they find?'

'They said after New Year, he was getting quite frantic; was telling people there were *shadows* after him. You know, black ops shit. Thought he was on an MI5 kill-list or some-thing. Anyway, a lot of us assumed it was paranoia but, after yesterday, who knows? Anyway, he pulled out his book, waved it about, almost as if he thought it was a gun and was getting people to back off. Damn near almost started a scrum of backbenchers before he put it away and left.'

'Do you know who was after him?' Declan frowned. 'With you being so important and all that?'

'No, but let's be honest, I'm sure you've written a list out by now and had to find more paper,' Baker smiled. 'Dammit, I *am* going to miss you, Declan. If there's anything I can do to help—'

'I already said—'

'I know, but maybe I can put you on some Honours List or something? That could help you a little?'

'I'm fine,' Declan smiled. 'I appreciate the offer. But I think if you were to give me anything right now, or even help me out, the optics wouldn't look great.'

'I can see that,' Baker nodded at this. 'Although I will say, it depresses me a little to think that you'd turn your back on me at such a vital moment.'

Declan chuckled. 'At what point did I ever give you the impression I was on your side?' he asked. 'Let's be frank. You've been a pain, you've been a friend, but you've also been an enemy to me over the years. I think I've saved your life enough times to equal out the issues, but when you worked for Gladstone, you weren't exactly on my side.'

Charles Baker accepted the comment.

'They reckon there'll be a vote of no confidence in the next six months,' he said. 'I'm an unelected leader without a mandate, and people are out for me already; Tamara was one of the main ones. That she's now about to resign helps me, but makes me wonder why such a thing went out.'

'Do you think whoever's got the book is helping you?' Declan asked. He hadn't considered that option.

'That's a question you're going to have to ask Karen Pine, the writer of the last piece,' Baker said. 'After all, she's the one who broke it.'

'You think she was helped?'

'Oh, I know she was helped,' Baker replied. 'There's no way she was intelligent enough to do it herself.'

Baker rose. 'I have a meeting, unfortunately,' he said. 'It was good to see you, Declan. Don't be a stranger. I'll make sure you are invited to a variety of different events. We can hang out; it might even be nicer once you're no longer investigating me.'

As Charles Baker left, Declan sat, considering the conversation.

Edward Sinclair had been the "stick" for the Conservatives. Was this why he was trying to get the book back? Could he have been involved?

One thing was for sure. Karen Pine needed to be brought in and questioned.

He glanced at his phone; it'd buzzed during the conversation, but he hadn't looked down at the message.

Now he did. It was from Anjli and about Karen Pine.

'Well shit,' he muttered to himself as he left the terrace, possibly for the last time.

13

HOUSE OF SHARDS

THE YOUNG WOMAN HAD BEEN WAITING FOR HIM AS HE returned into the Houses of Parliament, not saying anything, but simply turning on her heel and walking off, expecting Declan to follow.

Declan grinned; she'd probably been warned against talking to him, and it was a good suggestion. However, Declan was almost at the edge of the central lobby, when a *new* man arrived, nodding to the woman as she stopped, finding him blocking the way.

'It's okay, Lauren, I'll take him from here,' he said with a smile, nodding back at Declan as he did so. He was young, maybe thirty years old, his mousy-blond hair neatly parted on the side. His suit was basic and off the shelf, a far cry from the tailored suits that many of his contemporaries wore; more likely something from *Next* or *Marks & Spencer's* than Savile Row. And he had a youthful face, one that was relaxed and open as the woman frowned at the request.

'But I was told—'

'Honestly, Lauren, and please take this with love, but I

don't care what you were told,' he smiled at her, but there was no warmth in it. 'Baker's said his piece, and your job is over. Now it's time for others to chat to him. And, as I said, I'm taking Detective Inspector Walsh to the door.'

He leant in.

'Or the new MP for Bethnal Green and Bow could come and have a chat?'

The female aide shrugged, turned around and, without even saying goodbye to Declan, walked off, probably glad that her job was over.

And, this done, the young man turned to face Declan.

'Sorry about that,' he said. 'I thought I'd just quickly say hello. Name's Bonner. I'm the MP for Hackney East.'

'Labour?' Declan had already assumed this by Bonner's subtle usage of Johnny Lucas, one of Labour's more recent additions to Parliament.

'Of course,' Bonner replied as if the idea of another party to be a member of was incredulous.

'And you're a friend of Johnny Lucas,' Declan added.

'Well, I wouldn't say "friend," I mean, I've met him a couple of times at events,' Bonner said. 'I just wanted to say hello, and I know Lucas came with a rep, so I used it.'

'Because you wanted to say hello,' Declan nodded as they walked towards the Great Hall. 'And why would that be again, Mister Bonner?'

'I wanted to thank you, to be honest,' Bonner replied. 'I heard through the parliamentary grapevine it's your last week or something and, well, I've not really had a chance to speak to you, to give my thanks for you saving my life last year.'

Declan paused at the top of the stairs leading down into the hall.

'You were at the State Dinner?'

'I was one of the back tables,' Bonner nodded. 'But yeah, you saved a lot of us there.'

Declan didn't really know how to answer this; the story was known that Declan had stopped many MPs at the Queen's State Dinner from eating a dessert that had been poisoned. But the fact of the matter was that Declan had been banned from the building, and by the time he'd got into the hall, the food had already been changed, the culprit exposed, and the MPs saved.

Still, people remembered what they saw publicly, and that was the vision of a Detective Inspector running in, security behind him as he yelled at people *not to eat the dessert.*

'Well, you're welcome,' Declan smiled. 'Glad to help.'

'You definitely helped,' Bonner carried on down the stairs. 'I was new, only joined Parliament in the last election. So I was terrified anyway, even without death threats.'

'Well, you've said it now, no need to walk all the way down, only to walk back.' Declan decided not to mention only the Cabinet was being targeted.

Bonner smiled, pulling out a cigar.

'It's fine, I need to go outside. I could really do with a puff or two. Do you smoke?'

Declan looked at the cigar. It looked to be a short, stubby thing, not the cigars he remembered seeing Winston Churchill smoke in news images.

'No, I'm fine,' he said. 'But I didn't think you could smoke here?'

'Oh, there's a little area we can go to outside, where the paparazzi can't take photos,' Bonner said, rolling the cigar between his fingers.

'This is a Hoyo De Monterrey Epicure No.2,' he explained

proudly. 'It's a Robusto, quite a light taste to it. I like to use it as a pallet cleanser.'

'For a Labour MP, you're sounding very middle class,' Declan mocked. 'Next, you'll be talking about your favourite port. And I don't mean Folkestone.'

Bonner chuckled.

'Yeah, I suppose,' he said. 'I never used to smoke these. It's the people you end up talking to that corrupt you into these vices.'

He looked up at the Great Hall.

'Churchill smoked, you know, all the time,' he said. 'He preferred the Cuban Romeo Y Julieta the most. He'd smoke between eight to ten a day, and he believed they aided his steadfast leadership during the Second World War. It was so well known, the long cigar he smoked is now called a "Churchill." Poor bloody Kenneth Clarke never had a range named after him.'

'I wasn't saying anything against it,' Declan replied, 'I'm sure smoking cigars is lots of fun. Just not my thing.'

He smiled.

'Although I did notice the names you mentioned were both Tory politicians. Are you sure you're in the right party? Perhaps you should be walking across the aisle, the same way that Charles Baker did?'

'Well, look how that's gone for him,' Bonner now smiled back. 'I'm one of the most right-leaning centrists in the party, but I'm not yet ready to bleed blue.'

Declan noted the "yet" in the comment, but chose not to mention it. And, as they walked through the Great Hall, Bonner paused.

'Sorry if this is a little personal, but why are you leaving?' he asked. 'The impression I got was that you liked your job.'

'I do,' Declan replied. 'But it's a budget thing.'

'I work with Civil Servants, I know all about those,' Bonner nodded. 'All my life seems to be involved with budgets and cuts these days.'

'Oh, what do you do, then?' Declan asked, more out of politeness. 'I mean, I'm aware you're an MP, but I'm guessing you're part of some ministry somewhere?'

'I'm one of the Junior Shadow Under Secretaries in Agriculture and Fishing,' Bonner made a face. 'As you can guess, it's every bit as exciting as the title.'

Declan laughed. He warmed to Bonner; the man was fresh, and didn't seem to have an agenda, which was nice. But the fact he didn't *seem* to have an agenda meant there probably *was* an agenda somewhere, and it was about to rear its ugly head.

'What's this actually about?' he asked, with possibly a little too much world weariness behind it.

'I was told you were a good detective,' Bonner sighed. 'Looks like you've proven them correct.'

He looked around the Great Hall, as if checking they weren't being listened to.

'I was wondering how your case was going?' he asked. 'With Hunt Robinson?'

'Why would you want to know that?' Declan replied cautiously.

'I've worked with him a couple of times. I know he's got a bad rep, but I never saw it.'

'You're the first person I know to say something nice about the man,' Declan said and Bonner shrugged.

'To be honest, I've already said I'm the new guy in town,' he replied. 'When you're the new guy, you need to make your friends where you can, and sometimes your friends are the ones that other people don't like.'

He scuffed his foot on a brass plate on the floor absently as he considered his words.

'Someone like Hunt? He's good for me. He's given a few titbits, and told me what's going on here and there. Basically gave me a heads up when I've needed it. Helped my "brand," so to speak.'

Declan wanted to write this down, but knew that if he pulled his notebook out, talking to an MP in the middle of the Houses of Parliament, somebody somewhere would see it and it'd be made even more of a story.

'Did you know Hunt Robinson well?'

'*Did* I know?' Bonner raised an eyebrow. 'You make it sound like he's dead. I heard he was just attacked.'

'Force of habit,' Declan said. 'Usually I'm talking to people about bodies.'

'Well, I've only met him a handful of times. But I'd say I'm a pretty good judge of character,' Bonner replied. 'There's scuttlebutt saying he did this to himself?'

'I don't know,' Declan said, deciding not to confirm or deny anything right now. 'Did you ever see his book?'

At this, Bonner laughed.

'The bloody book,' he said. 'God, that's a great bit of PR, isn't it?'

'How do you mean?'

Bonner stared at him for a few seconds, as if confused about what he'd just said.

'Well, it's not real, is it?' he eventually continued. 'I mean, come on. A magical book that has all the secrets? Nobody has such a thing. It would have to be like twenty books deep by now.'

He considered his next words, backtracking slightly as he spoke.

'So, my thinking is, he probably had *a* book. At some point, that is. And there probably was a book that had secrets. But now, he just uses the *legend* of the book. "He's Hunt Robinson. Don't piss him off. He'll probably have a secret about you in his book, and he'll use it on you." Something like that.'

Bonner scratched the back of his neck as he pursed his lips.

'I think he probably had a handful of secrets from back in the day, and he's dined on those for the last two, maybe three decades.'

'So, you never saw the book?' Declan repeated.

'I've seen a book, but whether it's this mystical grimoire? Who knows,' Bonner smiled, continuing to the door again. 'I know the stories people are claiming are apparently from the book, and none of them are as exclusive as you think. Lucy-Rachel Adams's little theft sprees? I heard that was taken from his book, but I saw that on Tattle two months ago.'

'Tattle?'

'It's a website, a forum. People put blind items up about celebrities, things they've heard. You know, no names, completely anonymous. And then other members of the forum will try to guess who it is, or they'll add their own stories. And seventy percent of the time, the stories are pretty much correct. You can go on there. You can work out who these people are. And every time something happens, Tattle was talking about it months ago.'

'Do you go on Tattle a lot?'

'Absolutely,' Bonner replied, as if it was a stupid question to ask. 'I go on them all. I'm a member of Parliament. Half the stories on these sites are about my peers. I read those, subscribe to Popbitch, hell, I'm even on three Parliamentary WhatsApp groups purely aimed at MP gossip.'

He grinned.

'Even when they don't have names, I can pretty much work out who they are.'

Declan wanted to write this down but decided instead to just check out the names when he got back.

Bonner shrugged, nodding in passing to an older woman, hurrying past.

'There's a vote in ten minutes,' he said, leaning in. 'The Tory whip's trying to pull everyone in on it.'

'Anything important?'

'Nah. Just migrants. Which is important, but the vote's all about the points. It's just box-ticking.'

He stopped, realising what he'd been talking about, and returning to it.

'The one thing about super injunctions is they stop the press talking about things, but it doesn't stop the public chatting about stuff.'

Declan watched Bonner for a moment.

'So, you're saying that you don't believe Hunt Robinson has a book of secrets, and instead is using sites like this Tattle, or others to gain the gossip he wants?'

'No, not at all,' Bonner backtracked. 'He's a good journalist. I've seen that from working with him. And he has good people hunting secrets for him. What I think he does, is he gets the stories, knows what's going on, has seen what else is happening, and then he just tells people he has the full thing, using what he knows as breadcrumbs, as he holds it over them. It's just currency for getting bigger stories.'

'And now someone's taken it.'

'Good luck to them. If it exists, and it's real, then we're gonna have a shitstorm happening. If it's not real, then I'll just keep checking sites like Tattle because that's where the stories will come from ... just like they always do.'

They'd reached the door to the Great Hall by now, double doors within a great glass arch. Bonner looked at his watch, and then with great reluctance placed his cigar away again.

'Listen, I've got that boring Commons bill to be in too, so I have to leave you now,' Bonner said. 'But I just wanted to say thank you for helping and, you know, being one of the few people speaking up for Hunt Robinson. He's not the bad guy.'

'You're sure?'

'A lot of people usually say if you don't like Hunt Robinson, it's because he's got something on you.'

'But not in a book,' Declan smiled.

'What do I know?' Bonner shrugged 'I'm still the new boy on the block.'

Declan raised a hand, a subtle gesture to stop Bonner from leaving just yet.

'A quick Parliament question,' he said. 'You hearing anyone talking about the Bannisters? Or the "Romans," as they seem to be known?'

Bonner looked confused.

'Jay and Alfie Bannister?' Declan added.

At this, Bonner's face brightened as he understood the question.

'Nah, they're before my time, although there's talk of a memorial. Not sure why,' he said. 'I've only been here four years or so. And I'm all about blackmail material, not old stuff.'

He winked.

'I'm ten years younger than Blair was when he became

Leader of the Opposition,' he said. 'I'm here for the long game.'

'Say hi to Johnny for me,' Declan said.

Bonner frowned, and then, as if realising what Declan meant, nodded.

'Yes, absolutely,' he replied. 'Good luck, DI Walsh. I hope you find what you need in your next job.'

This said, Bonner, the MP for Hackney East and the junior shadow Undersecretary for something to do with fish and farms, walked back towards the House of Commons, and a bill he wasn't bothered about.

Declan watched him leave, a slight frown creasing on his forehead. There was something here he wasn't getting; some parts of the jigsaw which were missing when it came to Bonner. He didn't know what it was, but he had the feeling that the young man had been standing in the Central Lobby waiting to speak to Declan since he had arrived for his meeting with Charles Baker, and that never bode well. And the fact he claimed he'd been going for a smoke, but had to have known there was no way he could smoke a cigar in the time before the vote was needed, felt that had just been an excuse to meet Declan.

But was it to speak to him, or size him up?

Sighing, Declan nodded to the doorman, and left the Great Hall with more questions than he'd arrived with.

14

CHECKING OUT

HUNT ROBINSON WAS STANDING BESIDE HIS HOSPITAL BED, NOW dressed in a new set of clothing most likely brought by Janine the previous day, when Monroe and Anjli arrived at the hospital ward.

'Come to give me a sendoff?' he asked, quite jovial for the time of day and the circumstances he was in. 'They finally allowed me out. I can go home.'

'I don't think you'll be going home just yet,' Monroe replied, stepping forwards. 'Mister Robinson, I'm—'

'I know who you are, DCI Monroe,' Robinson smiled. 'I know all of you media-friendly police types.'

'I'm a media-friendly police type?'

'Yeah, you've done enough things to get you in the papers. And I've known about you for a while. You're even in my book.' Robinson winked. 'Not as a major character, though. More as a side character, standing around, you know, being in the room when things happened.'

'That sounds ominous,' Monroe stated, his voice emotionless. 'Maybe you should tell me a little more.'

'Oh, I don't think I will,' Robinson carried on getting his items together. 'I think I'll leave that to whoever you get to do your memoirs. Because, let's face it, you'll not be writing it yourself, too many utterances of "jings!" and "hoots, mon!" for the average reader.'

Monroe ignored the insult, glanced at Anjli, and then frowned as he turned his attention back to Robinson.

'You seem remarkably chipper for a man who yesterday was worried his entire world was falling apart,' Anjli interrupted, stepping forwards to join Monroe now. 'Do you have information on the book's location?'

'No. Do you?'

'Actually, we might,' Monroe replied. 'Have you seen today's newspapers?'

'Yeah, I saw,' Robinson's eyes narrowed, as he realised this possibly wasn't the conversation he was expecting to have.

'Karen Pine put out another story. I wonder where she'd got that from? Maybe she got it from your book?'

'It's a possibility,' Robinson nodded warily. 'She's always been snapping at my heels.'

'But where would she have seen the story?' Anjli asked, looking at Monroe with mock confusion. 'She would have had to hold the book, flick through the pages to see it?'

'Ah, yes, she probably read it while Mister Robinson was sleeping,' Monroe replied earnestly, glancing back to the now annoyed Robinson.

'Are you insinuating that I had an affair with a rival journalist?' he snapped. 'Are you sure you want to go down that route with a man well versed in libel and slander cases?' He shrugged. 'Bring it on. I could do with some payouts.'

'Oh, I don't think we need to worry about that at the moment,' Monroe grinned a dark, humourless smile. 'You see, me thinking you've had an affair is the last thing you should be worrying about right now.'

He looked back at Anjli, a conflicted expression on his face.

'I just don't know what we arrest him with,' he said, almost sadly. 'I mean, if you fake a suicide, then you get mental health assistance. Likewise, if you actually try to kill yourself, for real. If you fake an abduction or a kidnapping, well, that's mainly wasting police time. But what do you arrest someone with when they fake an attempted murder? Are they the victim, or the suspect?'

Robinson's face paled.

'I don't know where you're going with this,' he said. 'But I really – um, I really believe you should—'

'Shut up and listen to me, laddie,' Monroe snapped, even though Robinson was clearly the same age, if not slightly older. 'We know you met Karen Pine on Monday evening. We know you walked into St Bride's minutes before it closed—'

'And that's a crime, is it?' Interrupting, Robinson looked from Anjli to Monroe, and then back. 'It's a crime to visit London, to speak with people?'

'It's not a crime, but you have to admit it's suspicious, when you're claiming to everybody that you have amnesia caused by some kind of drug cocktail, and that you were held somewhere before a ritualistic murder,' Monroe replied, his voice cold.

'Well, I've got amnesia,' Robinson said, but he was flustered, more nervous now. 'I don't know what I did. I could have done anything on the Monday. All I remember is waking up in the crypt.'

Anjli nodded sympathetically at this.

'I get that,' she said soothingly. 'So let's have a little chat about a few things. First off, we have CCTV footage of you walking to The Albion pub on Monday to meet with Karen Pine. In your hand was a carrier bag, with a book-shaped item within it. One Karen left with, almost an hour later.'

'I don't know what you mean ... meeting Karen? Come on. I don't think that would have happened—'

'You left a note in your office arranging the meeting,' Monroe added. 'Although we can't yet work out if you were telling her to meet you, or she was telling you to meet her.'

'You've been in my office?'

'Oh, aye, your wife let us in. Let us look around, do whatever we wanted. No "jings" or "hoots mon" needed.'

He leant closer now as Robinson scooted backwards, falling back onto the bed.

'We saw your phone was there, as well as your satchel, so no need to worry. Oh, your wallet too. How lucky was that, eh? However ... your book seems to be missing, but then we think that's what you brought to Miss Pine.'

'Who, as we said a minute ago, left with the same bag and what looks to be the same book,' Anjli added. 'Interesting how Miss Pine, the woman who was possibly given this book by you the day before you were found almost dead and amnesiac, releases a story *from* your book today.'

Robinson hadn't expected this conversation. He'd been totally unprepared for it. And Monroe actually felt sorry for him.

'You did good, laddie,' he said. 'You had us looking for quite a while. But unfortunately, even the best stories have unreliable narrators. And you seem to be the most unreliable of them all.'

Anjli pulled her notebook out, reading from it.

'You were poisoned with something that only gives you

stomach ache. You were tied with a rope we know you had to tie yourself, because you left your own blood on it. And we've had a chat with the church, and they found a baseball cap in their waste bin, beside the gift shop, which we're expecting to reveal your DNA.'

She leant over the bed, staring down at the now terrified Hunt Robinson.

'So how about you actually stop whatever this is and explain why you've led us on such a dance?'

'It's just – it's not what you think,' Robinson stuttered. 'You should speak to Karen Pine, she'll—'

'Ah yes, that's the other problem we have,' Monroe said. 'Karen Pine is dead, stabbed in the back last night with a kitchen utensil. Lack of defensive wounds gives us the impression she knew her killer.'

He sniffed.

'Now we know it's not you, because, well, you're in here,' Monroe's voice lowered as he continued to watch Robinson. 'Our police officers looked around the premises and unfortunately, they can't find the book of secrets you're worried about losing. You know, the one you gave her in The Albion on Monday evening. Which means that whatever plan you had with Karen Pine, some way to boost her career, giving out stories you couldn't be seen to be releasing ...'

He sighed, leaning back.

'Well, I assume that's out the window now, because someone else has your book, and I don't know how friendly they are to you.'

Hunt Robinson opened and shut his mouth several times; no sound came out as he did.

'Karen's dead?'

'Aye, we found her this morning, when we were bringing

her in for questioning,' Monroe nodded. 'Let's just say at the moment we don't have many suspects; as to what's going on here, your little runaround's now turned into a fully-fledged murder inquiry – of which you seem to be one of the prime suspects.'

'Wait, you said I was innocent! I was in hospital at the time!'

'No, although I said you were in hospital at the time, I didn't say you were innocent,' Monroe waggled his finger as he shook his head. 'You see, Mister Robinson, you could have easily outsourced this to someone else. It's not the first time you've done such a thing.'

'We're still trying to find Digger Doug right now, so if you have anything we can use here, we'd really appreciate it,' Anjli added.

At the name, Robinson's shoulders slumped.

'Someone's out to get me,' he replied, his voice soft and almost broken. 'I don't know who it is. They've got my phone number. They contacted me before I went to Ukraine.'

'Did you recognise the number?'

Robinson shook his head sadly.

'I'm a journalist, so I get a lot of sources contact me from phones they can't be traced on,' he explained. 'And I also know the other side of the coin, how to work out where the number comes from. And I checked into this. It's a burner number. It's somebody who doesn't want to be found, and trust me, I've looked. I even had Doug hunt the number down, try to find them.'

'Did he?'

'No. Yes. I don't know,' Robinson replied. 'All I know is he spent a week trying, told me he'd worked out they were coming from a cell tower near Whitehall, and then stopped taking my calls. I have no idea why.'

'He worked out who it was, and it scared him?' Anjli suggested. 'Whitehall suggests the Government.'

'Or it's St James's, and the Royals, they hate me too. Or even whoever it was paid him off. It's not the first time he's ended a job with me because he gained a bigger offer to piss off,' Robinson shrugged, dejectedly. 'I don't pay a lot. So I get it.'

'What is it they wanted?'

'They want me to reveal a story for my book,' Robinson replied.

'The Bannisters?' Anjli asked, and Robinson spun to look at her as if he had been electrocuted.

'How did you—' he stammered. '—I mean, what did ... who—'

'We're quite good at our jobs,' Anjli said. 'We notice things happening. Like that Commander Edward Sinclair was connected to the Roman case, and that "Romulus and Remus" were nicknames for the Bannister brothers.'

'We also know there seem to be a lot of leads taking us to the Bannisters and a helicopter crash ten years back,' Monroe continued. 'But what we can't work out is why you would fake your own attempted murder, and pretend that your book was stolen.'

'Because if I did that,' Robinson sighed, 'then they might think I didn't have it, and they might leave me alone.'

'They might leave you alone, that's a telling statement,' Monroe glanced at Anjli. 'Leave you alone and not reveal the secret they have on you? I'm guessing that's what it is?'

Robinson shrugged.

'Let me guess, they came to you, and said "give us what

we want, the story that tells the truth about the Bannisters, or we reveal your mistresses to the world, reveal your time with Karen Pine, your drug addiction ..." I could carry on.'

At these, Hunt Robinson started to cry.

'God, man,' Monroe muttered, his eyebrows knotting as he stared at the man in front of him. 'What the hell is this? You're Hunt Robinson, pain in everyone's arse. You've been in war zones. Why the hell are you crying at this?'

'Because my career is over,' Robinson sniffled. 'There's no way I can get back after this. When he finds out I faked my death, that I did all this ... I'll be a joke.'

He shook his head.

'This was all done so I could have some kind of plausible deniability, you see.'

'And Karen Pine was there from the start?'

Robinson nodded.

'She suggested it. She could tell I was in a bind, told me to meet her, that she'd do this for me. It didn't hurt that she'd get her byline name on some good stories in the process, but I didn't ... I could never ...'

He sobbed harder now; great wracking sobs from the heart that caused Monroe to reach across to some tissues beside the bed, and pass them to him.

'She's dead, and it's my fault,' Robinson wiped his eyes with a tissue, staring down at the bed.

'Aye, laddie, I think it is,' Monroe said sadly, straightening as he spoke. 'So how about you, and I, and Detective Inspector Kapoor here have a little stroll to the station and see what we can find out?'

Awkwardly, he leant closer and patted Robinson on the shoulder.

'Don't worry,' he said soothingly. 'At the moment, nobody

else knows you did this – as far as they know, you were the victim of an attack.'

And, to drive the point home, he patted his notebook.

'It's just in our little books,' he said, nodding at Anjli. 'And with your help, we can solve a murder, tear out those pages, and it all goes away.'

Robinson looked up at Monroe, desperation in his eyes, and for a second Monroe didn't recognise the bastard journalist nobody likes.

'You really think so?' he pleaded.

'No, laddie, but it's a nice thought to keep in your head as the world turns to shite around you,' Monroe shrugged. 'Come on, grab your things. Time to go.'

———————

15

MARIGOLDS

KAREN PINE LIVED IN A SMALL SEMI-DETACHED HOUSE NEAR Baron's Court tube station, on the Piccadilly Line, just south of Kensington and to the west of the *Daily Mail* offices in Hammersmith. It was an old house, built sometime around the turn of the century, and looked like it could have done with some serious, tender loving care over the last few years.

Many of the nearby houses had been recently renovated, possibly for profitable flips by younger entrepreneurs. But the impression De'Geer had as he stared up at the building was that Karen Pine had either lived here a very long time, or inherited something very old – and done nothing with it.

Once inside, the latter seemed to feel a lot more likely. The house felt like it had been time-locked from the seventies, or even the early eighties. The wallpaper was a beige and white series of hexagonal squares that couldn't have been left by choice; the burgundy carpet was worn, and even the light fittings were decade-specific; it felt like this was more of a museum than modern-day property. Weirdly, when De'Geer checked one of the lights, he saw it had a smart bulb in it, likely connected to either the house's Alexa, or maybe one of the other various Home Hub Ads that now controlled people's lives.

Perhaps she liked the way it looked, he wondered to himself. *Perhaps she liked the retro style. It was back in vogue, after all.*

There was the fact that Karen Pine was also a woman in her late fifties, and possibly didn't care that much about this sort of thing anymore. From the conversation he had had with her editor before arriving, he got the impression that Karen Pine spent more of her time in the office than she did in the house.

Walking through and nodding to Cooper, who was currently checking the living room, De'Geer found himself at the door to the kitchen where a PPE-dressed forensics officer passed him a disposable PPE suit to put on. He noticed Doctor Marcos, arriving shortly before him was already in her custom grey one, already kneeling down on the floor. And, not for the first time since he'd joined forensics, De'Geer wondered how he too could gain a custom PPE suit. Not for the colours or the individuality, it was simply that being just over seven feet tall, the average PPE suit, although fitting, was very ... snug in certain places.

Doctor Marcos looked up, seeing him pulling on the PPE.

'I hope they found you an extra extra-large,' she said. 'Some of the other female forensics get all giggly when they see you in a tight one.'

De'Geer grimaced, knowing that Doctor Marcos had said this deliberately to embarrass him, and also to wind up Cooper, who even though was in the next room, could hear everything that was being said.

'What do we have?' he asked as he pulled on his mask and hood. Walking over to her, his plastic boot coverings made a squeaking sound on the stone flooring of the kitchen.

'Well, she's definitely dead,' Doctor Marcos said. 'Case closed! I can go home now, right?'

De'Geer smiled.

'I never doubted you for a minute, boss,' he said.

Doctor Marcos, in response, nodded at the body; it still hadn't been moved since it had been found.

'Poor bloody Cooper,' she said quietly. 'I can't believe she was the poor bloody copper to find this.'

She looked back at the door and nodded silently to herself.

'We'll have a chat with her later,' she said. 'She really should chat to her therapist, the amount of dead bodies she keeps bumping into here. You know, it's pretty unnatural.'

'How would you mean?'

'Well, the average copper doesn't really see that many dead bodies in the grand scheme of things,' Doctor Marcos explained. 'You're keeping the peace, not hunting corpses everywhere. Yet the Last Chance Saloon seems to find them around every sodding corner.'

'I get that,' De'Geer nodded, as Doctor Marcos smiled at him.

'It's why you came, wasn't it? A bit more action? I'm assuming Maidenhead was a bit dull for corpses, and things like that.'

De'Geer shrugged, the slightest hint of a smile on his lips.

'Well, apart from the fact that Hurley had a serial killer, then yes.'

He glanced back at the body.

'The knife's been taken?'

'It's already gone to be checked,' Doctor Marcos rose from

her crouching position. 'But I can tell you now it wasn't brought into the house. It matches the set of knives against the wall over there.'

She pointed across the kitchen, at a magnetic strip on the tiles above the sink. Attached to the strip were a selection of metal kitchen knives, ranging from a meat cleaver all the way down to a tiny paring blade. There was an obvious gap where the chunky chef's knife would have been.

'Blood was on the handle. But whether there're finger-prints or DNA, I'm not sure,' Doctor Marcos continued. 'I had a sniff, and although I could smell the iron tang of blood, I thought I could smell a bit of latex, so I worry that they wore gloves, maybe marigolds.'

'Marigold rubber gloves?' De'Geer was impressed. 'You could tell that from the smell residue?'

'No, you idiot, there's one marigold glove on the sink, a left-handed one, and no right-hand glove,' she said. 'The killer could have grabbed it, put it on, and then picked up the knife to kill Karen Pine. What does that suggest, Sergeant De'Geer?'

'This was an opportunistic kill,' De'Geer considered the question. 'If they were intending to murder her, they would have brought a weapon with them. Or, they would have at least brought gloves.'

'Well done,' Doctor Marcos said. 'So now we know some-one's in the kitchen with Miss Pine, and at some point, they grab a knife and slam it into her back. What else does that tell us?'

'She knew her killer. I don't know about you, but I wouldn't feel comfortable turning my back on someone I wasn't sure about, especially long enough for them to put on a pair of gloves—'

'One glove.'

'Sorry, yes, put on one glove and stab them in the back. So, somebody she knows turns up. Right-handed. She lets them in.'

'Forensics on the scene when I arrived, claimed the time of death at around five this morning,' Doctor Marcos looked from De'Geer to the body, and he followed her gaze. Karen Pine had been wearing a dressing gown when she died. He assumed underneath it was a pair of pyjamas or nightdress – he hoped so, anyway, as the last thing he wanted to do was turn the body over to find the victim slept naked.

'So, five in the morning, someone turns up and Pine opens the door,' Doctor Marcos was already working through the scene in her head. 'It's early, earlier than most normal people would arrive, so she knows something's wrong. She brings them in. She immediately comes to the kitchen, maybe to make a coffee. The kettle, for example, is not in its usual spot.'

'How do you know that, boss?' De'Geer frowned at this. 'You've not been here before.'

'No, but it's one of those kettles you place on an electronic base,' Doctor Marcos pointed. 'It's beside the sink. I think she was filling it, maybe placing it down beside the counter as she was murdered.'

'So five am, Someone comes in, she makes them a coffee, and they kill her. You think this is about the book?'

'It makes sense,' Doctor Marcos looked around the room. 'But why come so early? What time did she leave for work?'

Doctor Marcos raised her voice.

'Cooper!' she shouted. 'Get your diminutive arse in here, please!'

PC Cooper walked through the door, a slight hint of a smile on her face.

'Ma'am?' she deadpanned.

'Do you have anything from when you spoke to her editor about when she would turn up for work?'

'She's usually in the office by six to six-thirty,' Cooper read from her notebook. 'She likes to be there before the breakfast shows start, so she can get an idea of what's going on. The editor also said she likes to read the papers before she starts her day.'

'Okay, so it's a half hour journey to walk there from here, maybe twenty minutes if you hurry,' Doctor Marcos was counting back on her fingers. 'That means she's leaving here, say, six. So with showering, breakfast, coffee in the morning, five o'clock could be a time she'd be waking up at.'

'Oh, it is, doc,' Cooper nodded. 'I can tell you without a doubt her wake-up time is five.'

'And this is because?'

'Because I looked in the living room,' Cooper pointed back into the room she'd just exited. 'She has a lot of self-help books. But not ones that make you feel better about yourself, the ones that are all about entrepreneurs and go-getters, and how they work their days, and pretty much most of them I know tell you to start your day at five in the morning.'

'And how would you know that without reading them?'

Cooper shrugged. 'Because I've read them,' she said. 'When I was at Hendon, I was big into productivity. I recognise a lot of the books.'

'Impressive.'

'Oh, and she has an alarm clock in her bedroom, which has the alarm set for zero-five hundred.'

'And you couldn't have started with that?' Doctor Marcos replied.

'I wanted you to think I was very clever,' Cooper smiled.

'I would have thought you were more clever if you hadn't told me that.'

'I know, but I just can't help being honest,' Cooper looked at De'Geer now. 'We found her phone as well, but we can't get in it without her fingerprint ...'

Doctor Marcos knew exactly what Cooper was insinuating.

'Technically, we shouldn't be doing it, but she is a murder victim, and there might be something there,' she said. 'Bring it over.'

Cooper had it in a plastic evidence baggie, and passing it over, the baggie half open and held by her blue latex-gloved fingers, Doctor Marcos pressed the dead index finger of Karen Pine against the sensor, and then passed it back to Cooper.

'Let me know what you find,' she said as, with a nod, Cooper left to get started, leaving De'Geer and Doctor Marcos alone in the kitchen, looking back down at the dead body.

'So five am, she gets up,' Doctor Marcos was working through the timeline again. 'Somebody turns up at the door. She has a chat with them. They stab her, they leave ... what does that suggest to you?'

'That somebody knows she gets up at five,' De'Geer suggested. 'If it was before that, the five am alarm upstairs wouldn't have been turned off. Also, if somebody turned up at, say, four o'clock and she was talking to them, she would have made the coffee earlier; she wouldn't have been in here, unless there was a top up being made, and there are no dirty cups.'

'Agreed,' Doctor Marcos nodded. 'This is definitely somebody turning up when they knew she was waking up. This is definitely someone she knows. She hasn't had a shower yet, so she just woke up, still in her pyjamas. They come along and ask her for help. And now we're in a situation where they can kill her and be out of here before most people are awake.'

She started looking around.

'No way any motion-detected video doorbells would pick her up if she walked away. I didn't see any speed cameras around, but even those wouldn't really pick her up unless she was running faster than thirty miles an hour, so maybe Billy can do something with that...'

She started muttering to herself, so low that De'Geer couldn't hear.

'We won't find anything on the body,' she said. 'The killer stabbed her. She fell. The killer would have then left, maybe wiped the blade, but I don't think so, because they left it in the body. This was an opportunistic action at best, so maybe we can hunt for a missing marigold glove, and hope we can find some DNA on the inside, but then again Karen Pine could be the kind of person who has a cleaner, and this could have been ...'

She slammed a fist on the kitchen table.

'Dammit!' She cursed. 'Everything's still in the air, and I hate it when it's like this. Cooper!'

'Yes, Ma'am?' Cooper walked back in, still looking at the phone.

'What do you have? Give me something to work with here.'

'It might take a while,' Cooper was still scrolling as she

spoke. 'She's made a lot of phone calls in and out; a lot of unknown numbers calling her, and her calling them.'

'That could be anything,' Doctor Marcos mused. 'Journalists have confidential informants, they're bound to be talking to people on burners, getting information ... especially as she was trying to confirm stories she was putting out there. What else?'

'There are a couple of messages,' Cooper said, frowning. 'But it's a little strange. It was sent from Hunt Robinson's phone.'

'Why's that strange?' De'Geer asked.

'It was sent Tuesday afternoon,' Cooper looked up. 'When he was in hospital.'

Cooper turned the phone around to show Doctor Marcos.

FROM: HUNT ROBINSON.

If you're going to do it, do it right. Or I will take the book back and do it myself.

'Interesting,' Doctor Marcos said as she read the message.

'But we know the phone wasn't in Hunt's possession,' De'Geer replied. 'We saw it when I went with the Guv to his house, and the only person who was anywhere near it was Janine Robinson.'

Doctor Marcos nodded.

'Just because he wasn't near the phone, didn't mean he couldn't send the message,' she pointed at the message as she replied. 'The message is blue, and it's an Apple product. Therefore, it's probably being sent through *iMessage,* which is what Apple products use. If you have an Apple phone and you message somebody else with an Apple phone, sometimes it doesn't use the network – instead, it goes through the Wi-Fi, or something along those lines.'

Cooper turned the phone over to look at it.

'But it also means that if you have that person in your contacts list, you can text them from your computer, your laptop, your iPad, anything on the Apple ecosystem, right?' she asked.

'Hunt Robinson could have sent that message on Tuesday afternoon,' Doctor Marcos leant against the kitchen counter. 'He might not have the phone, but De'Geer wrote in his report she had a large handbag with her, large enough for a possible laptop or tablet - so his wife could have brought him his computer to work on, and as soon as he was logged on? He could have used it to send a message.'

'Should I change the passcode so Billy can check it?' Cooper asked.

'Well, we've probably broken a dozen rules moving it from chain of evidence right now, but sure,' Doctor Marcos replied. 'I think we're done here for the moment. The rest of the magic happens in the lab.'

She grimaced to herself.

'And to think, I was moaning yesterday about a lack of bodies to examine,' she grumbled. 'I should have known I jinxed myself right then. Anything else?'

'Actually, yes,' Cooper brightened, disappearing into the side room. A moment later, she emerged with a small cream notebook.

'Don't tell me that's ...' Doctor Marcos widened her eyes.

'No, not at all,' Cooper shook her head quickly to dispel any thoughts. 'But it's definitely something. There's only one page written on, and it's not in Karen Pine's hand.'

'How do you know?'

'Because she has notes everywhere,' Cooper replied, opening it. 'It's a list of titles. "Tamara Banks Nazi." "Marcus Leigh piss party." "Peter Morris shagathon." there's another three after but the handwriting's a bit terrible.'

De'Geer took a look.

'It looks like it's rushed,' he frowned. 'Hurried writing. It also looks like Hunt Robinson's writing. Well, from the notes we saw in his office, anyway.'

'Tamara Banks was outed yesterday, and I recognise the other names,' Doctor Marcos placed the book in a large, clear evidence baggie. 'This is more than an ideas pad.'

She looked back at the body.

'And I think Karen Pine was killed because of it.'

16

FAMILY AFFAIRS

JANINE ROBINSON SAT ANGRILY IN THE INTERVIEW ROOM, glaring at Declan and Bullman, sitting across the table from her, an elderly female solicitor sitting beside her.

'I don't appreciate a police officer turning up at my door, and dragging me here,' she snapped. 'Could someone please explain to me what's going on? I mean, yesterday I had your DCI turn up with some Viking in a police uniform, and today I have two more officers turn up and bring me here. This is inexcusable.'

Bullman stared at Janine coldly.

'It would have been easier if you'd been at the hospital,' she said. 'You know, staying with your husband. We could have brought me in together.'

'My husband?' Janine frowned. 'What's he got to do with this? Why is he being brought in, and why should I be at a bloody hospital?'

'Because you told our officers that's where you were going,' Declan replied.

'Yes, yesterday!' Janine exclaimed angrily. 'It's Wednesday now. I'm not going to stay overnight in a bloody hospital! All he does is lie in his bed and snore.'

She looked at Declan, assuming that as the younger of the two, he might actually be friendlier.

'Look, I don't know what's going on here. But all I do know is I saw your colleagues yesterday. I let them in, no problems. They had a wander around. Didn't ask for a warrant, anything like that, I gave them everything I knew. And then I went to see my husband,' she shifted in her seat. 'Then last night I came home, went to bed and woke up this morning at the banging of my door.'

'I apologise for any inconvenience,' Declan said, nodding at Bullman. 'Shall we begin, then?'

Bullman, taking the hint, leant forward, pressing the button on the recording unit.

'Interview with Janine Robinson, eleven fifty-eight am,' she said, checking her watch. 'In the room, Detective Inspector Declan Walsh and Detective Superintendent Sophie Bullman, and Mrs Robinson's solicitor--'

The solicitor leant forward.

'Marjorie Bond.'

The solicitor returned to a sitting position as Bullman leant back in her chair, staring at Janine.

'I echo my colleague's apology,' she replied. 'And I do apologise if we're more blunt or frustrated than we would usually be. It's just that the case has changed slightly.'

'Let me guess, Hunt's been a massive prick again?' Janine said. 'Has my husband decided to do something else that's stupid?'

'Well, we currently believe that he did this to himself,'

Bullman replied. 'This whole abduction, loss of his journal, and attempted murder was all part of some elaborate theatre he did to save his own neck, passing the book to someone else.'

'That sounds like him,' Janine said. 'But why am I involved? I know I'm his wife and all that, but I wasn't anywhere near him.'

'No, we know that,' Declan said. 'But that's not why you're here. You're here because of Karen Pine.'

'That whore,' Janine grumbled. 'What the hell has she said? Whatever it is, it's lies, I tell you.'

'She's not said anything,' Bullman replied. 'She was murdered in the early hours of this morning. We're still waiting for a time of death.'

Janine was about to shout another argument, but stopped, her eyes opening in astonishment.

'The bitch is dead?' she asked. 'What, you think I did it?'

'You have motive,' Declan replied. 'She had had an affair with your husband. She was also possibly the person who had stolen his book.'

'I didn't know what they were doing, if anything,' Janine quickly blurted out. 'I was at the Wellness retreat. I didn't know what was going on. I didn't know she had the book, I didn't know he had even lost the bloody book. Nobody tells me anything.'

'And I suppose it's hard learning about anything in the outside world, while in these Wellness retreats?' Bullman continued. 'I mean, with the fact they don't allow televisions or phones?'

'My client—' the solicitor started, but Janine waved her down.

'I can answer this, I don't have secrets,' Janine told her

before looking back at the others. 'I was in the dark. I didn't know what my husband was doing; as far as I was concerned, he was in a war zone. Whatever he decided when he came back, some insane plan, as you say, to do this to himself using Karen as his surrogate? I wasn't anywhere near it.'

'We never said that Karen was a surrogate,' Declan replied.

'Well, I guessed it would be her, as they were always together.'

'That's why we'd like to speak to you,' Bullman leant closer, resting her elbows on the table. 'We'd like to know why you came home.'

'What do you mean, why I came home? I've already talked to your detective friends. I was told my husband had been attacked.'

'And who told you this?' Bullman pressed on. 'Because you've been uncontactable.'

'The Wellness retreat must have gotten a message and told me,' Janine shook her head.

'No,' Declan contradicted. 'We've checked with them, and they seem to be quite certain that in the middle of the morning yesterday, you decided you wanted to come home, almost as if you felt something was wrong.'

Janine went to argue, paused, reconsidered her statement, and then slumped.

'I knew he was having an affair,' she said, her voice softer now, more resigned to the conversation.

'Mrs Robinson...' the solicitor warned, but Janine ignored the warning.

'With Karen Pine?'

'Yeah, I mean, I knew about Karen, but I also knew there were others.'

'Is this including this Lesley you mentioned to my colleagues?'

Janine nodded.

'It was embarrassing. It'd been going on for years. Someone had told me they'd seen him with Pine, and I was annoyed.'

'Did you have an affair as well?' Bullman asked, and Janine stared at her, unable to answer. 'It's just we understand you had a fling with Commander Edward Sinclair at Christmas?'

At this, Janine paled.

'No comment.'

Declan watched Janine carefully.

'My client's personal life—'

'Has cause for investigation in connection with the death,' Bullman replied. 'Which you know, Marjorie.'

She looked back at Janine.

'You knew your husband was having an affair. So why come home on a Tuesday?'

'Because he wasn't expecting me until Thursday,' Janine replied. 'I thought he'd arrive on Sunday night, get his shit together Monday, write whatever pieces he needed to finish for the paper and drop them off, and then Tuesday would be "playtime." He'd ask to have some time off and spend it with his other half. Well, his *other* other half, anyway.'

'You expected to come home and find them in bed together.'

'Yeah, why not?' Janine shrugged her shoulders. 'I'm not exactly expecting much here, am I? My husband isn't an angel, after all. And then, while driving down the motorway, I remembered the phone, and that it had been turned off. I thought I'd check it, just to make sure I hadn't missed anything important.'

She gave a little smile.

'Maybe he'd been killed in a war zone, and I wouldn't have to worry about this after all.'

Declan accepted the response; he didn't know how he'd feel if Anjli had been unfaithful to him. Or how Anjli would feel if the roles were reversed, but he did remember how he felt when Liz had started dating again.

'So then what?'

'Then my phone started going crazy, all the messages turning up at once, all telling me my husband had been stabbed and left in the church.'

'And still you came home?'

'Of course,' she replied. 'He was stabbed and left in a church. He wouldn't have had time to go home and remove anything incriminating before they took him to the hospital. I thought that if I couldn't find him in bed with someone, then this was my perfect opportunity to get back and find the things that he always hid from me.'

She looked at the desk, almost deflating as she recalled the moment.

'But there was nothing there. And, from what I could work out, my husband hadn't done anything in the days following his return from Ukraine.'

'Well, apart from hiding in the church and stabbing himself,' Bullman muttered, loud enough for Declan to hear, but not loud enough to reach the recorder before she continued. 'How well do you know Karen Pine in passing?'

'They had an affair years ago when they worked together,' Janine straightened in the chair. 'Then she left the paper, moving to the *Daily Mail,* and he got really pissy about it, because as far as he was concerned, she was his, and his alone. So, he spent the next couple of years trying to destroy her, find ways to get her removed ... and then a few months back, they suddenly became the best of friends again.'

'What happened a few months back?' Declan was noting this all down as he asked.

'God knows; he went to some Westminster Christmas party, and then the next thing I know, he's having coffee with her.'

'Did you go to the party?'

'No. Yes. I don't recall. Probably. I would have been drunk.'

'He told you he was having coffee with her?'

'Oh God, no,' Janine laughed. 'It was in his diary. I don't have access to it – well, I don't *officially* have access to it. I placed my facial recognition into his phone years back. He doesn't know, but I can log into his apps. And I've known his password long enough to know how to get through most things. I check it now and then, so I get a vague idea of where he is, and what dodgy shit he's up to.'

'Dodgy shit?'

Janine kept silent, and Declan knew even though she hated this man, she wasn't going to reply to anything that could get both of them into trouble.

'My client—'

'Yeah, yeah, don't get your panties in a twist. How did you know he was meeting Karen?' Bullman asked. They had the hindsight of knowing it was Pine he'd met, but unless he'd used her name, he could have been meeting anyone.

'He used the initials,' Janine spat. 'Sherlock Holmes over there in hospital thought that I wouldn't be able to work out that "KP" was Karen Pine, like I'd think he was meeting with that bloody peanut company instead.'

'So you know about the meeting at The Albion?'

'The Albion? Was that where they met?' Janine shook her head. 'No, I just knew he was seeing her.'

'Did you know about his decision to go to the St Bride's crypt afterwards?'

'What, this whole theatre experience he sorted out for us? The one man martyrdom of Hunt Robinson? No,' Janine folded her arms, leaning back on the chair. 'To be honest, I returned home wondering what was going on as much as you did.'

Declan glanced at Bullman, looking to see her take on this as Janine finished. Currently, her story sounded legitimate.

'When you went to see Hunt, did you take him anything?'

Janine nodded.

'Change of clothes, for when he got out, his Kindle, he likes to read things, and his laptop,' she replied. 'He likes to keep working.'

'The officers that came yesterday said his phone was in his office,' Bullman added.

'Yes.'

'You didn't take it for him?'

'No,' Janine's lips thinned as she replied. 'I wasn't giving him ways to text his girlfriend.'

'But you gave him his laptop?'

'Yes, but he needed that for work.'

Bullman shifted in her chair, narrowing her eyes.

'You hate him, but you'd still make sure he could work?'

'You ever been married?' Janine asked sadly. 'I might dislike him, and think he's a prick, and furious I've been made a fool of, but I still love him. I still want him to be okay, even if I dream of him falling off a building.'

She smiled.

'Holding Karen bloody Pine's hand as he does so. Although I suppose that's in bad taste now she's, well ...'

She made a throat-cutting gesture.

'I should go to St Bride's,' she smiled grimly. 'Check if someone's put her photo on the Journalist's altar. I always check it, you see. Usually hoping Hunt's on it.'

'And if it's there?'

'I'd take one of the candles and set fire to the damned thing. It's an altar for journalists, not hacks who steal stories and husbands.'

Declan was feeling this interview was going off topic now.

'Do you know of anyone who'd want Karen Pine dead?' he asked, trying to bring it back on track.

Janine's smile faded.

'This isn't about her though, is it?' she replied. 'It's about the book. It's always about the book. She took it from Hunt, as you said, and now it's missing from her house. She was killed for that toxic dirty bomb of a journal.'

'Did you ever look in it?'

Janine looked conflicted, as if she didn't want to admit to this, but eventually she nodded.

'A couple of times.'

'Can you remember any of the stories?'

'Honestly, no,' she shook her head. 'Hunt's handwriting was worse than a doctor's. Bloody spider crawl. He talked about it to me, once.'

'He did? How?' Bullman leant closer.

'Not on that,' Marjorie the solicitor said, pointing at the

recorder. 'I'm not having these on record spoken by my client.'

'Interview paused at twelve-oh-seven,' Bullman said, pressing the "pause" button. 'There. We're now off the record.'

Janine was nervously and likely unconsciously rubbing at her wrists as she spoke.

'He had a top ten,' she said. 'It'd change constantly, as the people in his book got bigger or smaller. He'd sometimes get drunk and do a countdown, like they used to do on "Pick of the Pops." Even sang the sodding countdown music. You remember that? *"At the Sign of the Swingin' Cymbal"* by Brian Fahey and his Orchestra?'

'You know it?'

'I grew up with it,' Janine shrugged. 'I used to love Alan Freeman, the presenter.'

'Can you remember any of them?'

Janine nodded.

'Lucy-Rachel the klepto was a popular one for him, then there were a ton of Yewtree ones; he was super pissed when Rolf Harris was outed, he genuinely thought that would be his retirement piece.'

'I would have had more respect if he'd not just sat on it,' Declan muttered.

'Oh I know,' Janine replied. 'But he wasn't wired with a conscience. Anyway, there was that YouTube Preacher who hung himself, he was there for a while, Charles Baker was on the list—'

'Can you remember what for?' Declan couldn't help himself.

'No, but I remember the Tory Nazi,' Janine added. 'Tamara Whatsherface. And the footballer, Marcus Leigh? He

had a big thing on him while he was at Man City. Put out a
super injunction last year, banning publication of any details
of an alleged "blackmail plot" over a group sex incident in a
New York hotel, that was filmed on a mobile phone. Apparently, he had some Swedish women piss on him.'

Janine thought for a moment.

'And of course, Romulus and Remus, the bloody
Bannisters.'

At this, Declan leant closer.

'What did he have on them?' he asked. 'Is this to do with
the helicopter? The affairs they were reported to be having?'

Janine sadly shook her head.

'I genuinely don't know, and after they died, he stopped
talking about it,' she said. 'We hadn't been together long
then, we got together just after. But at the same time, he still
had it in his charts.'

Declan glanced at Bullman.

'Can I have a word, Ma'am?'

Nodding at Janine and her solicitor, Bullman rose from
the chair, indicating for Declan to follow her. Once outside,
she looked at him.

'Thoughts?' she asked.

'She knows more,' Declan said.

'Gut, or facts?'

'Both,' Declan looked back at the now closed door. 'She
mentioned the book, saying with confidence it'd been stolen
from Karen Pine's house, but we never told her that. Just that
we thought Karen stole it.'

'I picked up on that, too,' Bullman nodded. 'Also, she has
no alibi for five this morning. She could have been the one
that killed her.'

'I could get someone to check the house for anything?'

Bullman shook her head.

'I think we're done here for the moment,' she said. 'Hunt's coming in, so we'll hold her too, maybe put the two of them together and see what happens?'

'Sure, boss,' Declan smiled. 'If you want another murder.'

———

17

PRIVATE EYELIDS

THEY HADN'T INTENDED TO ARREST HUNT ROBINSON, SO THERE was no squad car for him. However, as they exited the hospital, Anjli knew that her own police vehicle, a white Hyundai IX 35, was perfectly fine and anonymous enough for them to use. Because, as she glared out of the window at the main entrance outside the hospital, she could see there were a gaggle of photographers looking for the story.

And the irony here wasn't wasted on her, that the "story" was the man who usually *hunted* for the story.

But, knowing that they were waiting, Anjli had changed her plans; they needed to find a way that didn't involve walking out with a hospital blanket over Hunt's head, as much as she'd like that, and because of this had quickly made sure that they could exit out of a quieter, more secure entrance.

As they walked along the corridor that led to the car park, however, Anjli paused, noticing someone standing down one of the side passageways.

She peered closely, walked over to Monroe, and gently held him by the arm to stop him from carrying on.

'Guv, you know how to drive, don't you?' she asked softly.

'Of course I do, lassie. I just choose not to,' Monroe replied. 'Why? You decided you don't want to be the chauffeur today?'

'It's kinda like that, actually, sir,' Anjli implied, passing him the keys to her car. 'Please don't crash.'

Hunt Robinson turned and frowned.

'What, so even *you* don't want to be seen leaving with me?' he asked, a twinge of hurt in his voice.

'It's not what's waiting for me outside, it's just I have something to do inside,' Anjli said, nodding down the corridor. Hunt couldn't see down there, but Monroe could, and saw the man standing at the other end, trying his best to keep to the shadows.

'You know who that is?' Monroe asked.

'I think it's Digger Doug,' Anjli said softly, so that Hunt Robinson couldn't hear. 'If it is, I'd like to have a quick word with him, if that's okay.'

Monroe nodded, accepted the car keys and, with a playful 'come on, laddie,' started leading Hunt Robinson away as Anjli started making her way down the side corridor.

The man at the end was slim, bespectacled and balding. He was short but not too short, middle-aged, and if she was being honest, looked like any average member of the public; if he was in a lineup, you wouldn't be able to pick him out. If he was in a crowd, you wouldn't be able to notice him. He was as average as you could get.

It was only as she got closer, she realised that his slim build was actually quite muscled for his age. *He looks like a gymnast,* Anjli thought as she smiled. It seemed to her that, by making sure he fitted in anywhere, Doug Reynolds, aka Digger Doug spent more time making sure his own image was a lie, than he did working for others.

Seeing her walk towards him, he straightened.

'Detective Inspector Kapoor,' he said, nodding. 'Congratulations on your promotion.'

'You talk like we've met,' Anjli replied, stopping a few feet away from him. 'But then your reputation precedes you as well. I'm guessing you did some kind of incredible detective work to find this out?'

'Nah, I saw you on TV at Christmas,' Doug replied. 'And I'd heard that you'd been promoted. Your boss is leaving this week, isn't he?'

Anjli's smile was more strained now, but she still kept it on.

'He's not my boss,' she replied. 'DI Walsh has never been my boss. We work together as a partnership.'

'Oh yeah, of course. But you know, when you were a detective sergeant, he *was* technically your boss,' Doug grinned. 'I'm just ribbing. Look, I'm here for serious reasons.'

'Oh, I know why you're here. You're curious why we're arresting your client.'

'I know exactly why you are arresting my client. I'd say it's because he faked his own abduction and attempted murder,' Doug laughed. 'There are things you need to know, and he won't tell you about those. But there are things involving me, and I don't want to be part of this.'

'Any particular reason why?'

Doug shrugged.

'I've done a lot of dodgy shit for Hunt Robinson over the years. I found things out that nobody should know,' Doug was admitting things, and Anjli was almost convinced that, although admitting criminal doings, Doug was actually showing off. 'I've broken super injunctions that are supposed to be airtight. I've poked around houses and hotels when a door was locked—'

'And if things come out about Hunt, then things come out about you as well,' Anjli finished the sentence. 'I see what you're saying. You want immunity?'

'I'm looking at my options.'

'That depends on what you can give us.'

'Maybe we could discuss this over coffee? Somewhere less, well, corridor-based?'

Nodding at the suggestion, Anjli started walking back towards the main corridor.

'There's a coffee shop I noticed in the main reception. Would you like to go for a drink?'

'I'm guessing that you can't get back to the station,' Doug commented, walking behind her. 'Your car being taken by your Guv'nor and everything.'

Anjli didn't respond, just carried on walking to the coffee shop.

'Do you know where the book is?' she asked.

'Karen Pine has it,' Doug replied matter-of-factly. 'It was part of a deal they made. Karen would take the book and she would release stories.'

'What kind of stories?'

'Whatever stories moved the needle,' Doug shrugged, nodding at a nurse as they walked past. 'The whole point was to give the belief someone else had the book, and that poor Hunt Robinson was nothing more than a victim, like the others.'

'Who was pressuring him?' Anjli asked. 'We've been told

they wanted a particular set of papers aimed at the Bannister brothers.'

Doug didn't say anything, sitting down at the cafe's table.

'Nothing for me, you grab what you want,' he said. 'I've had enough caffeine today to last a week.'

'Early start?' Anjli asked, watching Doug carefully. She'd received a text from Doctor Marcos, and knew that whoever killed Karen Pine had been up at the crack of dawn.

Doug grinned.

'I'm an investigator, but I've worked *with* the police a lot and I've worked *against* the police a lot. So I know exactly what I need to have with me, receipt wise,' he replied. 'Whenever I come to speak to someone, I can tell you now, Detective Inspector, that I can cover every minute of the last twenty-four hours, if you so require.'

'Oh, I'm sure we'll so require,' Anjli replied. 'Hold that thought.'

She was going to continue, but there was something that had caught her eye; a man, suited, sitting at another table in the cafe, was murmuring to himself. That they were in a hospital meant this wasn't as surprising as it could have been, but it was the fact that, as the man spoke to his invisible friend, he was touching his ear.

Like you would, if talking to someone on an earpiece.

'Have you felt like you were being followed?' she asked, sitting down and leaning close to Doug. 'No, don't look around. I'm not sure if it's someone watching us, or just here with their thoughts.'

'Is it the guy in the suit?' Doug asked, keeping his eyes locked on the wall opposite. 'I clocked him when we walked in.'

'Look familiar at all?'

'No, but then that doesn't mean I haven't seen him before,' Doug leant back on the chair. 'Mid-forties, buzz-cut peppered hair, navy-blue suit, no tie?'

'That's the one.'

Doug smiled.

'I've never been tasered in the balls in an MI5 black site,' he replied quite jovially. 'It could be fun.'

Anjli made the smallest of groans; Doug Reynolds was probably right.

'Okay, we need to do this quickly,' she said. 'Did you take the book?'

'Karen Pine has the book.'

'Karen Pine is dead,' Anjli replied, watching Doug's face for any expression of surprise. There wasn't one.

'It was early this morning, wasn't it?' Doug smiled. 'That's why you made the "early start" quip. You think I might have done it?'

'Did you?'

'I have the receipts to show I was nowhere near her house at five this morning.'

'How did you know it was five?'

'Because I know what time she gets up, and if it's after six she's already at the *Mail*, or heading there,' Doug's lips thinned as he continued, and Anjli could see he was getting angry.

He'd also not asked what happened.

'The thing I really hate about people is their morbid curiosity,' she said. 'You know, how people want to know the gory details.'

'You don't need to tell me that,' Doug smiled, although it hadn't reached his eyes yet. 'That's my whole life.'

'And yet you didn't ask,' Anjli continued. 'I said she was

dead, but not how. You guessed it was early morning, fine, I get that, but you haven't asked how she died, or if we know who did it. It's as if you don't care.'

'I don't,' Doug was shifting in his seat now, irritated. 'And I shouldn't be targeted as a suspect because of it.'

'And yet you made a big thing about your "receipts," showing you were covered for the last twenty-four hours,' Anjli leant back now. 'As if you knew you'd need it.'

'Do I?'

'Yeah, I'm starting to think you do,' Anjli nodded slowly.

'Fine then. How did she die?'

'She was stabbed in the back with a kitchen knife,' Anjli replied. 'How tall are you again?'

'I didn't do it, Detective Inspector.'

'Okay then, let's say for the moment you didn't,' Anjli was still watching the man at the other table. 'Who would?'

'There's countless people who want—'

'Bullshit,' Anjli interrupted. 'I didn't want the textbook response. I wanted you to be honest with me. As an investigator. Karen Pine took the book from Hunt Robinson, and only a handful of people would know that. You included. Who would be the others?'

Doug went to reply, but then froze.

'Shit,' he muttered. 'You're right. Only people who knew the attack was fake would look at Karen. Especially the moment the Tamara Banks story came out.'

Anjli considered this. Declan had spoken to Sean Ashby, Sinclair had been at the scene, Monroe and De'Geer had spoken to Janine Robinson ...

'Sean Ashby. Edward Sinclair. Janine Robinson. Any of those possible suspects? In your experience?'

'I've worked for Sean, he's a good man ... I don't think

he'd do this, although he deals with a lot of unsavoury types. MPs, you know the drill,' Doug shook his head. 'Janine was at a retreat, so she wasn't around, and Sinclair ... yeah, I could see him wanting to do something like this.'

'You think the City of London Police Commander would murder for the book?'

'For what's in it, yes,' Doug was now distracted, staring across at the man at the other table. 'He's gathering his things. I think we're about to be taken.'

'Oh, for God's sake, wait there,' Anjli rose from the table, walking over to the man who, now seeing Anjli walking towards him, straightened.

'Detective Inspector Anjli Kapoor, City of London Police,' she said, sitting down in front of him, flipping open her warrant card and showing it as she did so. 'Visiting someone?'

The man looked as if he really didn't want to speak and went to rise—

'Nuh-uh,' Anjli shook her head. 'Not unless you want me to arrest you.'

'For what?' The man's voice was deep and Scottish.

'Anything I damn well want,' Anjli said, nodding at the earpiece. 'How about you tell me who you are, who you work for, why you're here and why I shouldn't be putting cuffs on you right now?'

The man went to argue this, but then sighed, his posture relaxing.

'Peter Foyle, SO14,' he said.

'SO14? That's Royal protection, isn't it?' Anjli frowned. 'Why the bloody hell are you here? Why aren't you off protecting Charles, or whatever you usually do?'

'Believe me, I'd rather be doing that,' Peter replied softly.

But unfortunately, I've been sent on some bloody wild goose chase—'

'Let me guess, to find a missing book?'

Peter nodded.

'I know Hunt Robinson's here,' he said. 'And I know he lost the book. I thought if I camped out, I'd see someone worth investigating. Like the investigator you were talking to.'

'Were?' Anjli glanced back, and swore.

Doug Reynolds was gone.

'He left the moment you rose,' Peter replied, and there was a hint of amusement in the voice. 'I do hope you didn't need him for something.'

'How did you know he was an investigator?'

Peter shrugged.

'I know he's Doug Reynolds,' he said. 'He was here earlier, on the phone, to someone named Lesley. Said his name then. I know Hunt had an investigator named Reynolds.'

Anjli almost swore again.

'Maybe we could discuss this over coffee? Somewhere less, well, corridor-based?'

Bloody Digger Doug had led her here. He'd seen Peter Foyle, clocked him as authorities, made sure Peter knew his name, and then went to find Anjli.

He then brought Anjli to the same place.

But why? If he wanted to escape, he could have just left before speaking to Anjli. They hadn't discussed anything new, and if anything, he gave more than he gained. So why aim Anjli at …

He was aiming her at Peter Foyle. He knew she could get more, as police, than a simple investigator could.

'I think he, in some roundabout way, wanted us to meet,'

she smiled. 'So, Mister Foyle, why don't you tell me why the Royal Family are worried about a little book of secrets?'

Peter Foyle grimaced.

'It's delicate,' he said.

'It always is,' Anjli smiled.

18

OLD COLLEAGUES

After Janine had been taken back to a holding cell upstairs, Declan had returned to his desk, sitting down at it and now staring at the Funko Pop police officer that he'd had on the desk since he'd arrived, wanting more than anything to just punch it off the desk in frustration and anger.

The only reason he hadn't was because it had been a present from Jess a few years earlier, and she was currently in the same room as him.

'You okay, Dad?' Jess asked, looking over from where she'd been sitting with Billy.

'We go three steps forward. And then four steps back,' Declan grumbled. 'We know Hunt Robinson faked his attack. We know he passed the book to Karen Pine. We know Pine was murdered and that the book was taken. Whoever knew she had the book, is in the wind.'

Monroe leaned out of his office, looking over at Declan.

'Hey, laddie, you've got a walk in downstairs, specifically asked for you,' he said with the hint of a smile. 'Think you might want to have this one ... now, rather than later on.'

Declan frowned as Monroe went back into his office. Monroe wasn't usually someone to make cryptic comments like that. And so, with a nod, he rose from the chair and made his way down the stairs to the main reception.

He didn't know who to expect. Usually, when someone came asking for him, it was a lackey sent by Charles Baker or someone connected to the case, who would be there to give away some timely clues to help him, but always at a cost.

He wasn't expecting Tessa Martinez.

Although she'd spent more than a year in prison, she hadn't changed. If anything, she looked better. She was toned and slim, her hair now short, and she wore a pair of jeans and a chunky fisherman's jumper under a *North Face* jacket.

He nodded at her as he walked through the door and into the reception area.

'I thought it best not to go in,' she said. 'I don't know yet whether police stations burst into flames if I enter them properly.'

'I didn't expect you to come to see me,' Declan replied cautiously, unsure where this conversation was going.

'Why? Worried your girlfriend is going to kick the shit out of me again?' Tessa grinned. 'Don't worry, I'm not here to cause a ruckus. I deserved everything Anjli gave me.'

'That's surprisingly candid.'

Tessa shrugged.

'I was mentally unwell. I was stressed: PTSD, painkiller addiction, yada yada yada. I could go on as long as you want.'

She stopped.

'How're you doing?' she asked with a more concerned expression. 'You look like shit.'

Declan carried on to the front door.

'Let's have this conversation outside,' he said.

'Of course, I'm not welcome in police stations.'

'Not at all,' Declan gave a small smile in return. 'I just need a coffee – or, to be perfectly honest, a really strong drink.'

'IT'S GOOD TO SEE THIS PLACE HASN'T CHANGED,' TESSA SAID AS they sat in the main bar of *The Old Bank of England*. Declan sat with a pint of Guinness in front of him. Tessa had opted for a pint of cider, now taking a long draught of it.

'I'll tell you one thing,' she continued. 'There are certain things you realise that you crave when you're in prison.'

'Cider?'

'No, not really. I didn't drink at all while I was in there.'

'I didn't think you could drink in prison, anyway?'

'Oh, you're so innocent,' Tessa grinned. 'I find that adorable still, in a kind of lost puppy dog way.'

'What did you miss?' Declan ignored the comment.

'Things like this. Sitting in a pub, listening to people talking while sipping a drink with a friend—'

'Oh, is that what we are now?'

'Do you not class me as a friend? I wondered. After I helped you with Jess, and your couple of visits, you haven't spoken to me for months.'

'I sent letters to you, asking how you were, but you've not replied to a single one,' Declan replied, stiffening slightly. 'I'm not the one who cut ties here.'

Tessa nodded, resting her head back against the top of the booth.

'I didn't think I was getting out,' she said. 'My lawyers told me they had a case, and your character reference helped. I'm not going to go into it, as it's too long to talk about – but basically, I thought I'd be stuck in there another five, ten, God knows how many years. I couldn't do that to you.'

'Do what, exactly?' Declan asked.

'You liked me, Declan, and it was obvious. But you also liked Anjli, and I could tell that even back then, months before you decided that you fancied each other.'

She laughed at Declan's surprised expression.

'It was obvious; everyone could see it, and I knew that if I kept contacting you, if I kept chatting to you, you'd become that person,' she shook her head. 'You know, the one that never moves on, and stays waiting, tying a yellow ribbon around the old oak tree and all that.'

'So you stopped talking to me so that I could get together with Anjli?'

Tessa shrugged.

'Yeah, in a way,' she said. 'I mean, we barely knew each other. We'd met for how many days before I was arrested? And maybe we spoke a handful of times after that. You were a friend. But you weren't like really close or anything.'

She winked.

'And there was also the fact you used to fancy me when you were a teenager.'

Declan reddened. It was true when teenage Tessa Martinez had been known as one of the *Magpies*, teenage Declan had found himself having a crush on her. He'd even had a poster of her on his wall. It was something that once learned, Bullman had used to make his life miserable.

'And now you work for the newspapers,' he said, trying to change the subject.

'Now I work for whoever wants to pay me,' Tessa replied. 'Let's be honest. I'm an ex-criminal. I didn't plead not guilty. I can't claim I was innocent. I accepted what I did, and I accepted any charges I was given, any punishments that I'd receive.'

She looked away for a moment, recalling the court case.

'Sean Ashby, he was a good man. Came to me from your recommendation—'

'I recommended he talked to you to get your story, I didn't think he was going to offer you a job.'

'Well, he did,' Tessa took another mouthful of the cider before continuing. 'When he heard my appeal succeeded, and my sentence cut short, he contacted me, said they needed a couple of people who knew their way around investigations. And even though I had done terrible things, I *was* one of the *Magpies,* and I had worked well in the police services until painkillers and everything else going on stopped it.'

'How are you now?' Declan hadn't wanted to ask.

'I'm clean,' Tessa replied. 'That was one good thing prison did. They have some great programs for detoxing. I realised most of the pain had gone years ago, but my body just convinced me it was still there because it needed the drugs.'

She glanced at the pint in her hand.

'I'm not obviously completely clean. I will still have my own vices, but nothing of that level anymore.'

'Good to hear,' Declan nodded. 'So, are you here to talk to me about the job?'

'Actually, no,' Tessa said. 'I'm here to talk to you about Hunt Robinson.'

Declan hadn't expected this. Even though he knew she'd had a connection to Robinson, he really didn't think that this would be a case they'd be working together.

'What do you know?' he asked.

'I used to deal with him back in the day,' she said. 'Reginald Troughton, all the secrets about him ... Hunt found out. I'd been told about it by Bruno Field, and asked to see if there's anything I could do, you know, to calm him down, but what could I do?'

Declan recognised the name Bruno Field. At one point he'd been the manager of the *Magpies*, and had worked for Norman Shipton when he was in the Fisheries department.

'Were you police at the time?'

'Yeah, but not high enough to do anything. Luckily for us, the *Magpies* weren't exactly that big a name anymore. As far as Hunt was concerned, outing Reginald as a fraud wouldn't sell copies of his papers. Better to wait. And then Hunt contacted me when I was arrested. He wanted my story. He wanted to get it out there, because now he could connect it to what he had. Everybody now knew about the *Magpies*, but he still claimed he had other stuff, things that could be used against the government. I didn't want to know.'

'So what else do you know?'

'I used to work with Bruno a lot while Norman Shipman was in the Labour backbenches. I wasn't doing it day to day, but there were occasionally things that needed police officers, perhaps a firm but gentle hand and sometimes I'd be brought in to assist, when my "name" brand could help them.'

'Even though you were in Manchester?'

'I wasn't always in Manchester, Declan,' Tessa said. 'There was a time I was based in London. Before you came out of the military police. We're talking about fifteen years ago. I was young at the time, maybe seven years out of being a *Magpie*, and still trying to hide the fame. The books were still selling, and I was helping the Labour Government, because I felt I owed it to Norman and Bruno; both had helped me in my career after I'd left.'

'How was Bruno involved?'

'Well, with the *Magpies* no longer taking up his time, he was more of a crisis manager for other people,' she said. 'As well as Norman, he'd been working with the Tories he still knew from the before times. And they were back in power, so he wanted to stay with the people who could get him places.'

She stopped, taking another drink, and Declan couldn't work out whether this was because she was thirsty, or needed time to think.

'But at the same time, there was a problem that covered both parties,' she continued. 'Charles Baker had walked across the Commons a few years earlier. There had been a few issues, he was up for a minor cabinet role and I was tasked to find out what had happened. You know, what would make Blair boy Charles Baker leave.'

'Alfie Bannister pulled Charles Baker across.'

'You already looking into the Bannisters, then?'

Declan nodded. There wasn't any point in not telling her; she'd find out, anyway.

'The Bannisters died in a helicopter crash ten years ago,' he said. 'It's believed that Hunt Robinson knew something more about this, and had connections to the cleanup case. Robinson knew it wasn't just the two brothers in the crash, that there was at least one television presenter and a couple of aides in there as well, two of which were romantically connected to the brothers, and something that, if it came out would have caused great problems to both parties.'

'There's more, but I really can't mention it,' Tessa nodded.

'Can't, or don't want to?'

'Official Secrets Act levels of can't,' Tessa replied. 'There's more here. I can say that one of the "aides" wasn't an aide. But that's it.'

Declan noted this down as Tessa continued.

'Baker had been unhappy with what Jay had been doing on the Labour bench.'

'Yet it was Baker that introduced Jay to Emily Kim,' Declan replied.

'I don't think Baker knew how far things would go when he introduced them,' Tessa shrugged. 'After a couple of years, Jay was a running joke around Westminster. So, whenever there was a party involving wives, people would wonder whether Jay would bring his wife or his "wife" with him. Bruno was running the crisis management side to make sure nobody could talk about it. Super injunctions were bouncing around left, right, and centre. Charles Baker kept out of it by now, as he'd moved across a year or so after he shit the bed with Jay and Emily, Alfie Bannister bringing him under his own wing.'

'I bet Jay wasn't happy about that.'

'Wouldn't know. Alfie, at the time, wasn't talking to Jay.'

'When did they start talking again?'

'Probably a couple of years before they died. Their dad passed away, they were at the funeral. I think it was there they hatched the plan for the Roman campaign.'

'I know about that,' Declan looked up from the notepad, realising he'd been neglecting his Guinness, while Tessa's pint was almost empty.

'Are you looking into Edward Sinclair?' Tessa asked, the question surprising Declan.

'You knew Sinclair?'

'No, but I saw his name turning up on enough things to realise he was trying to get something out of them. Pushing for career options. His family are donors, I think Sinclair expected an easy route to the top.'

'Well, he's definitely had that,' Declan muttered.

'I was told by others that he was a gobshite of the highest order,' Tessa grinned. 'Shortly after that, I was moved to Manchester. Once the government got into power, they didn't really need me, and Shipman was yesterday's news. So, 2011, off I trot. I didn't hear anything else again, until obviously 2013 turned up, and the helicopter crash, and I knew the press that came out about the thing had Bruno's fingers all over it.'

'Because of something you can't say.'

'Yeah. Sorry about that,' Tessa sighed, straightening in the chair. 'Look, Dec. I'll be honest, I didn't think I was getting out. Now I am out, is there a chance for us, perhaps?'

'Tessa, I'm with Anjli.'

'Yeah, but come on, she apparently has some billionaire after her, right? And she's pissed at you because you didn't tell her that you're leaving.'

Declan grimaced.

'You're talking to Sean.'

'I didn't need to. I'm a detective, Declan, and I don't have to be in a police station to solve crimes.'

'Anjli and I are having moments, but then all couples do,' Declan said. 'Do I have a jealousy of Eden Storm? Sure, but we spoke recently and I think he's got somebody else in mind.'

'But if she told you that she loved him, now—'

'I'd fight for her,' Declan replied without a moment's hesitation.

'Good to know,' Tessa nodded. 'But know now, Declan, if she hurts you, I will do to her what she did to me. And if you do have any problems, I'm here. And I can be there for you.'

She paused, frowning, as a new thought came to mind.

'You know Janine worked for them, right?'

'What do you mean?'

'Janine Robinson, Hunt's wife. He met her through Bruno, he was at some party in Westminster.'

Declan frowned.

'What was Janine doing?'

'She was a Civil Servant. Some kind of PR clerk lackey I think, working with the Government.'

Declan shook his head, stunned by this.

'And she knew the Bannisters?'

'Absolutely. She worked with Alfie at some point, I know that for a fact.'

Declan knew there was something here with this new piece of news, but he couldn't work out what it was. If she'd got to know Hunt with the sole plan of taking the book, she could have grabbed it at any point, and she never needed to marry him to do that.

'One last question,' he said. 'If Janine Robinson worked for the Conservative Party ten, fifteen years ago, is there any chance she met Sinclair?'

'God, you should have a chat with your mate in the Liberal Club,' Tessa laughed. 'He'll tell you everything you need to know. Although as I said, she worked with, not for.'

'Is that an important difference?'

'Ask a Civil Servant and see what they do,' Tessa winked as she finished her cider and stood up.

'Give Jess a hug from me,' she said. 'I wasn't able to do it across the visiting room desk.'

And with that, she left Declan alone.

Declan sighed, finishing his own drink, wiping the foam from his mouth as he considered what she'd told him.

There was something bigger going on with the Bannisters, and Hunt had been desperately working to find out what it was. It had to be something so bad it eclipsed the corruption of MPs. But whatever that was, he had no clue.

And, whatever was going on with Tessa Martinez, he was equally as clueless.

'Great start, you idiot,' he muttered as he rose from the chair, heading out of the pub.

It was time to chat with an old family friend.

19

SWANKY CLUBS

'I wondered when you'd come and see me, Declan,' Anthony Farringdon smiled as he sat in his usual place in the National Liberal Club. To Declan's surprise, he was dressed more casual than usual. His jacket was hanging over the edge of his chair, and his military tie was loosened.

'Is it casual dress day?' Declan asked.

Farringdon shrugged.

'I'm allowed to loosen my tie once in a while,' he said. 'I'm not a stickler for rules.'

'Oh, I hadn't realised,' Declan played innocent at this, and Farringdon laughed.

'You know, once you leave, you can still come and play with us,' he said. 'There's an open membership for you here if you want it. It was your father's, but I never really pushed it.'

He waved for a server to come over.

'But, now you're leaving, I'm sure we can do something for you.'

'Thank you,' Declan said, 'I appreciate it. But I'm not here about job offers.'

'No, you're here to ask about the Bannisters, aren't you?'

Declan wasn't surprised that Anthony Farringdon knew why he was here. The man had spent years controlling security for the Houses of Parliament and Number Ten.

'If you've got anything you can tell me, I'd greatly appreciate it.'

Farringdon leant back in his seat, thinking back.

'I was head of security at Whitehall for a long time,' he said. 'And I saw a lot of things in my time, we both know this, I've helped you enough times about things that happened within those doors. But I never got involved with the grubby stuff.'

Declan understood what Farringdon was talking about; although he had helped him with a knowledge of Charles Baker and other MPs during the Victoria Davis case, he never really got involved in the grimier side of it. He knew who was seeing who, but he didn't dig into it.

'I get that,' he said. 'And I'm not asking for salacious details, but I'm trying to organise a timeline in my head and I can't work it out. I've got a man with a book of secrets, who faked his "almost" death yesterday, purely to arrange some narrative where the book was missing, and he did this because he hoped by pretending he didn't own the book anymore, people wanting the pages from the book would no longer be able to hassle him. So he passed the book to somebody else.'

'And they were the person who put the terrible piece up today about Tamara Banks?'

Declan nodded again.

'Then you should be giving them a bloody medal,'

Farringdon said. 'She was an odious woman, and I'm glad she's going to be resigning.'

He leant closer.

'The piece the *Daily Mail* did was good, but it didn't even scratch the surface of the atrocities that woman has done while she's been in power. Horrid woman. Do you know if they're going to be releasing any more stories about politicians? I do like it when I see people I dislike burned.'

'Well, that's the problem,' Declan leant forward to match Farringdon. 'I think there might be more stories coming out, but we don't know who's doing them. Karen Pine was given the book, but she was murdered early this morning, and the book was taken.'

'Ah,' Farringdon said. 'And now you need to work out who took the book from the person who took the book.'

'In a way, yes,' Declan chuckled at this. 'We're guessing this is all connected to what happened ten years ago, with the Bannisters and their deaths.'

'Which I'm guessing you only know the official story.'

'Is there an unofficial one?'

'Dear boy,' Farringdon smiled. 'There's always an unofficial one.'

Declan shifted in his chair.

'Why don't we start with you telling me what you know in relation to the helicopter crash?'

Farringdon nodded, shifted in his seat, and placed his two index fingers together on his chin as he considered this. Declan knew that one of the advantages that Anthony Farringdon had was an eidetic memory. He could pretty much recall anything that had happened in the years that he worked for Westminster, with picture-perfect clarity. It was a good skill to have, especially when Declan would call on him for answers.

It was probably also a very good skill to have if you needed to blackmail someone.

'What do you know?' Farringdon asked. 'Let's start there.'

'We know that both brothers died in the crash,' he said. 'I also know there were three other unidentified bodies that weren't mentioned to the press. But this is what confuses me.'

He leant forward.

'Why wouldn't they have been announced in the news? There was a helicopter crash. Six people died, including these two brothers and the pilot. Why keep three complete identities out of the press?'

He held a finger up, pausing Farringdon from answering yet as he continued.

'Let me say before that, I know one of the three was Emily Kim. And I know she was having an affair, I think with Jay. Charles Baker told me as much earlier on, so I can get why one of them wasn't announced. And I know one was Penelope Hallett, who was a secretary of some kind.'

Farringdon gave a subtle half nod to this. 'Jay was never happy with what he had,' he said. 'He was on a fast track to Number Ten, the golden boy, once the *previous* selection of golden boys managed to shit the bed. That is, once Andy Mac and Shaun Donnal proved themselves not to be next Prime Minister material. And Charles Baker running across the Commons like a startled lamb. The pundits started to look at Bannister.'

Declan nodded at this. He was also aware that the reason Donnal, Baker, and McIntyre had started to fade out of the public spotlight was because they were all being blackmailed by Frankie Pierce, all believing that they had murdered Victoria Davis.

'So, Bannister's the heir apparent,' Declan said. 'And he's shagging Emily Kim on the side.'

'Oh, he was shagging several people on the side,' Farringdon chuckled. 'Emily was just the unfortunate one to be there for the long term, and who was the flavour of the month when the helicopter crashed. He had a voracious appetite, shall we say? It was one reason why I know people tried to avoid him.'

'Baker?'

Farringdon considered the question.

'When Baker walked from one side of the Commons to the other and joined the Conservative Party, people believed it was because of Jay Bannister's excesses. The man was a friend of Baker's, which meant that Baker heard everything. But there were a lot of other reasons.'

He took a mouthful of his drink, placing it on the coffee table.

'Labour had been in power for a while, and was stagnating. Tony Blair had already made his deal with Gordon Brown; that when he eventually left, Brown would replace him, and Brown wasn't the centrist that Blair was. People were wondering whether Blair, with the stink of the 2003 Iraq war hanging around his neck, could beat the Conservatives a third time, especially with the newly minted Tory leader, Michael Howard, who was a veteran of the Thatcher years, and believed by the party to be a return to that "glorious era," and so on.'

Farringdon sat back in his chair.

'The problem that Baker had when he ran away in 2003 was he hadn't realised that of the Bannisters, Jay, was actually the sensible one,' he whispered. 'Alfie Bannister made Nero look like a Puritan. He was always being investigated by the whip's office on reports of prostitutes and drug abuse and a dozen different things ... the man believed he was untouchable. Poor bloody Baker, when he turned up, probably took him ten minutes before he realised he'd gone from the frying pan into the fire.'

'Do you know who the other body was?' Declan asked.

Farringdon looked around the Liberal Club.

'Nobody knows who any of the three bodies were,' he said, 'on paper. Do you understand?'

'I do,' Declan replied. 'And if I find out who they were, the source that gives it to me would obviously gain full confidentiality.'

'The body nobody talks about was Stephanie Sackville.'

'I know that name,' Declan said. 'Wasn't she the Duchess of Dorset?'

Farringdon didn't reply. But his eyes said everything.

'Jesus Christ, one of the Royal Dukedoms?' Declan said. 'I heard she died in a plane crash in Europe.'

'That was the official statement,' Farringdon replied. 'It was deemed best by the Crown that the truth was, shall we say, massaged? She was a happily married mother of one, married to Edmund Sackville, the eleventh Duke of Dorset, something like thirtieth in line to the throne – and the fact of the matter was Alfie Bannister had been shagging her for a while.'

Declan now waved to the server.

'Can I get a whisky please?' he asked. 'Neat. No ice.'

'She died on the helicopter, while estranged from her husband, and it was decided it was probably best that people didn't realise how depraved a minor member of the Royal Family had become.'

'This wasn't just about people hiding affairs for upcoming politicians, or the hiding of an affair with a celebrity,' Declan nodded. 'This was now a royal matter. Was Penelope Hallett her press secretary?'

'It's harsh to say, but they were an upper-class nobody, and nobody cared about poor Penelope,' Farringdon replied, before stopping. 'They didn't even think to add her to the fake accident that killed her boss, just let her fall through the cracks, never to be heard of again. I can tell you who she *did* know, though. Edward Sinclair.'

Declan froze.

'How did he know a Royal press secretary?'

'They went to school together,' Farringdon replied. 'Edward plays himself very much as a working copper made good. But he was destined for greatness from the start. He was part of the polo set of the seventies and eighties, his parents were friends with Prince Charles, and when he joined the police, it was purely to place him in a position as Commissioner.'

Declan knew others brought in such positions; less "career copper," more "upwardly moving career copper." Every role he would have taken, moving up the ladder, was nothing more than positioning to give him enough experience to move to the next level in the shortest amount of time. Do a stint in crime for a year or two. Then do vice, move over to finance ... and so on.

'He was a promotional prospect from the start,' he muttered.

'Dear boy, he was a Sinclair. He was always going to be someone high up.'

Farringdon looked around the room again.

'I'm guessing he's digging his nose in. Makes sense. When we spoke last, I got the distinct impression he'd never forgiven the Bannisters for what they did.'

'What they did?'

'It was believed that the helicopter pilot, as forgettable as Penelope was, had been part of a party the night before, and was still ... under the influence, shall we say?' Farringdon mimed snorting something off the back of his hand. 'The line I heard was he was a coked-up hedonist. When the "accident" happened, Sinclair made sure he was involved in the case. He wanted to find out what was happening, maybe gain justice for his friend, but then at some point, he started to cover everything up. He made sure nobody knew.'

'Perhaps he wanted to keep the memory of his friend intact?'

'Well, that was probably his original intention,' Farringdon nodded as the server came over with a whisky, allowing Declan to take a large mouthful before continuing. 'But when you work with certain elements of the monarchy, the chances are he changed his tune quickly. Probably reminded of his family connections, or offered some kind of Lordship or something down the line, if he could keep things quiet about Stephanie.'

Declan now placed the empty whisky glass on the table.

'Jesus,' he said. 'And now someone's threatening to reopen it. No wonder he's doing backflips. All the work that he did, everything he positioned to make sure nobody ever found out about Stephanie, it could come out.'

'It could indeed,' Farringdon replied. 'So the question you have to ask is who has the most to gain from the story coming out? And who has the most to gain from the story staying hidden? The Royal Family would probably be annoyed if it came out now, but it was a decade ago. The Queen has passed away, Charles is King. An old scandal isn't really going to affect him, especially with his son going off and writing books, and doing documentaries about how bad the Royals are, and his brother hanging out with ... well, the *wrong sort*.'

He smiled.

'Although, with all the changes being made right now, a lot has been passed on to the twelve-year-old heir to the Dukedom of Dorset. Who looks just like his father. That is, he looks nothing like Edmund.'

'Christ,' Declan whistled. 'That explains a lot. Thank you. One more question before I go, though. Janine Robinson.'

'The journalist's wife,' Farringdon nodded. 'I know her, but never dealt with her that much. She was more Whitehall than Houses of Parliament. And she didn't really deal with the Prime Minister, but she was there. She was working with the Bannisters, Alfie in particular.'

'Did she meet Hunt Robinson here?'

'Again, I don't deal with tittle tattle, dear boy, that right there is a question you'd have to ask her.'

Farringdon sighed, leaning back into the chair.

'I apologise, I can't help you with her, but I can tell you for a fact she was in the room when it happened. In fact, it was when the Bannisters died that she left the Party. She was a staunch Royalist and was furious over what had happened.'

'Could she have been the one that passed the information to Hunt Robinson?'

'Oh, it's been an open secret for years she did that, dear boy. Woman was a sociopath, definitely had an axe to grind, and she was happy to let anybody fall under the blade. She was a very close friend of Penelope's too. Hunt Robinson was a tool she used in the same way that a surgeon would use a scalpel. But everything she told Hunt was then removed by Sinclair.'

'Did she know Sinclair?'

'Oh, I can confirm she knew Sinclair back in the day,' Farringdon nodded. 'For a start, I know they were sleeping together for a good six months.'

'I thought you didn't deal with tittle tattle?' Declan grinned.

In response, Farringdon shrugged apologetically.

'I know, but sometimes having a photographic memory is a curse, you know? I caught them once in a side room, having a bit of a fondle. I told them "don't do things like that where journalists can see you," and I never saw them together again.'

Declan rose from his chair.

'As ever, thank you.'

'You know your father had a file on Sinclair?' Farringdon enquired, and Declan stopped, surprised. He knew Farringdon had been aware that there were files in his dad's room, but never what had been in them.

Farringdon nodded.

'I know he had a file on him, because I was the one who told your father about him,' he said. 'Patrick had suspicions, even back then, that Sinclair had some kind of plan. It just wasn't out in the open. Please, when you next visit his grave, say hello to him for me.'

'I will,' Declan now started towards the main entrance of the Liberal Club's bar. 'And thank you again.'

As he left the bar, Declan considered the new information he had been given. *Janine Robinson hadn't lied, but she'd definitely massaged the truth somewhat.* She said she barely knew Sinclair, and there was no way she wouldn't have recognised him at a party a month earlier if they'd been so close a decade or more before. Besides this, the "simple affair turned into tragic death" that people seem to think this was, had now blossomed into some kind of wild conspiracy. In fact, he was so engrossed in his thoughts as he walked down the stairs towards the entrance of the National Liberal Club, he didn't notice the man at the bottom until he stepped out in front of Declan,.

'Ah, Walsh,' Commander Edward Sinclair said. 'I heard you were here. Can we have a chat? Just the two of us?'

'Sure, sir,' Declan replied. 'I'm guessing you have a lot to talk about.'

'Great,' Sinclair said, and waved to the door, where two uniformed officers appeared, as if by magic. 'Come with us.'

Declan suddenly realised this wasn't the casual chat he was expecting.

'Am I being arrested, sir?' he asked, frowning.

'Not at all,' Sinclair replied as the two police officers walked up either side of Declan. 'Well, unless you decide not to cooperate.'

So, flanked by officers on either side, Declan was led out of the National Liberal Club, and into an awaiting squad car.

20

ROYAL BLOOD

DECLAN SAT IN EDWARD SINCLAIR'S OFFICE, HIS FACE A MASK of fury, even though he was valiantly trying to hide his anger.

'I don't appreciate being dragged here, sir,' he said.

Edward Sinclair, sitting behind his desk, nodded at this.

'And I don't appreciate being treated as a suspect in an investigation,' he said. 'Look, Declan. I'm sorry if it looked like you were being brought here against your will—'

'I was, sir.'

'But I needed to control the narrative as quickly as I could,' Sinclair continued. 'You don't know how many people in that club were listening to you. I couldn't speak to you there. I needed somewhere I knew we were safe to talk.'

He waved around the office.

'Guildhall, for example.'

Declan tried to relax, but found he still couldn't.

'So, you wanted a little talk?' he asked.

'Declan, I like you,' Sinclair said. 'Your leaving is the police's loss. Just like the death of your father was a tragic loss, too.'

'I don't recall seeing you at his funeral, sir.'

Sinclair shifted in his seat, and then rose, walking over to a sideboard.

'I didn't go,' he replied. 'We weren't talking at the end. But that doesn't mean I lost respect.'

He poured out two glasses of water, passing one across to Declan.

'I'm not the bad guy here,' he said. 'But I do want to be in the loop.'

'I got the impression, sir, you wanted to control the loop.'

'Candid,' Sinclair returned to his chair.

'With all due respect, sir, I leave in a couple of days,' Declan replied. 'I don't really have anything to lose here.'

'You might not, but your attitude and your decisions today could cause a ripple effect onto others,' Sinclair sipped his water. 'How's your daughter doing? She's started work experience today, right?'

Declan stiffened.

'If you're threatening my—'

'Oh calm down, for Christ's sake,' Sinclair shook his head. 'Bloody hell, you really are quick to anger, aren't you? No wonder the Temple Inn unit reports read like a Tom Clancy novel.'

Declan sat back, but his anger was still simmering under the surface.

'You're just like your father,' Sinclair muttered.

'Thank you.'

'It wasn't a compliment.'

'I'm aware, sir.'

Sinclair didn't reply to this, instead deciding to concentrate on his water some more.

'I can sit here and drink water with you, sir, or you can tell me why you dragged me across London,' Declan eventually said. 'Because as I said, I don't have that much time left before I'm gone, and I'm trying to catch a murderer.'

Sinclair sighed, looking up at the ceiling.

'I'm in a bit of a tough spot here, and I could use a friend,' he said. 'Are *you* a friend, Declan?'

'Depends on the context, sir,' Declan replied. 'But I will say, I'm probably the only person in the City of London police who'll tell you the truth, as I don't really have an agenda ... apart from maybe Monroe.'

Sinclair grimaced at the name.

'Let's talk hypothetical,' he said. 'Because this conversation isn't happening.'

'Yes sir,' Declan replied. 'Are we talking the hypothetical that you were involved in the coverup of Jay and Alfie Bannister's deaths, or are we talking the hypothetical you were having a fling with Hunt Robinson's wife, who you dated for months back before she was married?'

'How dare you!' Sinclair rose now, slamming the palms of his hands onto the table in rage. 'Who the hell do you think you are? I could—'

'With all respect, sir,' Declan loudly and forcibly cut through Sinclair's rant. 'First off, you said hypothetical, and second, we both know I wasn't lying. And, more importantly, both facts are being investigated right now.'

It was as if Declan had stuck a pin into Sinclair, the speed the man deflated.

'I'm not the bad guy here,' Sinclair muttered, his voice softer, and almost as if he was trying to convince himself of this.

'Then prove it, sir. Help us get in front of this,' Declan said. 'Give me what you have.'

Sinclair rose, walked to the sideboard, opened the drawer and pulled out a bottle of Bushmills. Opening it, he poured two measures, passing one glass to Declan, who was worrying about the amount of alcohol he was being expected to drink right now.

'I knew her back in the day,' he said simply. 'We had a fling. Nothing serious, we were both single, and we hung around the same scene.'

'How did you meet her?'

'Penny,' Sinclair said, and, thinking Declan hadn't a clue who he was talking about, he carried on. 'Penelope Hallett. She was a friend from school, she'd grown up with me, our families knew each other. And she worked with Janine.'

Declan already knew the name, but didn't want to write anything new down; he didn't think Sinclair would be happy if he pulled his notebook out right now.

'It was years back. Before either of us got married,' Sinclair added. 'And it ended quickly.'

'Did you call it off? Or did she?'

'Neither,' Sinclair said sadly. 'Circumstances did that.'

He walked back to his chair, sitting in it, sipping the whisky.

'The Bannisters' crash,' he said. 'Penny died, Janine was working for Alfie Bannister—'

Declan nodded.

'Penelope was Stephanie Sackville's press secretary, wasn't she?' he asked. 'And she was having an affair with Alfie Bannister.'

'How did—' Sinclair grimaced. 'That's why you were at the club. Bloody Anthony Farringdon.'

'You know him?'

'We met a few times in Westminster. He was always

sticking his nose in,' Sinclair muttered. 'Anyway, sure, when the crash happened, Penny died in it, but nobody was talking. So I put myself into the case, so I could—'

'Control the narrative?'

'Solve the case, Declan.'

Declan resisted the urge to make some glib comment here.

'So, you got involved? But from what I can work out, only the Bannisters were named. Penny, Emily Kim and Stephanie Sackville weren't ever mentioned.'

Sinclair looked uncomfortable.

'There were ... problems,' he said. 'Stephanie was a minor Royal. She couldn't be seen in some kind of hedonistic affair. And if she couldn't be named there, then Penny couldn't either.'

'And Emily Kim?'

'Well, if you're hiding one body, you might as well hide another. And then when you have two, well, three's not that big a jump.'

Declan leaned closer.

'Your choice? Or a call from high up?' Declan asked. 'Hypothetically?'

'You have to understand, I was caught in a bind,' Sinclair explained. 'Hypothetically. I was on a fast track to ... this.' He waved a hand around the office. 'To do anything to complicate that, or to cause anything that could jeopardise it, well, there were many people who would have been incredibly unhappy with me.'

'So you were being guided?' Declan asked. 'You had higher ups planning your future?'

'Everyone has blasted higher ups doing that for them!' Sinclair snapped. 'Look at you!'

Declan had been waiting for this, and smiled.

'Yes, sir, I understand you'd been unhappy with my rise,' he said.

'I couldn't give a monkey's about your rise!' Sinclair replied angrily. 'Just the way your father used his position to steamroller it through. It was nepotism of the highest order!'

'And yours wasn't?'

Sinclair didn't answer.

'I was told to drop the case,' he said eventually. 'I was told to keep to the story of a terrible accident. It'd help a fractured Government, and it'd stop more interest in another Royal scandal.'

'You'd keep the peace rather than solve the crime?'

'"*I do solemnly and sincerely declare and affirm that I will well and truly serve the Queen in the office of constable, with fairness, integrity, diligence and impartiality, upholding fundamental human rights and according equal respect to all people,*"' Sinclair intoned. '*And that I will, to the best of my power, cause the peace to be kept and preserved and prevent all offences against people and property; and that while I continue to hold the said office I will to the best of my skill and knowledge discharge all the duties thereof faithfully according to law.*" Did you ever swear the Constable's oath?'

Declan nodded.

'It doesn't mention anywhere about solving crimes,' Sinclair stated. 'It says *"And that I will, to the best of my power, cause the peace to be kept and preserved and prevent all offences against people and property."* And that's a different thing. By ensuring the story was kept over the salacious facts, I caused the peace to be kept. And I preserved and prevented.'

Declan shook his head.

'You can't use the words of an oath as a mission statement,' he replied. 'I know the book too, sir. And I can quote lines as well as you. How about "*Each sworn constable is an independent legal official, and each police officer has personal liability for their actions or inaction,*" instead? Personal liability, sir. This was on you and you alone, not the people who suggested you turn a blind eye. Not the people who promoted you to toe the line. You, and your inaction here.'

'Well, it's all hypothetical,' Sinclair muttered, and Declan realised there was an aspect of narcissism in his personality; Edward Sinclair would never admit he was wrong, no matter how strong the evidence against him was.

'Why do you want the book?' he asked. 'Was it because Hunt knew about this and wrote it down? Or because you're worried he's written other things about you in it?'

'There's three pages, hypothetically, that, if released, could end my career,' Sinclair replied carefully. 'I'd prefer them not to be out there. But while he's had the book, he's had sway over me. Now it's gone, and I worry it'll be released into the world. I've tried legal action, I've tried less-than-legal action, too—'

'You tried to turn Janine to your side.'

'How do you see that?'

'Because I believe you had a fling with her around Christmas,' Declan replied.

Sinclair grimaced.

'We met at a party a little while back, maybe Christmas? I can't remember,' he said. 'Hunt was showing the book off, as if he was worried people might have forgotten he had it. She was pissed at this, angry he was drunk again. I thought I could get back in with her, convince her to do the right thing, give me the book. But obviously things didn't work out. She'd found out he was having an affair—'

'Karen Pine.'

'Among others,' Sinclair nodded. 'She decided turnabout was fair play.'

'You thought you could use her, while she thought she could use you.'

Sinclair nodded.

'Hunt Robinson isn't a good man,' he said. 'He's a drunk who's pissed off major players. And the Royal family want him removed right now.'

'Removed as in …' Declan drew a finger across his neck.

'Good God, no!' Sinclair looked horrified. 'Like having his wings clipped! Blacklisted!'

'Oh. Well. Good.' Declan paused. 'Why is Hunt so important right now?'

Sinclair looked as if he didn't want to say anything, but then, almost as if a switch inside him went "ah, what the hell" he leant closer.

'You know why Stephanie was in the helicopter?'

'She was having an affair with Alfie Bannister.'

'Do you know how long it'd been going on for?'

Declan frowned.

'Why is it relevant?'

'Because when she died, she left behind a two-year-old son, and a one-year-old daughter,' Sinclair replied carefully. 'She'd been with Alfie for three years, on and off.'

Declan straightened.

'Are you saying her kids were … *his* kids?' he asked. 'I'd heard that her son didn't take after his father.'

'Let's just say that her son looks just like Alfie did when he was a teenager,' Sinclair replied. 'And if it was to come out that someone on the royal succession list was a bastard, the press would have a feeding frenzy right now.'

'Is this because of Charles becoming King?'

'Partly, but also because of a memorial that's being considered for the Bannisters,' Sinclair replied. 'Ten years on, there are still people around who remember the "real" them, and think this is insulting. These people could look to find anything that, well, destroys that idea.'

'And you've been told to stop the news coming out, while Hunt waves his book around again,' Declan nodded. 'What was it, a knighthood? A Lordship?'

'Why can you not believe I'd do it out of civic duty?' Sinclair asked.

Declan folded his arms as he considered the question.

'Maybe because I've met you, sir,' he said frankly. With this said he rose from the chair.

'Where do you think you're going?' Sinclair rose to face him. 'We haven't finished here.'

'You brought me here to find out what I knew,' Declan replied. 'And now you know we're looking at you. There's more to it, I'm sure, and we need to find out who killed Karen Pine and stole—'

He stopped as his phone rang.

'Walsh,' he said, answering it.

'Declan, it's Sean,' the voice at the other end spoke. 'I thought I'd give you a heads up. A story's come into us, it's making the rounds, so someone will take it. A footballer was in New York—'

'Is this Marcus Leigh?' Declan interrupted.

'Oh, you already know?' Sean seemed deflated. 'No worries. I'll send you the details, anyway. I'm not sure if it's relevant, but you said if anything out of the blue came through ...'

Declan disconnected the call.

'What is it?' Sinclair asked.

'Marcus Leigh, Man City footballer,' Declan said. 'Story's hit the press about him in an orgy in New York a few years ago.'

'So why the pale face?' Sinclair asked. 'Are you a City fan?'

'No sir, it's just that I heard the story earlier today,' Declan replied. 'From Janine Robinson, when she was telling us about a couple of secrets she knew in the book.'

He looked back at his un-drunk glass, wondering whether he should finish it.

'It seems whoever now has the book has started releasing stories from it,' he said.

21

TOO MANY COOKS

MONROE STOOD AT THE FRONT OF THE BRIEFING ROOM AND stared at the officers facing him.

Declan and Anjli were to the right of the room, while Billy and Jess were to the left. At the back were Cooper, De'Geer and Doctor Marcos, while Bullman was still in her office on the phone to Bradbury, likely still trying to save Declan's job.

'Well, this is a fine kettle of fish we have here,' he muttered. 'It's late in the day, but tomorrow's papers are definitely going to be outing Marcus Leigh, unless his solicitors can restart his super injunction.'

'And even if they do, it's out there,' Billy said. 'There's a dozen Reddit pages on it already, and that's just the clean ones.'

'We're definitely sure it came from the book?' De'Geer asked. 'Could it have been some other source?'

'It's literally word for word what Janine told us,' Declan turned to face the Viking sergeant. 'It's too similar to be a coincidence.'

'And the notebook we found in Pinc's house had it mentioned,' Cooper added. 'Unless we think "Marcus Leigh piss party" means something else?'

Monroe moved his mug of coffee from beside him and leant against the edge of the table.

'Okay then,' he said. 'We have both Robinsons upstairs for the moment. Let's decide if they need to stay there. Tell me what we have.'

'Where do you want to start?' Anjli asked.

'At the beginning,' Monroe replied. 'The Bannisters.'

'According to everyone we've spoken to, they weren't the golden boys they claimed to be,' Anjli continued. 'Both look to have been having possible affairs when they died, Jay most likely with television presenter Emily Kim, and Alfie with Stephanie Sackville, Duchess of Dorset. Which is now confirmed by Sinclair and Peter Hoyle from SO14.'

'Which is where the problems seem to start,' Declan added. 'Both Emily and Stephanie, as well as her press secretary, Penelope Hallett, and the pilot, died that day. Apparently, he was on drugs and his reflexes were slow.'

'So, now we have a terrible tragedy the press want to know more about, and the Royals don't,' Anjli continued. 'They send in Edward Sinclair to fix things. He's already invested because he was at school with Penelope. At some point he's "suggested" that perhaps it's better to remove the names rather than solve the crime, and hey presto, the Royal dies in the Alps.'

'But Penelope worked with Janine Robinson in Whitehall, they were apparently incredibly close, even though Penelope was based in St James, and Janine was angry at the lack of justice,' Monroe now added. 'So, seeing that Sinclair, who she's been sleeping with isn't really gaining the justice she wants, the wee lass tells the one person she thinks can sort this. Hunt Robinson.'

'Who doesn't, and instead banks the story to use later,' Billy grimaced. 'He does that a lot, apparently.'

'Okay, so the story festers, nothing happens, it's decided to leave the Bannisters as martyrs and life goes on,' Monroe leant further back on the desk. 'So what happens now to change this?'

'The Queen dies,' Cooper added from the back, reddening when everyone looked at her. 'And the whole royal line of succession is being changed. The Duke of Dorset is probably stepping down from any kind of public life, and his son is likely to inherit titles soon.'

'How do we know he's doing this?' Monroe looked back at Billy.

'Because he did an interview in Horse and Hound magazine,' he replied. 'Jess found it. He talks about his new interests and how his upcoming divorce is draining him, and he's passing everything to his son.'

'Divorce?'

'Married again five years ago, but it's been a bit volatile, sir,' Jess said. 'It's all over the Royal gossip boards.'

'There are Royal gossip boards?'

'Oh yes, sir. And a whole YouTube channel. They don't like her. The new wife. She's sick of being likened to Stephanie. But she's also fighting for the title.'

'How does she have a right to that?'

'She has a one-year-old son she claims is the rightful heir.'

'And she might be right,' Declan added. 'According to Anthony Farringdon, Stephanie conceived her other children around the time she was seeing Alfie on the side, and apparently the son, Hugo, looks quite "Bannister" in looks.'

'There's a cuckoo in the nest,' Monroe chuckled. 'So a vicious little divorce battle wouldn't go down well if it came out there was proof Alfie Bannister and Stephanie Sackville were in the same crash. So why not just pay her off?'

'She wants the title, and hates her current husband, I think she's rejecting everything because she knows what the title and land are worth.'

'We also have MPs who are angry the Bannisters are getting a ten-year memorial,' Declan added. 'There's talk of finding ways to scupper that. An affair with a minor Royal would do it.'

'The Royals are quite worried, I reckon,' Anjli said, shifting around in her seat. 'So worried they sent an SO14 officer to talk to Hunt.'

'Who no longer has the book.'

'So now we get to the next part,' Monroe gave a theatrical sigh. 'Hunt Robinson and his blasted book.'

He looked over at Declan.

'Or lack of one, perhaps?'

Declan rose, looking around the room.

'I saw Charles Baker today,' he started, instantly regretting it as he received a series of catcalls from the room, primarily led by Doctor Marcos, mocking the fact he had tea with the Prime Minister, and *wasn't he special*.

It wasn't the first time he'd had this, and he'd actually expected it, but not from his daughter, who had enthusiastically joined in.

'But that's not what I'm talking about here,' he quickly added. 'After that, I met a Labour MP, named Bonner.'

He looked at Billy, who, with some clicks, brought up a page from the Houses of Parliament's website.

On it, a smartly dressed young man, blond hair in a parting, smiled at the screen.

'It's actually "Bonneville," Guv,' Billy explained. 'Les Bonneville. MP for Hackney East. Won it in the 2019 election with a majority of four thousand.'

'Not Bonner?'

'It's a nickname, sir,' Billy added. 'Like People say "Mac" for someone named MacDonald, or "Fitzy" for Fitzwarren.'

'That last one sounds a bit close to home,' Monroe said, adding, 'eh, Fitzy?'

'I knew I shouldn't have mentioned that,' Billy bemoaned.

'Anyway, this "Bonner" said he'd been working with Hunt Robinson, trying to build his brand, and get known – which, if he only had a majority of four thousand, was probably a wise thing to do,' Declan continued. 'But he reckoned the book was an urban myth, something Hunt had kept in the early days, but something he'd let gain a life of its own, so he could threaten people.'

'And the stories already out of it?'

'Seen on a site named Tattle,' Declan continued. 'Apparently they've been blind items for years, and people work it out. Open secrets which super injunctions have issues with.'

Monroe nodded.

'Makes sense,' he said. 'That would explain why Robinson went to such lengths. If he's being blackmailed for pages he doesn't have, then he has to find a way to explain why he doesn't have them.'

'But similarly, he was waving the book around at a Christmas party, and showed it to his editor, so there's definitely something out there, even if it's nothing more than a prop.'

De'Geer coughed, and everyone looked back at him.

'Something in your throat?' Monroe cooed mockingly.

'Sorry, but I ...' De'Geer pointed at the screen. 'I have a friend called Les. It's short for Leslie. And it says there on the screen that although he's an MP, Bonneville is also Junior Shadow Under-secretary—'

'Oh, Christ,' Monroe nodded, looking back. 'Janine said Robinson was having an affair with a secretary called "Lesley." What if he was working with Bonneville, the name was never written down, and she got the wrong idea?'

'Have we talked about him before?' Jess asked. 'Sorry, Guv.'

'The MP?' Declan shook his head. 'Maybe you read about him?'

'Did he know the Bannisters?'

'Apparently before his time.'

Jess was still frowning and was fidgeting on her chair.

'You don't need to ask permission to return to your desk to check something,' Monroe smiled, and Jess gratefully leapt from the desk, running off into the office.

'Okay, so let's continue,' Monroe said. 'At Christmas, Robinson goes to a party in Westminster, the same one that Charles Baker's go-to copper, Declan Walsh goes to, but gets pissed, waves his secret book around in an argument, and then comes back terrified of something. Something he's even happy to go to a war zone to avoid.'

'We went through Robinson's phone records, and we have a text,' Billy said. 'Arrived Sunday. *"I'm still waiting Hunt. I want those pages. You have a week before I go public on you. And my book is better than yours."* Looking at the timestamp, it would have arrived as he was being driven home from the airport.'

'Burner phone?'

Billy nodded.

'Yes, but as Anjli learnt, Doug Reynolds was right when he said the cell tower it was pinging from was Whitehall. This was the same.'

'Okay, keep on with that,' Monroe replied, looking at Doctor Marcos. 'Any news on Karen Pine?'

Usually, at this point Doctor Marcos would rise, but this time she didn't, simply shaking her head, her lips pursed together in anger.

'No,' she said. 'And it's really pissing me off. The house was ransacked, but politely. Someone was looking for the book. We assume they found it because there isn't a book of secrets there.'

'We do have something from the house, though,' Billy added, looking back at Doctor Marcos. 'PC Cooper got me Karen Pine's phone.'

He pressed a button and a message conversation appeared onscreen.

> Why don't you use the footballer?

I felt Banks was a better choice. People hate her. And we know it's on the list.

> If you're going to do it, do it right. Or I will take the book back and do it myself.

'This was a conversation between Hunt Robinson and Karen Pine, spread out over a couple of hours on Tuesday,' Billy said. 'Now, Doctor Marcos pointed out this was an iMessage conversation, so there was every chance the text could have been sent while Hunt was convalescing, especially as Janine claimed she passed him a laptop when arriving.'

'Usually the balloons are a different colour, aren't they?' Monroe asked, ignoring the catcalls now aimed at him. 'Aye I know about technology. Piss off, the lot of you.'

'You're right, Guv, but it's not that relevant here, as Hunt couldn't have sent it,' Billy replied. 'On checking the phone, I saw they'd been sent when he was being operated on. The first was eleven-thirty in the morning, the second, the reply, around one, the third just before two.'

He looked around the room.

'When you spoke to Mrs Robinson, she said she could open his phone with facial recognition. There's every chance she could have sent all of these, as we have her arriving south of the Thames via the Dart charge just before eleven in the morning.'

'So Janine sent the messages. She was working with Pine, not Hunt?' Anjli frowned.

'She was also asking her about a leak that came out hours later by Pine,' Billy replied. 'And, around midnight last night, Karen called the number, but it went to voicemail.'

'What did it say?'

'I can't check without a warrant, but the message length was two seconds, so Pine probably disconnected the moment the phone started recording.'

'Hold on,' Declan said, frowning. 'The text there says it's on the list, not the book, right? What if they don't have the book after all? What if Bonner – Bonneville – whatever his name is was correct?'

'We saw her leave with it.'

'We saw her leave with a book,' Declan contested. 'Billy, do you have an image of it?'

'Already ahead of you,' Billy said as he brought up an evidence photo, showing the notebook next to a ruler, around A5 in size. Next to that was a zoomed in and pixelated image of both Robinson walking to the pub, and Pine walking from it, both with the book-shaped bag.

They were the same size.

'What if that was the book Pine was given, just with head-lines to look into?' Declan asked. 'We already know they were blind items on sites.'

'We also know something else,' Billy added. 'But it's not a hundred percent, so we can't use it. Though I looked into the first story, the one that started all this, when Pine scooped Robinson on the Lucy-Rachel Adams piece? Well, I used an AI program to learn how Hunt Robinson wrote, using his last years' worth of pieces for places like *The Individual*, and then did the same with Karen Pine.'

He brought up an image with two lines of data.

'As you can see here, when putting this piece through as well, the scoop was eighty-nine percent similar to Hunt Robinson's style. As if Karen Pine took the piece he gave your friend Sean, altered a couple of bits, and then posted it.'

'Sean passed Pine the piece?' Declan shook his head. 'I can't see him doing that.'

'Well, it's a conversation you might need to have with him, laddie. Right then, we need—'

Monroe stopped as Jess ran in, her eyes like saucers.

'I know where I saw it,' she said. 'Obituaries.'

'You're gonna have to explain more, lassie.'

'Billy had me looking through old news pieces connected to the Bannisters' crash,' Jess continued, her voice speaking at double speed, as if she was trying to get all the words out quickly. 'The names of the others never came out, but I found an obituary for the pilot who crashed the helicopter. It was Lewis *Bonneville*.'

'Bonneville's not a common surname,' Declan said. 'What are the chances—'

'That he's the brother of Les? I'd say a hundred percent,' Billy was checking MP records. 'Yeah. Lewis died when he was twenty-seven and was the older brother of the Right Honourable Leslie Bonneville by about seven or eight years.'

'Named "Bonner" by his mates,' Anjli muttered.

Declan rose from his chair.

'We need to get him in,' he said.

'For what?' Monroe rose to face him. 'For being related? We don't know how he's involved. We know he was working with Hunt, and that's it ...'

His voice trailed off as Bullman, her face a mask of anger, walked into the briefing room.

'You can all take the evening off,' she said, her voice tight. 'We're off the case.'

'You what?' Declan exclaimed, a hurried 'Ma'am?' following.

'Just been talking with Bradbury at New Scotland Yard,' Bullman continued. 'It seems the case has been moved to Bishopsgate nick, as we've been dragging our heels and asking the wrong kinds of questions to the wrong kinds of people.'

'You mean Charles Baker?' Declan looked around. 'This has to be him, right?'

'No, Declan, this was straight from Edward Sinclair,' Bullman replied coldly. 'Who apparently felt you were accusing him of being a major suspect only a couple of hours back. He's taken the case from us, and Bishopsgate is coming over to remove all paperwork tomorrow.'

'Tomorrow?' Monroe frowned.

And, finally, the slightest hint of a smile crossed Bullman's lips.

'Well, sure,' she said. 'None of you were here when I got in, were you? So I couldn't tell you to stop. I reckon we can get until midnight before the clock actually stops.'

'But you could call people on the phone ...' Cooper trailed off as she realised what was being said.

Bullman needed them to close the case in a matter of hours before Edward Sinclair covered everything up for a second time.

'We need to speak to Hunt Robinson and his wife before we lose them—'

'Already lost,' Bullman replied regretfully. 'I can fluff the paperwork issue, but they've already been removed from the cells.'

'And taken to Bishopsgate?'

'No, they've been let go, on condition they return if needed.'

'Bloody Sinclair!' Monroe snapped. 'Always sticking his nose in!'

Declan looked around the briefing room.

'We have maybe five hours, no confirmed murder suspect and no proof of any kind of conspiracy,' he said. 'How do we fix this?'

'By taking a leaf out of Hunt Robinson's missing bloody book,' Monroe hissed. 'We fake some news of our own. Your mate, the editor. He said he saw the book once, right? And I'm sure we can find a couple of people who can confirm it's the same one he showed at Christmas?'

'I believe so, Guv.'

Monroe nodded.

'Right then. Declan, go chat to the editor, I want a detailed description. Anjli, take De'Geer and go visit Bishopsgate. Make it look as if you're willing to cooperate.'

'And while we're there?'

'Get Sam Mansfield out of there, and bring him over here,' Declan smiled. 'If Monroe's thinking what I'm thinking, then we've got a job for him.'

———

22

ART CLASS

THE OFFICE HAD BECOME A WHIRLWIND OF CHAOS AS EVERYONE started their tasks. And, as the office emptied, Billy gave Jess a smile.

'It's always like this,' he said, walking to his monitor station and sitting down. 'I like the quiet when they all bugger off.'

'And you don't miss it?' Jess looked at the door longingly, wanting more than anything to go with one of the teams.

'Sure, now and then,' Billy was typing. 'But I'm the mastermind that keeps them all going. My computers are my team, and my team is better.'

'So, what does your "better" team say we need to do?' Jess smiled.

At this, Billy passed her a printout.

'This is Karen Pine's credit card receipt.'

'Are we supposed to have it?'

'If anyone asks? She said we could before she died.'

'So no,' Jess nodded. 'What am I looking for?'

'This payment,' Billy said, pointing at one from the

Monday. 'Two pints – one lager, one bitter, a sandwich, and a large wine.'

Jess saw it and frowned.

'Okay, so now I ...'

'Now you call The Albion, and look for someone who was there,' Billy said. 'Tell them you're calling on behalf of me.'

Jess started to understand.

'It's the pints, isn't it?' she asked. 'You don't think Hunt Robinson mixed, you think there were two pint drinkers there?'

'Worth a look,' Billy nodded over at Declan's desk. 'Use the phone there.'

Jess walked over to her father's desk, sitting down at it. She felt strange to be sitting there, working, and she felt wrong somehow, that she was being unfaithful to her father's memory by sitting at his desk the week he looked to be leaving.

No, don't think that, she thought to herself, forcing the other thoughts away. *He's not dead. You're not being unfaithful to any memory.*

She googled the number for The Albion and picked up the phone.

'Hello?' A female voice answered.

'Hello, are you The Albion?' Jess asked, instantly regretting the opening. 'I mean, are you The Albion pub?'

'Yes,' the voice said, a little strained. 'Can I help?'

'I'm Jessica Walsh, Temple Inn Crime Unit,' Jess squeaked. 'I'm calling on behalf of Detective Sergeant Fitzwarren, he was wondering if there was anyone there right now who worked the afternoon shift on Monday?'

'I did,' the woman on the end of the line replied. 'What's this about?'

'A particular order,' Jess said, looking at the piece of paper. 'Two pints, one lager, one bitter, a sandwich, and a large wine. Would have been between four and five.'

'Yeah, I remember it,' the woman replied. 'Two men and a woman.'

Jess wanted to punch the air.

'If we showed you photos, could you identify one of the people?'

'Look, we're busy—'

'I could literally be there in five minutes,' Jess was already standing up. 'I'm the work experience girl, but ...'

'But PC Esme Cooper will be with her,' Cooper said from behind, almost causing Jess to drop the phone. 'Come on, Jess. They'll wait.'

Billy was watching.

'A third person?' he asked, already sending photos to the printer. 'Here, take this with you.'

Jess pulled them off the printer; the first was Leslie Bonneville, the second Doug Reynolds, the third Sean Ashby.

'It'll be one of these,' Billy smiled. 'I'm going with one or two.'

Jess grinned, grabbing her jacket and running for the door.

'Didn't you say you were going with her?' Billy asked Cooper, who shrugged.

'I'll give her a minute before she realises,' she grinned. 'Come on, guv. We were like that once.'

As Cooper headed for the door and Jess, who'd stopped on the other side, Billy smiled to himself as he continued to work through his tasks.

'Not me,' he muttered.

SAM MANSFIELD STOOD IN THE RECEPTION OF THE Bishopsgate Police Unit and stared in confusion at Anjli.

'So let me get this straight,' he said. 'You're taking on my case, and they're taking one of yours? What are you, time-share police?'

Anjli shrugged, looking at De'Geer.

'Could you?' she asked, nodding at Sam. 'I need to have a chat with this miscreant.'

As De'Geer walked over to the front desk, passing a folder over to them, Anjli walked up to Sam.

'We're looking into your case,' she said. 'It looks bad for you. Really bad. Especially as you took the piss out of DI Walsh, apparently.'

'It's okay, he'll be over it in a couple of days,' Sam suggested. 'Of course, we'll also be saying goodbye to him because he'll be out in a couple of—'

He winced as Anjli punched him hard on the arm.

'Do you want us to be nice to you, or what?' she hissed. 'Because we're quite happy to be utter pricks to you in the time we have left before you're sent off to, quite frankly, a terrible holding prison.'

Sam narrowed his eyes.

'How nice?'

'Let's just say we need your help, and it would be noted during your trial that you assisted us with no expectation of any lessening of sentencing.'

'But there is an expectation,' Sam smiled. 'I'm guessing this is a forgery situation?'

'Quick turnaround,' Anjli nodded.

'What sort of "quick" do you mean here?'

Anjli glanced at her watch.

'About three hours, give or take,' she replied. 'DI Walsh is checking some facts, but we know certain things. And we're looking to create a fake diary, so it's mainly handwriting, not art.'

'What, because writing's not as hard?' Sam sighed. 'This is what I get, philistines—'

'I meant it's not being authenticated, it just needs to bring people to a table,' Anjli grabbed Sam by the arm, moving him out. 'What do you need for this?'

'A Big Mac meal, and chocolate milkshake,' Sam grinned. 'For creative reasons, I promise.'

Cooper and Jess stood at the bar in The Albion as the barmaid who'd answered the phone, named Heather, glanced at the photos.

'It weren't the pretty boy,' she said, tossing the picture of Bonneville down. 'This was the guy. And the guy he was with, he was the one they found at St Bride's, around the corner, wasn't he? Is this to do with that?'

Cooper took the images back, ignoring the question.

'We know two left, but we didn't see the third one leave,' she said. 'Did he stay long?'

'Oh yeah, ordered another bitter and a burger, and sat down to watch the match,' Heather nodded. 'Didn't seem to be in a hurry. Did he do it?'

'We're not at liberty to say anything,' Jess replied, staring at Heather. 'Thank you for your time.'

Heather nodded at another customer who'd just walked to the bar.

'Well, if you need anything,' she said, the offer unspoken but there. 'Oh, and one thing. He didn't leave by the door there, he went out the fire door about nine. I remember being angry about it, because it meant it didn't shut properly and anyone could have got in.'

'Where does the fire door lead?' Cooper asked.

'Bride Court, out the side,' Heather nodded.

Cooper thanked Heather, who'd already moved over to serve the newcomers as Jess texted the new information to Billy.

'Come on, we'll go through Bride Court,' Cooper pulled Jess to the main entrance.

'Don't we have to use the fire door—'

'There's an entrance beside the pub,' Cooper said as they exited the pub, walking down a covered alley to the side. 'This was where we found Robinson, the FedEx building is to the ...'

She stopped as a man emerged from the other end of the corridor.

'I understand you've been looking for me?' Doug Reynolds asked.

'There's no bloody way you knew that,' Cooper frowned. 'How did you ...'

Doug laughed.

'I was on my way to your station, saw you pop into the pub,' he said. 'Thought I'd wait. Out of sight, like.'

'And how did you know we're Temple Inn?' Jess asked.

'Because you're the daughter of Declan Walsh, and with your bright red hair, you stick out like a beacon,' Doug laughed. 'Shall we?'

And, his question asked, he turned and walked off.

'Well, your name precedes you,' Cooper shrugged as they followed. 'Although I'm not sure if that's a good thing or not.'

ANJLI WAS IN THE OFFICE WITH BILLY AND DE'GEER, SAM Mansfield sitting at a desk between them, the remains of a McDonald's meal in front of him when Jess, Cooper and Doug Reynolds arrived.

Sam was currently writing what looked to be random scribbles onto some A5 lined paper, before passing it back to Billy who, the moment he had it, was scanning it with his phone, the image appearing on his monitor screen. It looked quite industrious, and Jess wondered quietly what exactly was going on.

Passing another piece across to Billy, Sam looked up at the new arrivals and grinned.

'Well, hello, little girl,' he said. 'And who might you be? Surely someone as pretty as you shouldn't be doing police work. I'll have a coffee.'

He looked around.

'Is it too late for a coffee? Yeah? Maybe a herbal tea, then.'

'She's out of your league and half your age,' Anjli said, clipping him around the back of the head.

'That's harsh,' Sam replied sullenly, rubbing at his neck. 'How old do you think I am?'

'No, "how old you think she is?" should be the question you're asking,' De'Geer commented and the tone of the seven foot Viking was enough to stop Sam, holding his hands up.

'I'm just playing,' he said. 'I know she's Walsh's Mini Me. I'm just bored. This isn't as exciting as I thought it would be when you sprung me from jail.'

'You sprung him from jail?' Cooper asked, shocked.

De'Geer shook his head, ending that lie as quickly as it started.

'Mister Mansfield is helping us with our enquiries, using a particular set of skills,' he intoned calmly. 'But it's slow because we're waiting for information. We know it's a black Filofax, but we're not too sure about some of the other details, so we're filling out the back of it.'

'We're working on the main pages,' Billy passed over a printed Filofax lined notepaper page from the printer. 'Here. See? There's a lot of fonts out there for doctors' handwriting, random scrawls, things like that. I've taken several of Hunt Robinson's most recent news pieces and put them through a word processor, using that font. I've then taken these pieces, positioned them on a PDF template of the diary to place them all higgledy piggledy, and then printed them off.'

He showed it again, holding it up. It had been cut with a ruler and Stanley knife, and it was passable as writing on a diary.

'Looks just like the real one,' Doug said. 'What? I know the book we're talking about here. It's not real. Hunt made it last year.'

'We thought as much,' Anjli said. 'Why?'

'People were forgetting he had such a thing,' Doug shrugged. 'So he gave a show. Turned up to a Christmas bash, pretended to be pissed, held it up to let people have a squizz at it, then ran off. All to build the story.'

'So the book exists? The one we're making?'

'For about three hours,' Doug laughed. 'He tossed it into the Thames off Westminster Bridge before going home.'

Anjli frowned.

'Wouldn't Janine have seen that?'

'Nah, not really. Let's just say she went to a different home that night.'

'Cheeky!' Sam exclaimed before Anjli leant over and cuffed him.

'But you'd know how he writes his notes,' she said to Doug. 'Can you help?'

'It only needs to be seen once or twice, so we don't need to go too hard,' Billy added.

Doug picked up the paper, turning it in his hand.

'Your problem is it's too clean,' he said. 'You need to work out how to make it look like it isn't, well ...'

'Crap,' Sam said, taking it from him. 'That's the problem with these police types. They don't understand how art works.'

He shook his head sadly at Billy.

'Look at you. I bet you use AI on things. God, creativity is being removed by you guys.'

'Says the forger,' Billy smiled.

'I do *not* forge,' Sam replied indignantly. 'I provide my own interpretation of classic pieces. And if somebody wants my work, they can have it at a very reasonable price.'

'It helps that your interpretation of these classic pieces happen to look *exactly like* these classic pieces, though,' Anjli said with mock innocence.

Sam didn't reply. Instead, he took his straw out of the chocolate milkshake, and let the contents inside it drip onto the desk.

'Hey!' Anjli shouted. 'Don't do that. It'll make the desk all sticky!'

'That's the point,' Sam replied calmly, using his finger to make a large circle of milkshake on the desk. 'Why did you think I asked for it?'

'Because you were hungry?' De'Geer suggested.

'Well, there is that,' he said. Taking the base of the milk-shake's disposable cup, Sam Mansfield rubbed it into the sticky mess on the desk, and then, on the side of the paper used the base to create a sticky brown half circle over the printed words.

'There,' he said. 'Now it looks like someone accidentally placed a mug of coffee on it.'

He then took a finger, stuck it into the remains of the now-empty Big Mac box, and on the corner of the paper wiped a long stain of burger sauce.

'As I said,' he explained, turning the paper over and repeating the same thing on the other side. 'When you make your forgeries, you make them pristine, soulless. Nobody thinks of putting the little details in. Why would you forge something and leave it in this book if it's been made dirty?'

He looked up.

'Come on, that's not rhetorical, class is in session.'

'Because you don't care what it looks like if it's for your-self,' Jess replied.

'Ding! The kiddie corner understands better than you!' Sam exclaimed. 'You'd keep it, if it was something no one would be seeing.'

He passed it back to Billy.

'There you go. Tell me it doesn't look better.'

'Yeah, okay, it does,' Billy reluctantly replied. 'Now we just need to do this for another thirty pages.'

Anjli looked at Doug.

'You here to help us?'

'Why would you think that?'

'Because you helped Hunt,' Billy said. 'You tried to mediate the problems with him and Karen Pine, didn't you?'

'For all the good it did her,' Doug nodded sadly.

'And because you aimed me at the Royal Protection officer,' Anjli added. 'It wasn't to escape, you could have done that anytime. It's because you know what's going on; that your long-time friend Hunt is in trouble, and you've been trying to help them.'

She smiled.

'We also know that you're probably the only suspect so far in this case who didn't murder Karen Pine. As you said, you have the receipts. Or were you lying?'

'No, I wasn't,' Doug nodded. 'I can tell you who *did* kill her, though.'

'I think we already know,' Anjli replied. 'So write it down on a bit of paper, and at the end of all this, we'll see if you were correct.'

Doug looked over at Sam.

'I saw the book when I was at the party,' he explained. 'It's close to this. There are some coloured tabs, too. You can gain a lot from the recent newspaper articles, the ones that were written about the football guy and the Nazi politician, but I can give you some other things. Hints and titbits I found for him over the years that aren't out there. I can pepper these pages throughout the book, with some things on them that'll really make people believe they're true.'

'See?' Sam said with a smile on his lips. 'Now this doesn't sound boring.'

'Should we call DI Walsh back?' Cooper asked. 'He was going to get a description too, and if we already have it now—'

Anjli shook her head.

'Declan's doing more than just getting a description,' she said. 'He's on a fishing expedition.'

She looked at Doug.

'What was on the cover?'

Doug frowned as he thought.

'It had "Vox populi" on it, in silver pen,' he said. 'It means—'

'Voice of the People,' De'Geer finished. 'What? I know Latin. So what?'

'Text that to Declan,' Anjli said to Cooper. 'He'll be able to use that. And Monroe is already planning his next thing.'

'What about Hunt?' Doug asked. 'He's been sent home, hasn't he? I'd been checking Bishopsgate when I started coming to you. Janine doesn't need him anymore. And she's … well, I can't say, in case I invalidate the name I'm about to write on a piece of paper.'

'Don't worry,' Billy said, passing another printout to Sam. 'Our boss has an idea about that as well.'

'Hey,' Sam looked over at Anjli. 'If you really want to screw with them, I've got some thick flash paper in my jacket, which you've taken and stuck in an evidence box somewhere.'

'Flash paper?'

'Oh yeah,' Sam said. 'Look, I'm getting the impression here that you want to do something with shock and awe. And you probably want things to stop them looking too closely at this forgery, right?'

'Flash paper,' Billy nodded with a smile. 'Can you set it up to be remote activated?'

'What, like a spark at the bottom that sets the entire thing off? Probably.'

Billy looked back at the printer.

'We've got this set for A5, which is roughly photo sized,' he replied. 'Could you print an image onto flash paper?'

'You thinking of a particular image?' Anjli asked.

'Janine Robinson mentioned Karen Pine when she was being interviewed, said if she saw her on the Journalists Altar, she'd set fire to the image,' Billy grinned. 'So let's give her something good to set fire to.'

Sam was considering this as Billy spoke.

'Normal stuff is a no-no as it could overheat, but the thicker stuff is made for printing on, so sure, I've done ID cards with it, I think it's worth a try,' Sam said, looking back at Anjli. 'You see? This isn't boring. If police work was like this, I would have joined.'

'They wouldn't take you.'

'Of course they would,' Sam replied, 'I've got a warrant card and everything. I'm a Detective Inspector, you know.'

Anjli shuddered.

'Please don't tell us things like that,' she moaned softly. 'We're trying to help you reduce your sentence, not help you dig a bigger hole. The judge would have a field day.'

'I'm a judge, too,' Sam smiled. 'It's amazing what you can do with Photoshop and boredom. And if someone calls me on it; quick flame and poof! The ID's gone, with no evidence left. Now, if someone wants to get me my things, let's set fire to some shit!'

———

23

HOLD THE FRONT PAGE

'Declan,' Sean said, quite surprised as Declan walked into the office. 'If you'd have told me you're turning up, I could have met you downstairs.'

'Don't worry,' Declan said. 'I'm not snooping around.'

He smiled sitting down opposite Sean, the desk a barrier between them.

'I'm actually here for a favour,' he said.

'You are?' Sean frowned. 'What sort of favour do you want?'

'Well, you told me you'd seen the notebook,' Declan said. 'I was hoping you'd remember what it looked like. How thick it was, maybe even what brand it had been created by.'

He looked at his own notebook.

'I have you saying: "black thing, looks like a Filofax" earlier on.'

'Yeah, I can remember that,' Sean nodded, already looking for paper. 'You looking for a better description for the hunters?'

'No, we think we've got the book,' Declan smiled. 'Don't

tell anyone, but we have *a* book – picking it up tonight – but knowing it's *the* book would help immensely.'

'What's in it for me?' Sean was fixed on Declan as he spoke, and Declan had noted a shift in his positioning the moment Declan had stated he knew where the book was.

'If you can provide us with a very detailed idea of what the book looks like, then we'd give you the exclusive rights to what happened,' Declan shrugged. 'And perhaps once I'm no longer in the police—'

'You'd give me your story,' Sean grinned.

'I don't know, Sean,' Declan replied, shifting in the chair. 'Kendis always said you were a bit bloodthirsty when it came to getting what you wanted.'

'Oh, I'm the blood-thirstiest when there's a story involved,' Sean was already writing. 'When do you need this by?'

Declan settled back in his chair, and Sean noticed this.

'Oh, *that* short a deadline then,' he said, scribbling frantically down. 'It's in shorthand. I hope you can understand it.'

'Actually, I can,' Declan rose from the chair, stretching. 'It's been a few years but Kendis used to write love notes to me in it.'

'Well, I'm not writing anything romantic, but I'll do what I can. It'll take a couple of minutes. It was about the size of an A5 Filofax, as I said before, black leather ...'

He faded off as he continued writing, forgetting to talk as he was scribbling, and Declan took his moment to look around the editorial office. He hadn't been here for a while; in fact, the last time he'd been in an office of Sean's, it had been at *The Guardian.* This office was bigger than the one he had there, which made sense if he was the editor of the paper rather than a features editor.

There was a sofa to the side, and Declan walked over to it. The view from the large window behind it showed London's night in all its glory. And as he stood there, he paused, sniffing.

There was a smell, like burning, but not quite. Looking around, he saw a coffee table with an ashtray.

'I didn't think you're allowed to smoke in the office anymore,' he said.

'I'm not,' Sean said. 'But now and then, you know how it goes ...' He carried on writing as Declan looked back at the ashtray.

It wasn't a cigarette in there; it was a cigar stub, with a *familiar* cigar band around it.

'Didn't take you down for a cigar smoker,' he said.

'Oh?' Sean looked up, pausing the writing 'Sure, yes, I have one now and then.'

'I'm a bit of a cigar aficionado myself,' Declan lied. 'What brand do you smoke?'

'I think it's Montecristo ...'

'Good brand,' Declan nodded. He didn't mention the cigar's band wasn't that of a Montecristo. In fact, it was that of a Hoyo De Monterrey, one he knew Leslie Bonneville smoked.

'Here you go. All done,' Sean said, grinning as he looked up, passing Declan the note paper. 'I hope you can use it.'

However, he held it as Declan went to take it, making Declan wait a moment.

'I want the story when it's done,' he said,

'Oh, I think you'll be definitely hearing about the story,' Declan replied with a smile. 'Do you still monitor the Westminster beat?'

'Not for a while. After Kendis died, I lost my taste for it.'

'Did you ever deal with an MP named Leslie Bonneville? Bonner for short?'

Sean leant back in his chair and frowned.

'Labour MP, I think?' he mused. 'No, I don't think so.'

'Then I'd tell your staff to stop letting him smoke his cigars in your office when you're not here,' Declan replied.

At this, Sean's smile disappeared.

'Good to see you, Declan,' he said. 'Don't be a stranger.'

Declan took a photo of the notepaper, and sent it to Billy with a message saying it was in shorthand before folding the original up and placing it into his pocket – but not before reading a message from Cooper.

'One more thing. How did Karen Pine get Hunt Robinson's Lucy-Rachel Adams story?'

'You know how these things go,' Sean mouth-shrugged. 'Sources speak to multiple reporters, someone comes out—'

'No, I meant how did Karen Pine get Robinson's actual story?' Declan asked again. 'We know he wrote the piece in the *Mail*. It's not Pine's syntax. And we also know he sent you hard copy, not email, so it couldn't have been sent to the wrong place, as he placed it on your desk.'

Sean paled.

'I have no idea—'

'Come on, Sean, at least do it right and say "no comment" if you're going to lie to me,' Declan hissed, leaning closer. 'Bonner was here today. I can smell the smoke. Does he come here often? Did you tell him about the piece?'

'Bonner works with Hunt,' Sean replied. 'He came today to offer his services.'

Declan nodded, watching Sean carefully.

'I don't think I'll be working for you after all,' he said. 'I need to trust my employers. And I don't know if I can do that with you. Tell your friends – we have the book.'

'You sure?' Sean smiled darkly. 'It looks like you were looking for details to make a fake.'

Declan knew Sean would ask this, and with Cooper's text, he knew he could call his bluff.

'Vox populi,' he said. 'Voice of the people. That was on the corner of this book, apparently. On the cover, in silver. I didn't read your notes, but did you add that? Because you never told me it.'

'No, I'd forgotten that,' Sean admitted. 'It was on there, yeah, now you mention it.'

'Great then. If it's real I might upload the stories within it myself,' Declan replied coldly. 'What will the police do, fire me?'

And, before Sean could say anything, Declan walked out of the office.

———

TESSA INTERCEPTED HIM BEFORE HE REACHED THE ELEVATOR, following him into it as the doors closed.

'I saw you met Sean,' she said. 'Was it—'

'Are you involved?' Declan interrupted, spinning to face her. 'Is this another bloody conspiracy I'm going to end up arresting you for?'

Tessa looked stunned at the outburst.

'What's that supposed to mean?'

Before Tessa could say anything else, Declan reached across, pressing a button on the elevator panel, stopping it between floors.

'Are you part of this?' he asked. 'I know your editor is now.'

'Part of what?' Tessa still seemed clueless, but Declan knew how good an actor she could be when needed.

'Hunt Robinson, the whole thing.'

'No!' Tessa replied. 'Why would you think that?'

Declan watched Tessa carefully as he spoke.

'Because Hunt Robinson gave Sean a document,' he said. 'A physical copy of an article he'd written, exposing Lucy-Rachel Adams – and that same document appeared in a rival newspaper while he was in a war zone.'

'It could have been a coincidence—'

'We checked the syntax, Tessa. It's almost word for word how he wrote, and nothing like Karen Pine, whose byline it was under.'

Tessa slowly nodded, understanding now.

'And you think Sean did this?'

'He's the only person who could have,' Declan replied. 'Hunt doesn't email, he probably doesn't believe in paper trails or something, and instead only uses physical copies. Like the one he left on Sean's desk before he went to Ukraine, and that Sean spiked.'

Tessa thought about this for a second ... and then swore.

'I don't think it's him,' she said. 'There was this guy, turned up a couple of weeks back. I was coming up to see Sean, but he was at an editorial meeting. I remember seeing this guy walking out of Sean's office, though. Like he owned the place. I didn't know who he was, and I assumed he was a publisher or someone connected to the guy who owns the paper. But he had a sheet of A4 in his hand.'

Declan opened up his phone, scrolling through the Westminster page until he found a photo of Leslie Bonneville.

'Was it him?' he asked, showing it.

Tessa nodded.

'Who is he?'

'He's a Labour MP who's been talking to Sean,' Declan replied. 'I know that because he's been smoking his cigars in the office. But more importantly, he's the younger brother of the pilot who crashed the Bannisters' helicopter into a mountain.'

Tessa paled.

'I can't talk about that—' she started, but Declan held a hand up to stop her.

'It's okay, I know what you can't talk about,' he said. 'That one of the people who died was the Duchess of Dorset, perhaps? Or maybe the fact that Alfie Bannister is the true father of the current heir to the dukedom?'

'Maybe,' Tessa smiled. 'I can't confirm or deny what you've said, Declan, even if you're on the nose.'

Declan smiled in response.

'I don't want to put you into any problems,' he said. 'But Sean, whether by accident or deliberately, started this whole thing.'

'What do you need me to do?'

Declan pressed the ground floor button again, and the elevator shuddered to a start.

'I need you to return to Sean and tell him you had a word with me,' he explained. 'Tell him you were conversational, but at the same time gained information. Tell him I know where the book is, and I needed his description so we could confirm it wasn't a fake.'

'And where's the book?'

'Tell him it's taped under one of the marble pews, in the crypt where Hunt Robinson was found,' Declan replied.

'Mention that the church is closed right now, but there's a security pass at eleven tonight, so a window to confirm this.'

Tessa nodded.

'You want him to tell the MP guy?'

'I want to find Karen Pine's murderer,' Declan replied. 'They were there looking for this book. They're not going to wait until morning, or allow a locked door to stop them from finding it.'

'And the others?'

'Oh, we've got that organised,' Declan said as he left the elevator. 'Don't you worry about that.'

'REJOICE!' MONROE SMILED AS HE WALKED INTO SINCLAIR'S office. 'Your problems have been solved, your questions answered. Your Messiah has arrived!'

Sinclair leant back in his chair, observing Monroe carefully.

'You know you're off the case now, right?'

Monroe sat opposite him and shrugged.

'I know,' he said. 'But we'd found this out before you told us to go away, so I thought I'd let you know.'

'So, what have you done?' Sinclair asked. 'Because I'm not expecting much. The bar is quite low when it comes to you, Alex.'

'We know where the book is,' Monroe shrugged.

'Karen Pine had it.'

'We thought that, too. But then when she was found murdered, the book was missing.'

'Because whoever killed Karen took the book.'

'No,' Monroe smiled. 'We checked the whole place. It'd

been looked through, and there was a book with headlines in. The same size as we saw her take on the CCTV. However, it wasn't *the* book. It seems the book never left the church.'

'What are you talking about?' Sinclair asked, frowning. 'Do you mean the crypt?'

'Robinson secured it under the seating with some gaffer tape,' Monroe replied. 'He finally told us today, before you let him go.'

He settled in his chair, smiling at his superior, with a smugness that belayed what was being said.

'Apparently, the plan was to make out that someone else had it, and allow Karen Pine to put out a couple of "easy to find" stories; ones out there already but known to also be in the book, and let them play out until whoever was after him no longer thought he had it.'

'And he could return to grab it. Yes, it sounds plausible,' Sinclair said. 'But why tell you?'

'Because he's scared, still,' Monroe looked at the sideboard. 'Any chance of a wee dram? Declan said you had the good stuff in here.'

'Stick to the point, Monroe.'

'Well then, sir, it seems he has this conspiracy theory, that members of the Royal Family want him dead, and ... uh, well ... you're leading a crusade.'

'Me?'

'Yes, sir. And now he knows Bishopsgate's taken over the case, and you'll most likely have more of a say on what's going on.' Monroe stared mournfully at the sideboard, as if imagining the drinks inside. 'He decided he'd rather come clean right now. Only problem is St Bride's is closed for the day, security don't do their rounds until about eleven tonight, and we know that we don't have the time to get it, because as you so wisely stated, we're no longer on the case.'

He rose from the chair.

'Anyway, the churchwarden opens up at around seven, so get some people in there lickety-spit, aye?'

'I appreciate the heads up,' Sinclair nodded. 'I'll tell Bishopsgate to go tomorrow, after it opens. There's no point causing any problems with the churchwarden.'

'Good idea, sir,' Monroe turned to leave.

'Alex,' Sinclair said, pausing him at the door. 'When Declan leaves, you know, for good, you won't be getting more budget; so expect to gain diminishing returns until there's no more use for you.'

'Oh, so I always expect that,' Monroe smiled from the doorway. 'Good luck with your knighthood, or whatever they're giving you for selling your soul for thirty pieces of silver.'

And with that said, Monroe left the offices of Commander Edward Sinclair.

Sinclair leant back in his chair again, staring up at the ceiling, considering what had just been said. And then, checking his watch, he rose from his desk and grabbed his coat.

He needed to pass this on. He needed to know what *they* wanted.

And he needed to gain his three pages back before *they* did.

WHEN THEY'D ARRIVED BACK AT THEIR HOUSE IN KENT, HUNT had gone to bed, claiming that the actions of the last few days had completely wiped him out. Janine had resisted the urge to point out the reason he was so tired was because he'd stabbed himself in the gut and tied himself to a pew for seven hours; she knew he was aware of the stupidity of his actions. And, if he didn't, she'd make damn sure he learnt over the next few weeks.

Or at least until she got a damned good divorce lawyer.

When she left him in the bedroom, she planned to spend the evening downstairs instead. She found it calmer and nicer to not be with Hunt in general, and for a change, they were in the same building and she didn't need to listen to his whining.

Sitting at the kitchen table, checking her phone, she considered her next options. After all, there were still things that needed to be done.

There was a buzz on her phone, she'd placed it on silent so as not to alert Hunt of any calls, and, closing the social media app she'd been checking, she read the message.

Then, rising, she checked her watch, working out timings in her head.

She could just make it if she left now.

'Darling? Are you awake?' she asked gently from the bottom of the stairs, but there was no answer. Hunt had obviously sparked right out. Which was good.

And so, without waking her husband, Janine Robinson grabbed her jacket, keys and phone, and left the house, walking off into the late night.

———

HUNT ROBINSON HADN'T BEEN ASLEEP. HE'D BEEN LYING ON HIS bed, listening.

He'd received a message, too.

FROM: LES BONNEVILLE

They found your book. No need for secrets
anymore. Now I get what I need.

Hunt sighed. So the mysterious, unknown blackmailer
had been Bonner. How pedestrian.

There was a second message, one that explained what the
first one meant.

Hunt it's Doug. You might get some strange
messages tonight, as someone's playing a
Hail Mary. Send me the details of anyone
who texts you about the book.

Robinson stared at the message. There was no book, just
loads of files in his office. The only "book" had been the one
Karen Pine had demanded. And even then, it was nothing
more than headlines. Unless they meant the prop for the
party?

He'd heard Janine leave, though, and now things were
starting to come into focus. He was realising who the true
perpetrators were here.

Rising carefully, still holding his side, he called the
number that had texted him.

'Doug? It's Hunt,' he said. 'I know everything, and I could
do with a friend. Are you one? The message made out you are
...'

After a moment, he smiled.

'I could do with a lift, too, if you're around,' he said. 'I'm
about to nail down a damn good divorce reason.'

He stopped, however, as the doorbell downstairs went.

'Hold on,' he said as he started down the stairs gingerly, walking to the door. 'I think Janine's outside. She's forgotten her key or something—'

He laughed as he opened it, watching Doug Reynolds turn off his phone.

'I was told to come here,' Doug said. 'It seems people are ahead of us. Ahead of me.'

'Who the bloody hell told you to come here?'

'A pain in the arse Scottish DCI,' Doug entered the house, walking past Robinson. 'Come on, settle down. I need to tell you everything.'

———

24

SHENANIGANS

It had been a wild idea, but then the best ideas at the Last Chance Saloon always were. With Sam Mansfield's help, the facsimile had been secured under one of the pews in the downstairs crypt before the ink had even dried.

Sinclair had been the first to arrive.

It had been just after eleven, as per the time Monroe had suggested. The security guard had walked around the outside of the church; Sinclair had watched him from the shadows of St Bride's Court. Then, the guard opened the main door to the church. He didn't walk in; he was just shining the torch around the entranceway, before closing the door, preparing to lock it back up.

'Guard,' Sinclair said, walking towards the now cautious security guard. 'I'd prefer you to keep that open. Commander Sinclair, City of London Police.'

The guard pulled his glasses on to check the ID shown.

'You're out late,' he said, checking his watch. 'Church opens—'

'The church is open now, thanks to you,' Sinclair said,

pushing the door open. 'I need to check something connected to the person we found here yesterday morning. You heard about that?'

The guard nodded, wide-eyed.

'I shouldn't ... I can't leave it unlocked.'

'Does your walk continue back here?' Sinclair asked.

'Yes, sir. I return in about half an hour.'

'Then that's fine,' Sinclair gave a smile, placing his hand on the guard's shoulder. 'I'll do what I need to do inside and hold the fort until you get back. Then you can lock back up and we'll call it a night.'

'I don't know—'

'I'm the third-highest person in the sodding City of London police,' Sinclair snapped. 'And you will do this, or I'll get a warrant in and bypass you. I'll also have you pulled up on interfering with a police investigation.'

'All right, all right,' the guard muttered, stepping back. 'Go play in the bloody church. I'll be back in thirty.'

With that, the guard stomped off down the courtyard passage into the night.

Breathing out a sigh of relief, Sinclair checked his watch; it was five minutes past eleven. He had thirty before the guard came back, so he needed to be gone in fifteen, just in case the guard decided to be civic-minded and call this in.

Walking into the dimly lit church, Sinclair couldn't help crossing himself before turning and heading down into the crypt. He wondered if Robinson had known of the eleven pm check, and whether he'd been in hiding two nights earlier, as he walked through the museum area, turning on the lights as he did so. After all, he wasn't skulking; he was gaining vital evidence before someone else came and took it.

The fact he needed to pull out some pages first was irrelevant.

Walking into the crypt, Sinclair glanced at a mark on the floor, likely the remnants of the blood from Robinson's wound, still not fully removed. The crypt stank of bleach, so someone had obviously had a go at removing it. Almost gagging from the overpowering stench, he walked over to the back of the crypt, crouching down and feeling with his hand under the seats.

There was a lump, secured with gaffer tape.

Yes.

Sinclair carefully pulled the package away, finding a green plastic carrier bag with a book inside. Tearing the bag away from the contents, he found himself staring at a black Filofax, the words "VOX POPULI" written on the corner in silver sharpie pen.

Hunt Robinson's book.

Rising, he flicked through it quickly; it was filled with random scrawlings, and there was no time to make sure everything he needed to remove was gone before he placed it in evidence, as this would take more time than he had right now in a crypt. But he could do this at his own leisure in his office.

He paused.

Or should he do it now and re-secure it, pretend he hadn't been here? No, the guard would name him, and his prints were on the book. Best to say he'd acted on initiative.

And so, still holding the Filofax in his hand, Sinclair left the crypt and started down the walkway, back into the museum.

Someone was standing at the other end.

'The church is closed,' Sinclair said, silently cursing

himself for not closing the main door in his rush to get into the crypt. Anyone could have got in, and this seemed to be the case here.

'I know,' the figure replied, walking into the light.

'Leslie Bonneville?' Sinclair frowned. 'This isn't Westminster, Bonner. You seem to be lost.'

'I could say the same to you, Edward,' Bonner smiled, nodding at the book. 'Oh, you found it. Well done you. Could I have a peek?'

'Looking for dirt on your rivals?'

'Oh, I have that,' Bonner shrugged, stepping closer. 'I'd just like to see three pages inside the book, in fact. You can have the rest.'

'Any particular ones?' Sinclair opened the book. It was a piece on Marcus Leigh. *Poor Robinson, another story he never gained a byline for.* 'I could give you the first three?'

'I was thinking more about the pages on the Bannisters.'

'You too? Small world,' Sinclair wondered quietly if this meant Bonner was more ally than enemy. 'I'm looking for those three pages as well. What did *you* want with them?'

'I should be asking you that, Edward.'

Sinclair shrugged and held up the book, flicking through the pages so Bonner could see it.

'I think it's best for the country if they disappeared,' he said. 'You?'

'I think it's best if the country knew about them,' Bonner replied, reaching into his jacket pocket. 'It looks like we're at an impasse, then.'

'Not really,' Sinclair shook his head. 'I have the book, and you don't.'

'Yes, but I'm armed,' Bonner pulled out a wicked-looking knife from his jacket. 'And you're all alone, Edward.'

JANINE WAS ALREADY TIRED BY THE TIME SHE ARRIVED AT THE church.

The walk to the station had been long; she hadn't wanted to risk driving. And the train at that time of night had been slow, stopping at all the stations until she changed and reached Blackfriars. Then it'd been a quick walk – almost a jog up the hill to the church, as she knew she was aiming for the only time the church was open.

Luckily, the door was still ajar when she arrived.

Walking into the church, she could hear the faint sounds of voices downstairs. For a moment, she paused, wondering if the church had some kind of a special event on; one that was exactly where she needed to be.

Deciding to give it a moment to see what the people in the crypt did, she walked into the church, away from the steps into the crypt. She thought the pews and chairs would shield her if anyone emerged from the crypt, probably in the same way her husband hid here two days earlier.

She realised at this point she was walking towards the journalist's altar, and at the front was a familiar image.

'You're bloody kidding me,' she said as she walked over, staring at the photo of Karen Pine. It had been printed out and stuck on card, but it was her, with "in memorial" written underneath.

'Screw you,' she hissed, taking one of the lit tea lights from the side. She hadn't even considered wondering why the tea lights would still be lit in a closed church; so intent was she with doing what she'd always promised to do, holding the tea light's flame to the base of the photo, hoping it'd catch light—

There was a burst of light, a flash of energy as the photo literally exploded into a ball of flame, causing Janine to stagger back, dropping the tea light to the floor as she rubbed at her eyes, the light of the fireball burned onto her retinas for a moment. Then, calming, she looked back at the altar, and as her heart skipped a beat, and her hand clamped onto her mouth to stop herself from screaming aloud, she looked at the remains of the card.

The photo was gone; but behind it, in charred handwriting, was a message.

YOU'LL BURN IN HELL FOR WHAT YOU DID.

Janine stared at the message, recognising the handwriting; it was Karen's, of that she had no doubt. Staggering back, as if she expected something to rise and attack her, knocking over two of the chairs as she did so, she backed against the wall, the only thing stopping her from backing any further.

'You're dead!' she shouted out. 'I killed you! Leave me alone!'

There was noise from the crypt, and suddenly Janine saw two figures emerge up the stairs. For a moment she thought they were demons, crawling out of hell to drag her down, but then the rational side of her brain regained control as she saw Edward Sinclair and Les "Bonner" Bonneville emerge. Sinclair held the book, while Bonner held a knife; that was all she needed to see to know what was going on there, as Bonner now positioned himself beside the door, closing and locking it before anyone else could enter or leave.

'What the bloody hell are you doing up here?' he hissed at Janine. 'You trying to bring the police here?'

'They're already here,' regaining her composure, Janine straightened, staring at Sinclair.

'Yeah, he's definitely not being police tonight,' Bonner smiled. 'Just check his hand.'

Janine walked slowly towards Sinclair.

'I need to look at the book,' she said. 'I always believed it was fake, that Hunt was lying, but if—'

'Let me guess, if the helicopter crash is in here, then you really need the pages?' Sinclair scoffed. 'Join the queue behind Bonner, and expect to wait a long bloody time.'

Janine glared at Sinclair.

'Of course, you're here because of that,' she said. 'You never wanted justice. You just wanted a peerage.'

She spun to face Bonner now.

'And you—'

'Don't you dare start on me!' Bonner snapped back. 'You didn't have your brother die in that crash!'

'Ten years ago!' Janine shouted. 'Ten years! You've been an MP for what, four of them? Not once have you tried to raise a committee about this! You've just cosied up to Hunt to see what you could get! Why now?'

'Because the memorial—'

'Oh, don't give me that bullshit!' Janine was on a roll now. 'The memorial, the memorial, the bloody memorial! You could have forced this at any time! Even if you claimed you didn't want to do it during Elizabeth's reign, she's been gone months now!'

She stormed up to Bonner, ignoring his blade as she poked him in the chest.

'You did this because there's an election coming up,' she

hissed. 'You did this because the Tories are in disarray and your bloody Labour paymasters aren't far behind. You wanted to throw a ton of people under the bus so you could rise in the party. This isn't about your brother. It was never about your brother. It's about you.'

'And this wasn't about you?' Sinclair said, his voice emotionless. 'Sure, Penelope was a friend, but we heard the rumours. How you'd been one of Alfie's early conquests, and how you were pissed he'd moved on.'

He mock-sighed.

'But I suppose you can't compete with a princess.'

'She wasn't a princess, she was a duchess, and a pretty shitty one at that,' Janine muttered. 'And for ten years she's been seen as this noble figure, almost deified as they did Diana. And don't you dare belittle my relationship with Penny. She helped me settle in when I joined the Civil Service, before she moved. She was like a sister to me. I want the truth out there.'

'And I'm working for people who don't,' Sinclair finished. 'So here's how it's going to go. I'm taking this book, and I'm removing a small percentage of it, right now, and setting fire to the pages—'

'Bullshit,' Bonner shook his head. 'You'll keep them for leverage, just like Hunt did.'

'Can Hunt arrest you? Destroy your lives?' Sinclair replied icily. 'Because if you keep back-talking me, I'll make sure you hit the cells, publicly, quicker than you can say "blackmail my peers for political gain," okay?'

Janine glanced back at the journalist's altar and shook her head.

'I'm not the only one going to hell,' she muttered.

'And what the hell does that—' Sinclair asked, but didn't

finish as Janine wrenched the blade from Bonner's unsuspecting hand, and dived at the Commander, the two of them falling to the floor.

'Why won't you die?' Janine screamed as she tried to force the blade down.

The church lights flickered, as if there was a power fluctuation, and one by one, the pictures on the journalist's altar burst into flames in quick, bright flashes of light.

Janine, seeing this, fell from Sinclair, blade held up, staring at the altar.

'You're not taking me to hell!' she cried out. 'Karen deserved what she got! She was working with Bonner!'

Bonner was standing, looking around, his eyes narrowing.

'Shut the hell up!' he hissed. 'These aren't ghosts! This is smoke and mirrors, meant to distract us ...'

He stopped and clapped his hands.

'Oh, well done,' he said, looking around. 'Come out, come out, wherever you are. Olly Olly oxen free!'

There was the sound of a wooden door creaking open, and a figure appeared in the doorway, with what looked to be a waste bin in their hand. Slowly, they walked forwards, savouring the moment, and now in the lights of the nave, their face was revealed.

'I think you'll find there are a lot of ghosts in here,' Declan said. 'And we're just entertainment for them. So, who wants to go first?'

25

GHOSTLY CONFESSIONS

THERE WAS A BANG ON THE DOOR BONNER HAD LOCKED; THREE sharp raps upon it.

'Could you open that, please?' Declan said, placing what looked to be a small metal bin onto one of the chairs beside him.

Bonner, smiling at Declan's arrival walked to it, unlocking and opening the door to reveal Sean Ashby and Tessa Martinez.

'Sorry we're late,' she said. 'I had to bring him here.'

Sean didn't look happy to be there, as he walked into the church.

'I know you like your theatrics, Declan,' he muttered. 'But this is taking stagecraft denouements to a new level. Even Poirot would turn in his grave ... if he was real.'

Declan shrugged.

'Thanks for coming tonight,' he said, smiling as he turned his attention to each of the people in the nave of St Bride's, one by one. 'It saves us a lot of time, and we don't have much.

We officially lose the case to him—' he pointed at Sinclair '—in about half an hour.'

'You've got nothing,' Janine muttered.

'We'll come to you in a moment,' Declan smiled. 'First, I'd like to talk to my boss.'

'Declan, I can explain,' Sinclair replied. 'DCI Monroe informed me of the book's location, and I knew someone would try to take it. So I came to pick it up, and Leslie Bonneville came at me with a blade.'

'The one Janine Robinson has?'

'She took it from him.'

'That's careless,' Declan smiled at Bonner.

'Arrest him, please.'

Declan frowned at the order.

'Oh, I will be,' he said. 'But not for you. In fact, all three of you will be—'

'Four!' Bonner pointed at Sean. 'He discussed the book with me! Confirmed what it looked like after I saw Hunt with it at the party!!'

Declan sighed.

'Yes, the book,' he said, holding out a hand. 'Sir?'

Sinclair clutched it to his chest.

'No,' he replied. 'You can't. It's mine.'

'Actually, it's mine,' an unfamiliar voice spoke, and Hunt Robinson entered from the same door Declan had, helped along by Doug Reynolds. 'And I'd like my property back.'

Before Sinclair spoke, Declan held a hand up.

'Sir, we all know this is a tense situation, so let's sort out the story, yeah?' he asked. 'I leave in two days. I don't care what happens. But I do care that Hunt Robinson gets his property back.'

'You have no idea what's going on, Walsh,' Bonner

snarled. 'Why don't you piss off back to wherever it is you're going to once the police dump your arse?'

Tessa sighed audibly.

'You know he's now going to explain everything, right?' She said. 'You're just goading him, delaying the inevitable.'

'Let me tell you what I know,' Declan said. 'I know it's more than just Jay and Alfie Bannister.'

He leant against the chair, the most relaxed person in the room.

'Ten years ago, Alfie and Jay Bannister, with their pilot, Lewis Bonneville, crash their helicopter in the Pennines. Boo hoo, terrible tragedy.'

'Be careful what you say about my brother,' Bonner muttered.

'Oh, I'll be saying the truth,' Declan replied. 'They crashed, according to the coroner's report, because of pilot error – the error being that Lewis, the pilot, was out of his box on cocaine and severely impaired. Drugs given to him by Alfie Bannister at a party they were all at before the flight.'

He looked at Sinclair now.

'But they weren't the only people there,' he said. 'Emily Kim, the TV presenter, who'd been an on/off shag with Jay for close to a decade was there. And with Alfie was Stephanie Sackville, Duchess of Dorset, and her press secretary, Penelope Hallett. Three names nobody knows. Apart from you.'

'I was told by the Crown to look into it,' Sinclair admitted. 'There's nothing wrong with that.'

'And why was that?'

'I knew the same people. I grew up in that scene.'

'With Penelope?'

'I knew her, yes.'

'You knew her too, right?' Declan asked Janine now.

'Working together in the Civil Service before she joined the Royal Household?'

Janine didn't answer.

'I don't know who it was that suggested you close the case quickly,' Declan returned his attention to Sinclair. 'But you were brought on at this point, weren't you? Then a Detective Superintendent, eager to move up the ladder ... and there you were closing down the case of your polo-set schoolfriend's murder.'

'It's not what you think,' Sinclair replied.

'And I don't appreciate people covering up murders,' Declan said as he now looked over at Janine.

'But, by now, the story had changed. No more was this some kind of drug-filled hedonistic crash, with the pilot coked out of his brain. Now it was a tragic accident, with three victims erased from history. You were a friend of Penelope's, and you knew what had been going on for a good few years now.'

A quick look back at Sinclair now.

'Enough time to place the parentage of both her children into doubt.'

As Sinclair glowered at Declan, he smiled, returning to Janine.

'You were vengeful this had been closed down, especially by Edward Sinclair, who you'd been seeing at the time. He might even have given you more information about the truth of this accident without realising. But you wanted the truth to be told.'

'He was stonewalling,' Janine muttered. 'I thought he'd be my white knight, and he turned into a snake.'

'So you looked for another white knight, and found one in Hunt Robinson,' Declan nodded. 'He was a journalist making his name, and you thought he could scoop the story, tell the world the truth. But instead, he wrote it into his black book. The one that all of you want.'

Declan nodded at the Filofax, still in Sinclair's hand.

'That one, in fact. So, now Hunt has taken his story, placed it into his book and he's using it to gain bigger stories. And, over the years, I'm sure he's repeatedly told Janine that he'll get around to this. That it's not time yet. And the years pass.'

'I was,' Robinson replied sadly. 'But things got in the way.'

'Things always got in the way, you feckless prick,' Janine shot back. 'Things like affairs, and your own drug-filled hedonism.'

'Why did you marry him?' Declan asked now, curious. 'I mean, nine years of marriage is a hell of a game plan.'

'Because I did love him,' Janine sighed. 'Young Hunt might have been a forgetful idiot, but he wasn't... this.'

She waved at Robinson.

'I married a different man,' she shrugged. 'It happens.'

'I'm sorry,' Hunt replied. 'I started the affairs because you were being cold to me. I thought you didn't love me.'

'I didn't,' Janine gave a humourless smile. 'Not by then. Good journalism instincts.'

As Robinson glared angrily at his wife, Declan turned his attention to Bonner now.

'In 2019, you become one of the youngest Labour MPs in London,' he said. 'But nobody cared about any connection to the Bannisters you might have, because you used a nickname that diverted from your surname. And your brother was forgotten when Sinclair swept everything away, anyway. You'd always believed your brother was an unsung victim, blamed in Whitehall backrooms for a crash that nobody investigated. And you too were angry and wanted the story out there.'

He looked around the nave now.

'And then, at a Christmas party, you heard about the tribute. That the Bannisters were having some kind of tenth anniversary memorial; possibly with a statue of them placed somewhere in Parliament. And suddenly, everything was brought back up again.'

'I couldn't live with this,' Bonner admitted. 'Those bastards, the Bannisters? They corrupted Lewis. He was a damned excellent pilot. And yeah, of course I wanted justice.'

'I get that,' Declan replied, seriously. 'But at the same time and unconnected, Janine had decided that she too, wanted to see something happen here. But the only person who could do it, didn't want to do it.'

Declan looked back at Janine.

'At the same party, Hunt arrived with you. And already there was tension because Karen Pine was there. She was a rival of Hunt, but she was an ex-lover—'

'You mean ex-mistress,' Janine muttered, glaring at her husband.

Declan shrugged.

'The party was integral,' he explained. 'It was where Sinclair, now a Commander met Janine again. And it was where Les Bonneville, using the nickname "Bonner" met Hunt Robinson for the first time, and realised this was the man who could help him, not only in getting his name better known but also in gaining justice. Especially when the statue was announced, and Hunt, using the party to remind people of his "brand," waved his book around, making a scene.'

'The fact we were all at a party isn't illegal, DI Walsh,' Sinclair replied.

'No, I can see that,' Declan smiled. 'And while Bonner and Janine looked at how to get the truth out, you didn't care. You'd moved on by this point, while Hunt just wanted the pay-out he'd been waiting for.'

Now Declan turned to face Robinson.

'At the start of the year, you started spending time with Bonner, not realising his true identity. Which, considering you're some kind of shit-hot journo, is frankly embarrassing. And during this time, your wife heard you'd been spending time with "Lesley, a secretary." She didn't realise that it was Leslie Bonneville, the MP and Junior Undersecretary, because to you, he was just "Bonner." But it was enough to think her husband was back to his old adulterous ways, which to be honest, you were – just not with Bonner here.'

Declan looked back at Bonner now.

'But you needed more,' he said. 'Hunt wasn't playing ball, and you needed to start a fire under his arse. You began trying to spook him, fake burglaries and muggings to make him think the book was under attack. And, while doing this, you courted *The Individual*'s new editor, Sean Ashby.'

'I'm a politician, it's what we do,' Bonner shrugged.

'Does "what you do" include convincing Ashby to send Hunt Robinson to a war zone, and stealing a story he wrote, passing it to Karen Pine, knowing they hated each other?'

Sean Ashby looked at Bonner in horror.

'And, does it include sending texts to him, convincing him you have secrets you'd release – secrets about his own hedonistic lifestyle, his affairs, his drug use, things that would make him unemployable? Things that would bring his honesty into question, which would then destroy the facts he had in his box, because who believes secrets from a man known for telling lies – if he didn't comply and give you the book?'

'It's whatever it takes,' Bonner's eyes glittered ominously. 'If he wasn't helping, he was in my way.'

'But there was someone else who got in your way,' Declan replied. 'You. Because after the party, Janine and Karen talked. And with this new mistress, this "Lesley the Secretary" appearing, the enemy of their enemy became their ally.'

'She was a tool, nothing more,' Janine snapped. 'I felt sick dealing with her. I wanted her to be gone.'

'Oh, we got that from when you set fire to her photo,' Declan smiled. 'But that didn't stop you priming her, convincing her to post the pieces, when she was in fact being used by you. And the Right Honourable Gentleman over there.'

'I never spoke to her!' Janine replied. 'Check my phone!'

'We did better, we checked Hunt's phone,' Declan replied. 'He sent messages to Karen while under anaesthetic, which is dead clever. So it had to be someone else, someone with access to his phone, who arrived at the house from a Wellness retreat, just in time to send the first one.'

Janine swore, looking at Bonner.

'Are you just going to stand there?' she snapped. 'Or do I drag you in too?'

'Karen was completely aware of what she was doing,' Bonner sniffed. 'She knew the plan from the start was to find a way to get the diary. I met her many times in Westminster. And the moment I knew Hunt had once been under her spell, I knew I had a way to get him.'

'And of course, Karen was more than happy to screw Hunt Robinson over,' Declan nodded. 'What I can't understand, though, is why he turned to her when he came up with this damned fool idea?'

'Because she told him to do it,' Doug said. 'I was there in the pub. She planned the whole thing out. Even gave him the knife to stab himself with. I said it was a mistake, but I was only there to keep things cordial.'

'Which I gave her,' Janine grinned evilly. 'I liked the idea that I stabbed him by proxy.'

'By then I was a mess,' Robinson admitted, glaring at Janine. 'Being married to that bitch didn't help. Doug was a mediator; Karen came to me. She claimed she didn't know she'd been passed my story, wanted to make amends.'

'By helping you stab yourself?'

'I've been stabbed before, I knew it wasn't as painful as people claimed,' Robinson replied. 'I said I'd give her some headlines to put out. We both won.'

He sighed.

'Apart from one thing. I didn't give her the book.'

'No, because that's here,' Sinclair replied, staring down at the book in his hand in confusion. 'You taped it—'

'No, we taped it,' Declan interrupted. 'We knew we needed something for you to believe in or you'd walk. Hunt Robinson didn't give Karen the book because there wasn't one. And that was the problem, because Karen took away a book with only a few stories in, ones already out there. Enough to give breadcrumbs, but not what Janine or Bonner wanted. And when Janine turned up at five in the morning to get the book, Karen tried to explain it wasn't there.'

He looked at Janine.

'You thought she was double-crossing you, hanging you out to dry for all this, and in anger, the heat of the moment and with a sudden opportunity, you stabbed her with a kitchen knife. We have forensics going through your house right now, and you pretty much admitted it to her "ghost" over there.'

Declan walked over to Sinclair, taking the book from his numb hands, walking over to the bin and tossing it in.

'It's a forgery. It's real. Which is it? I think enough people have died over this book, so let's just end it.'

'But we all saw the book!'

'No, you saw a book,' Declan replied. 'You wanted to believe it was the book. It's called apophenia, the tendency to see order in random configurations. Whoever got the book first would believe they had it, and the others would believe them, because they had no reason not to.'

As he said this, the back and front doors opened, police officers streaming in.

'Weirdly, although there are a ton of questions that'll be asked over the next few days and weeks, there's only one major crime, the murder of Karen Pine,' he continued. 'But she was a pawn in a larger game, aimed at Robinson by both Bonner and Janine Robinson. Only one of you struck the fatal blow, but you're both as responsible for her death. It's just a shame we can't charge you as accessories.'

As Cooper cuffed Janine, staring coldly at the floor as she did so, Sinclair turned to Declan, confused.

'So, there's no book?'

'No, not physically,' Declan said, looking at Robinson for confirmation. 'It's more a large filing cabinet.'

'You could have told the world,' Bonner said to Hunt Robinson, as officers led him out of the church. 'You would have been a hero.'

'Heroes are poor,' Robinson shrugged. 'I enjoy being rich and notorious.'

'Well, you're definitely the latter,' Declan smiled. 'You have Royal Protection keeping an eye out for you.'

'That's because I made a deal with them,' Robinson smiled. 'I give them the pages, they give me an exclusive when the next royal baby arrived.'

He looked at Sinclair.

'All that running around you did, the career you've ended, all for nothing. But that's about right for you, isn't it, Ed?'

Sinclair looked as if he was about to say something, his face reddening with anger, but instead, he turned and stormed out of the church. And, as the church emptied, Hunt Robinson looked at Declan.

'Come speak to me tomorrow, at home,' he said. 'You've helped me. So I should help you.'

'And how have I have helped you?'

Robinson laughed, nodding at Janine, being led out.

'You've given me a damned good divorce case,' he said, being led back out by Doug. 'An absolute banger.'

EPILOGUE

THE FOLLOWING MORNING, THE OFFICERS OF THE LAST CHANCE Saloon met in the briefing room, but it was a sombre affair.

'We solved the case,' Monroe muttered from the front of the room, leaning against the desk. 'But it's a bit of an anticlimax. We can't really throw anything against Bonneville or Sinclair, for a start.'

'Interfering with an investigation?' Declan suggested.

'Aye, that's literally it, but he's already pushing against that, saying how he believed our investigation was flawed,' Monroe sighed. 'And Bonneville? Well, he's claiming now he's outed as Lewis Bonneville's younger brother will no doubt start campaigning for his brother's redemption. While not pissing off the Royals, of course.'

'He held a knife on Sinclair!' Anjli exclaimed.

'Who isn't pressing charges,' Bullman said from the door. 'He knows if he does, people start to look into it, and that's the last thing he wants right now. And, from what I hear, he didn't do anything with it, as Janine Robinson took it.'

'And Janine's the only success here,' Anjli nodded. 'At least she's going down.'

'Aye, we have her in the area of Karen Pine's house thanks to the boy wonder and cell towers, and we think we found the marigold glove in her rubbish,' Monroe nodded. 'With her confession, it's just a matter of time before we have everything we need.'

'Hunt Robinson?'

'No point doing anything,' Declan replied to that. 'He has a pretty good case for trauma-induced activities. He was being blackmailed, was just back from a war zone ...'

There was a moment's silence in the room.

'I wanted something bigger for your last case with us, laddie,' Monroe said. 'Sorry.'

'I got to have a last moment,' Declan smiled. 'And it feels right that we started with a church, and me punching out Father Corden, and we ended with one.'

'Are you really going?' Jess, beside Billy, asked. She'd been grumpy all morning, mainly as she'd been sent home after the forging had ended and missed all the excitement.

'Last day's tomorrow, Friday,' Declan nodded. 'It's okay, we'll have a farewell bash. The Guv can give me the present you've all chipped together for.'

There was an uncertain mumbling around the room as the other members of the Last Chance Saloon realised they hadn't clubbed together for any kind of farewell gift, and Declan laughed, rising.

'Right,' he said. 'I'll be back in a bit, I need to go speak to a journalist.'

'You taking *The Individual* job?' Billy asked.

'Nah,' Declan said, shaking his head. 'I'm a copper. And although it'd keep me in London, I'd be bored. I'm speaking to DCI Freeman on Saturday, once I'm gone from here, to see if I can consult in Maidenhead.'

'And DCI Sampson?' Anjli asked.

'Was that you?' Declan replied, surprised. Anjli shrugged.

'Ports in storms and all that.'

'Well, I think the waters are choppy right now, but not too bad,' Declan smiled. 'I'm off to—'

He stopped as his phone buzzed. He stared down at the message.

'I'm off to see a journalist, and then I'm going to see Sinclair,' he said. 'How is he even in his office?'

'Because, as you said, laddie, he didn't technically do anything,' Monroe muttered. 'Cockroaches like him. They always fall upwards.'

Sinclair was waiting for him in his office when Declan arrived at Guildhall.

'I texted you an hour ago,' he said as Declan entered his office.

'I had a meeting before you in the City,' Declan said. 'Couldn't get out of it.'

'I'm sure.' Nodding for Declan to sit down, Sinclair sat back at his desk facing him, his face emotionless.

'Looks like you brought it in just under the wire,' he said with a slight smile. 'Well done, Detective Inspector, a good end to your final case, it seems.'

'Thank you, sir,' he said. 'Although I'm not sure if it's my final case or not. I'm speaking to a Thames Valley unit.'

'Oh?' Sinclair was surprised by this. 'I assumed you'd have taken up the offer of joining Sean Ashby's newspaper.'

'I don't feel like I'm the journalist type,' Declan shrugged. 'And I've had my run ins with enough private investigators over the years to know I'm not too sure if that's a job I wanted.'

He chuckled.

'Funnily enough, when I was being removed from Tottenham, a private investigator was my obvious choice. I suppose the Last Chance Saloon spoiled me in that respect.'

'So, what was the meeting you bumped me for?'

Declan pulled his phone out, turning it on and showing Sinclair a video message.

'This was posted on YouTube a few minutes ago,' he said.

On the screen was Hunt Robinson, beside a metal rubbish bin, in some courtyard in London. Beside him was Sean Ashby and Declan Walsh, there to the side as observers.

'*I'm Hunt Robinson,*' he said. '*You've probably read my pieces over the years, and you've read about my recent actions. These actions have led me to here, a defining moment in my life.*'

He reached into the bin, pulling out a handful of papers, showing them to the *camera before tossing them back.*

'*The contents of this bin are very personal,*' he continued on. '*They're the notes and papers I've called my "black book." It's something that almost got me killed, and I've decided I'm too old for that. And, to be honest, I've realised that over the years I've forgotten why I became a journalist. That I chased the truth, rather than the quick pay-outs and the front page by-lines. So, in front of my editor, Sean Ashby, and DI Declan Walsh of the City of London Police, both here as witnesses, I'm destroying them.*'

He looked to Sean, currently standing beside him looking irritated at this, probably because he was seeing exclusives and scoops sliding through his fingers, passed a flaming torch over.

'I hereby retire,' Hunt Robinson intoned solemnly to the camera before throwing the torch into the bin, where it burst into flames.

Declan paused the video, leaning back.

'He got the idea from me,' he said. 'It was filmed by Doug Reynolds.'

'That's a man out of a job,' Sinclair muttered, still staring at the phone, even though the video was no longer playing. 'Hunt was his bread and butter.'

'Not really,' Declan grinned. 'He was offered a job by Ashby. The one I'd been suggested for.'

'And Robinson was serious? About changing?'

'Who knows,' Declan shrugged. 'We'll see what his next big piece is.'

'So everything's gone?' Sinclair was finally realising the importance of the act. 'Including ...'

'Well, not everything,' Declan said. 'He kept a couple of things as keepsakes. And, before he did this, Hunt Robinson gave me a gift.'

Declan reached into his jacket pocket and pulled out three sheets of folded A4 paper. He passed it across to Sinclair, returning to his chair, as the City of London Commander picked up the papers, opening them, and staring at them in a growing sense of horror.

'As you can see, they're photocopies of three of the pages,' Declan said. 'The originals were given to me by Hunt Robinson before he destroyed the book – he thought they were something I could use.'

Sinclair flipped through the pages, reading and re-reading them, his face darkening.

'So this is blackmail?' he asked.

'No, sir, not at all,' Declan replied. 'But these are the notes he'd made of your investigation ten years ago, and although not naming the three bodies found, opens up enough avenues of enquiry for any committee to examine closer. And there are another three or four choice items, blind items he found on a website. They're about you, aren't they? He uses your name a couple of times, but I wanted to confirm.'

Sinclair placed the pieces of paper back on his desk.

'It's me,' he confirmed. 'But you knew that already. Are the originals burned?'

'No, sir. The originals were given to me by Robinson and I've placed them somewhere safe.'

Sinclair nodded.

'So, how is this not blackmail?' he smiled darkly. 'I mean, let's be honest. We're in the last hours of your penultimate day as an officer, and suddenly you pass me papers that, if they get out, could end my career. Me, the only person who could fix things for you, keep you employed, bring you to Bishopsgate, maybe keep you as a Detective Inspector.'

He leant closer.

'And it's not the first time you've done this, is it? We're all aware how you convinced the Prime Minister to keep DC Davey after you found out she was helping serial killer vigilantes, and even your own boss blackmailed the previous Prime Minister to keep Alexander Monroe on the team. This is your way of securing promotions isn't it? blackmail someone higher?'

'I get what you're saying, sir,' Declan replied coldly. 'And I'll agree, we have in the past done this, but this isn't what's happening today.'

He rose, pacing.

'You see, I could have gone to the Prime Minister and asked for my job. I could have gone to the Royal Court, showed them what I knew about the Duchess of Dorset and asked for my job. I could have done a dozen different things and each one would have ensured that I still worked as a copper in London. I could have transferred to Ireland, to Scotland, to the countryside. There's enough places for someone like me. But the Last Chance Saloon is my home. And if I can't stay there, then I don't want to be an officer.'

Sinclair leant back in his chair, watching Declan as he continued.

'And yes, sir, tomorrow I will indeed be leaving. But this? This wasn't me blackmailing you, sir. And I'm sorry you thought that. This is me passing you a message.'

'What sort of message?'

'A message telling you to get your house into order, because they're coming for you.'

Sinclair froze, his eyes narrowing.

'Who did you give these to?'

'The police, sir,' Declan said. 'I didn't think to act on it myself. After all, it's my last full day, and I want somebody to see this through, so I passed them to the relevant authorities, and I reckon they'll be coming to speak to you very shortly.'

Sinclair started to chuckle.

'You have a *Get Out of Jail Free* card here, and you're not using it? You're just here to tell me that my career's over as well?'

Declan moved towards the door.

'The one thing you've never got about me is I'm an officer of the law,' he said. 'And I'm a damned good one. Yes, I've had my adventures and yes, I've done things that many officers haven't. But at the end of the day, justice has to be served.'

He looked back at Sinclair.

'I was given something that Robinson genuinely thought

would help me. But I couldn't use it. It's not fair to use some-thing others don't have in my position. So, I wish you all the best, but having read those pages, and having worked with you these last couple of days, I can't say my respect for you has grown.'

With this said, Declan left the offices of Commander Edward Sinclair.

Sinclair looked down at the photocopied pieces of paper one last time.

And then, Commander Edward Sinclair picked up the phone.

———

DECLAN HADN'T RETURNED TO TEMPLE INN IMMEDIATELY; FIRST he'd walked around the surrounding streets, deep in thought. Then, he'd walked around the Inns of Court themselves, reminiscing about the time he found Reginald Troughton's body, or the time he'd been forced to run across the roofs to evade arrest. It wasn't exactly a case of "fond memories," but more a reminder of why he did this job, and what it'd mean to lose it all.

He didn't want to lose it, but it seemed the only way he'd keep his employment was to sell his soul. And as much as he wanted it, he'd seen too many times how that played out.

He'd arrived back in the afternoon and had mainly kept his head down, completing reports and making sure his admin was up to date. He didn't want Billy or Anjli lumbered with that, after all.

Jess had left around seven; she had a date with Prisha, and Declan gave her a hug and said he'd see her the next day. Monroe had offered a drink across the road, but

Declan politely refused; today was a day for reflection in the office.

He'd already decided he wasn't going home that night; he'd stay in one of the cots, where they often crashed out when on an all-nighter. He'd given himself the logic that as he was leaving the next day this was his last chance to do it, but there was a fear that if he went home tonight, he wouldn't come back tomorrow.

Anjli found him a couple of hours later and joined him, the two of them talking deep into the night. Anjli was worried that things would change between them once he was gone, but as he reassured her he'd never change, Declan was more relieved she wasn't going on about Tessa Martinez anymore.

They slept next to each other, like some police-based pyjama party.

AND THEN HE WAS WAKING UP AT SEVEN IN THE MORNING, STILL dressed, having finished off Monroe's whisky, after stealing it from the office around two in the morning. And by the time he'd woken up, showered, and changed into his spare clothes, it was almost nine.

Monroe was waiting for him as he walked slowly and wearily to the briefing room.

'My whisky?'

'I'll buy you a new one,' Declan replied, sitting down at his desk with a sigh. It wasn't a hangover; it was a strong melancholy that washed over him, as he realised every single thing that happened to him today would be the last time it happened.

However, Bullman had different plans, as she walked out of her office, looking around and spying Declan.

'Oi, Deckers,' she said. 'You started packing your box yet?'

Declan shook his head, confused.

'I was going to—'

Bullman held up a hand to stop him as she looked around the office.

'Call everyone here into the Briefing Room now,' she ordered Billy, who was already texting either De'Geer or Doctor Marcos, who'd both been downstairs.

Walking into the briefing room with the others, Declan frowned as he glanced at Anjli.

'Do you know anything about this?'

Anjli shook her head, just as confused and hungover as he was; even Monroe, walking ahead of them, looked unsettled as they sat in their usual places.

Billy was by the laptop, Monroe stood at the front and Cooper, currently alone, sitting at the back. With almost everyone here now, Bullman stepped to the front, now standing next to Monroe, addressing the team.

'Sorry to do this, but I've been having a chat with the superiors, and they've decided, Declan, that even though it's your final day, we don't need you today.'

'Ma'am?'

Bullman looked uncomfortable as she spoke.

'Yeah, sorry, they've said you can grab your stuff and leave, right after they bring some officers up to escort you out.'

'Now hang on!' Monroe reddened. 'This isn't on! It's his last day—'

'It's his last day,' Bullman replied, emotionless. 'And there's nothing to do now we cracked the case, so he might as well go home early. We'll still have a Walsh here. That is, when Walsh junior turns up.'

There was a long, uncomfortable pause.

And then, reluctantly, Declan rose.

'Yes, Ma'am,' he said, moving to the door.

'Ah, sit your arse down,' Bullman grinned. 'I'm just screwing with you. It seems you have a stay of execution.'

Declan sat back down, giving Anjli a confused look, as Bullman continued to address the room.

'Right then, we've had some news. Many of you will know Commander Edward Sinclair,' she said. 'I've just come off the phone with him.'

'What's he taking off us now?' Monroe muttered.

'Actually, he called to let me know he's decided, following this case, to retire from the force.'

There was a moment of stunned silence.

'Aye? Well, this is a surprise,' Monroe said, looking at Declan. 'Is it a surprise for all of us, though?'

Declan didn't say anything. He was still reeling from whatever had just happened.

'Do we know why?' Monroe continued to Bullman.

'Apparently, he's gaining a peerage soon.'

'And the police investigation?' Declan narrowed his eyes. 'The one they should be starting, with what I gave them?'

'Mysteriously stopped by Charles Baker.'

'Who was probably told to do this by Buckingham Palace,' Anjli muttered. 'After all, Sinclair has kept secrets for them for years. This is probably his retirement bonus, so he doesn't throw St James's Palace to the wolves if he's investigated.'

Declan shook his head.

'Bloody politics,' he grumbled.

'So who's replacing him?' Cooper asked.

'Well, apparently, there had been plans in place anyway,' Bullman explained. 'Detective Chief Superintendent Bradbury will be taking over his duties and moving to Guildhall with immediate effect.'

'Good for Bradbury,' Monroe nodded.

'It does, however, mean that there was a gap for Detective Chief Superintendent,' Bullman hadn't finished. 'I ... well, it seems I have been asked by Bradbury to assist him in this, and take on the promotion.'

There was a round of applause for this. That Bullman was moving up once more was a status to the Last Chance Saloon as much as it was to the officer being promoted.

Bullman smiled.

'Don't think you're getting rid of me. This is purely temporary until they can work out what to do next,' she said. 'And although I'll be at Guildhall, it's not that far away. And I will be here at least twice a week, so keep my office clean and don't do anything bad in it when I'm not here.'

She then looked at Declan.

'During this chat, Sinclair had a few choice words to say about you.'

'I bet he did,' Declan smiled.

'He said one thing he was allowed to do when he retired was to make some suggestions about his successors and their subordinates. Bradbury was one of them. Another was you, Declan.'

Declan shook his head.

'That can't be right, Ma'am,' he replied, confused. 'We ... well? It wasn't the happiest of chats.'

'That aside, he's written quite a nice report about you. It says he was wrong about his beliefs in relation to your abilities, and that you are an outstanding officer with full loyalty and devotion to the law.'

'Jesus, laddie, what did you threaten him with to get that response?'

'Whatever he did, it worked,' Bullman now grinned as she looked back at Declan. 'He suggested that you'd be promoted to Detective Chief Inspector.'

Declan chuckled.

'So I get promoted on the day I leave the force,' he said 'It's bittersweet, but I'll take it.'

'You're missing the point, Deckers,' Bullman said. 'You're not leaving the force. You're now the Temple Inn DCI.'

Declan did a double-take as he stared at Bullman.

'I'm sorry? Isn't Monroe the DCI here?'

'Well, with me gone, we're going to need somebody to take on my duties,' Bullman now looked at Monroe. 'I'm sorry, Alex, but you're going to be acting Detective Superintendent, and Declan will be acting DCI until everything's confirmed in a few weeks.'

Before anyone could reply, she addressed the briefing room.

'But what it means is the structure we have now will stay. I'll be in Guildhall, Monroe will be in my office when I'm not here, Deckers will be in Monroe's office and Anjli and Billy will – well, they don't change. Sorry. I could only fix the screw ups this time.'

Declan looked around the room.

'I'm staying,' he said. He hadn't hoped to even think such a thing. But now everything seemed open again.

'Bollocks to you staying, laddie, I've been made Detective Superintendent!' Monroe bellowed.

The cheering began then, with Anjli leaning over and

pecking Declan on the cheek, as Billy rose and ran at him, embracing him in a bear hug. Breaking from it, Declan nodded thanks at the smiling Bullman, before embracing Monroe.

'Looks like you're still my Guv, Guv,' he said with a smile.

'Only by the slightest of threads, laddie,' Monroe laughed.

Bullman patted Declan on the shoulder.

'Had to get the last "gotcha" in,' she said. 'You both deserve it. Although God help the City of London Police.'

The noise stopped abruptly though, as everyone realised there were three confused people standing in the doorway: Doctor Marcos, De'Geer and Jess.

'What the bloody hell did I miss?' Doctor Marcos asked. 'We've just picked up his leaving present. Are we not giving it to him now?'

Declan didn't think she expected Monroe to grab her and dance her around the room – and Jess seriously wasn't expecting a massive hug from her father.

'I'm staying,' he said to her with a beaming smile on his face. 'We'll have to return whatever you got me.'

'You are?'

'For the moment, it seems, yeah.'

'I can still boast to my friends my dad's a Detective Inspector?'

'Nope,' Declan laughed. 'From now on it looks like I'm Detective *Chief* Inspector Walsh.'

DCI Walsh and the team of the *Last Chance Saloon* will return in their next thriller

KISSING ᴬKILLER

Order Now at Amazon:

mybook.to/kissingakiller

ACKNOWLEDGEMENTS

When you write a series of books, you find that there are a ton of people out there who help you, sometimes without even realising, and so I wanted to say thanks.

There are people I need to thank, and they know who they are, including my brother Chris Lee, Jacqueline Beard MBE, who has copyedited all my books since the very beginning, and editor Sian Phillips, all of whom have made my books way better than they have every right to be.

Also, I couldn't have done this without my growing army of ARC and beta readers, who not only show me where I falter, but also raise awareness of me in the social media world, ensuring that other people learn of my books.

But mainly, I tip my hat and thank you. *The reader.* Who once took a chance on an unknown author in a pile of Kindle books, and thought you'd give them a go, and who has carried on this far with them, as well as the spin off books I now release.

I write Declan Walsh for you. He (and his team) solves crimes for you. And with luck, he'll keep on solving them for a very long time.

Jack Gatland / Tony Lee,
London, June, 2023

ABOUT THE AUTHOR

Jack Gatland is the pen name of *#1 New York Times Bestselling Author* Tony Lee, who has been writing in all media for thirty-five years, including comics, graphic novels, middle grade books, audio drama, TV and film for *DC Comics, Marvel, BBC, ITV, Random House, Penguin USA, Hachette* and a ton of other publishers and broadcasters.

These have included licenses such as *Doctor Who, Spider Man, X-Men, Star Trek, Battlestar Galactica, MacGyver,* BBC's *Doctors, Wallace and Gromit* and *Shrek*, as well as work created with musicians such as *Ozzy Osbourne, Joe Satriani, Beartooth, Pantera* and *Megadeth.*

As Tony, he's toured the world talking to reluctant readers with his 'Change The Channel' school tours, and lectures on screenwriting and comic scripting for *Raindance* in London.

An introvert West Londoner by heart, he lives with his wife Tracy and dog Fosco, just outside London.

Locations In The Book

The locations and items I use in my books are real, if altered slightly for dramatic intent. Here's some more information about a few of them...

St Bride's Church is a real church, and is indeed the location of the spire that inspired the "Wedding Cake" design. It's also where many families who left to travel to Roanoke worshipped, and was also where Mary Ann Walker, better known as Polly Nichols, both attended and where she married William Nichols, before she became infamous as one of the victims of Jack the Ripper.

You can visit the church, see the Journalist's Altar and visit the crypt during opening hours.

The village of Meopham, just south of the A2 in Kent exists, first recorded in 788, in the reign of King Offa, and John Major did indeed perform a "soapbox talk" at the cricket club (where he is a patron) in the 1992 General Election campaign. Meopham village is sometimes described as the longest settlement in England although others such as Brinkworth and Sykehouse make the same claim.

I often walk Fosco in Camer Park in Meopham, and have been looking to use it for quite some while!

Hurley-Upon-Thames is a real village, and one that I visited many times from the age of 8 until 16, as my parents and I would spend our spring and summer weekends at the local campsite. It's a location that means a lot to me, my second home throughout my childhood, and so I've decided that this should be the 'home base' for Declan.

The Olde Bell is a real pub in the village too, although owned by a hotel chain rather than man named Dave. It was founded in 1135 as the hostelry of Hurley Priory, making it one of the oldest hotels (and inns) in the world, and it was used as a meeting point for Churchill and Eisenhower during World War II.

Guildhall, where Commander Sinclair exists is the real location, and the building has been used as a town hall for several hundred years, while still the ceremonial and administrative centre of the City of London and its Corporation.

During the Roman period, the Guildhall was the site of the London Roman Amphitheatre, rediscovered as recently as 1988. It was the largest in Britannia, partial remains of which are on public display in the basement of the Guildhall Art Gallery, and the outline of whose arena is marked with a black circle on the paving of the courtyard in front of the hall. Indeed, the siting of the Saxon Guildhall here was probably due to the amphitheatre's remains.

It's also where I received the Freedom of the City of London in February 2023!

The Albion pub is on the corner of Fleet Street and New Bridge Street. A hundred years old, it was reopened a few years back with a return to the 1920s art nouveau style it had been created with.

Finally, **The Houses of Parliament** are real (obviously) and I've even attended the *Sherlock Holmes Society of London* dinners there. In addition, I've also attended SHSL meetings at the **National Liberal Club.**

If you're interested in seeing what the *real* locations look like, I post 'behind the scenes' location images on my Instagram feed. This will continue through all the books, after leaving a suitable amount of time to avoid spoilers, and I suggest you follow it.

In fact, feel free to follow me on all my social media by clicking on the links below. Over time these can be places where we can engage, discuss Declan and put the world to rights.

www.jackgatland.com
www.hoodemanmedia.com

Visit Jack's Reader's Group Page
(Mainly for fans to discuss his books):
https://www.facebook.com/groups/jackgatland

Subscribe to Jack's Readers List:
https://bit.ly/jackgatlandVIP

www.facebook.com/jackgatlandbooks
www.twitter.com/jackgatlandbook
ww.instagram.com/jackgatland

Want more books by Jack Gatland? Turn the page...

THE THEFT OF A **PRICELESS** PAINTING...
A GANGSTER WITH A **CRIPPLING DEBT**...
A **BODY COUNT** RISING BY THE HOUR...

AND ELLIE RECKLESS IS CAUGHT IN THE MIDDLE.

JACK GATLAND

PAINT
— THE —
DEAD

A 'COP FOR CRIMINALS' ELLIE RECKLESS NOVEL

A NEW PROCEDURAL CRIME SERIES WITH
A TWIST - FROM THE CREATOR OF THE
BESTSELLING 'DI DECLAN WALSH' SERIES

AVAILABLE ON AMAZON / KINDLE UNLIMITED

THEY TRIED TO KILL HIM...
NOW HE'S OUT FOR **REVENGE.**

NEW YORK TIMES #1 BESTSELLER **TONY LEE** WRITING AS

JACK GATLAND

THE MURDER OF AN **MI5 AGENT**...
A BURNED SPY **ON THE RUN** FROM HIS OWN PEOPLE...
AN ENEMY OUT TO **STOP HIM** AT ANY COST...
AND A **PRESIDENT** ABOUT TO BE **ASSASSINATED**...

SLEEPING SOLDIERS

A **TOM MARLOWE** THRILLER

BOOK 1 IN A NEW SERIES OF THRILLERS IN THE STYLE OF
JASON BOURNE, JOHN MILTON OR **BURN NOTICE,** AND
SPINNING OUT OF THE **DECLAN WALSH** SERIES OF BOOKS

AVAILABLE ON AMAZON / KINDLE UNLIMITED

EIGHT PEOPLE. EIGHT SECRETS.
ONE SNIPER.

THE
B⊕ARD
ROOM

HOW FAR WOULD YOU GO TO GAIN JUSTICE?

NEW YORK TIMES #1 BESTSELLER TONY LEE WRITING AS

JACK GATLAND

A NEW STANDALONE THRILLER WITH
A TWIST - FROM THE CREATOR OF THE
BESTSELLING 'DI DECLAN WALSH' SERIES

AVAILABLE ON AMAZON / KINDLE UNLIMITED

JACK GATLAND

THE
LIONHEART
CURSE

HUNT THE GREATEST TREASURES
PAY THE GREATEST PRICE

BOOK 1 IN A NEW SERIES OF ADVENTURES
IN THE STYLE OF 'THE DA VINCI CODE'
FROM THE CREATOR OF DECLAN WALSH

AVAILABLE ON AMAZON / KINDLEUNLIMITED

Printed in Great Britain
by Amazon